347 5
357-c

14 KiM

FREE FROM ALL DANGER

*Recent Titles by Chris Nickson from
Severn House*

The Richard Nottingham Mysteries

COLD CRUEL WINTER
THE CONSTANT LOVERS
COME THE FEAR
AT THE DYING OF THE YEAR
FAIR AND TENDER LADIES
FREE FROM ALL DANGER

The Inspector Tom Harper Mysteries

GODS OF GOLD
TWO BRONZE PENNIES
SKIN LIKE SILVER
THE IRON WATER
ON COPPER STREET

FREE FROM ALL DANGER

A Richard Nottingham Novel

Chris Nickson

Severn House Large Print
London & New York

This first large print edition published 2018
in Great Britain and the USA by
SEVERN HOUSE PUBLISHERS LTD of
Eardley House, 4 Uxbridge Street, London W8 7SY.
First world regular print edition published 2017 by
Severn House Publishers Ltd.

British Library Cataloguing in Publication Data
A CIP catalogue record for this title is available from the British Library.

ISBN-13: 9780727893963

Severn House Publishers support the Forest Stewardship Council™
[FSC™], the leading international forest certification organisation. All
our titles that are printed on FSC certified paper carry the FSC logo.

Typeset by Palimpsest Book Production Ltd.,
Falkirk, Stirlingshire, Scotland.
Printed and bound in Great Britain by
T J International, Padstow, Cornwall.

To the memory of the real Richard Nottingham and his descendants.

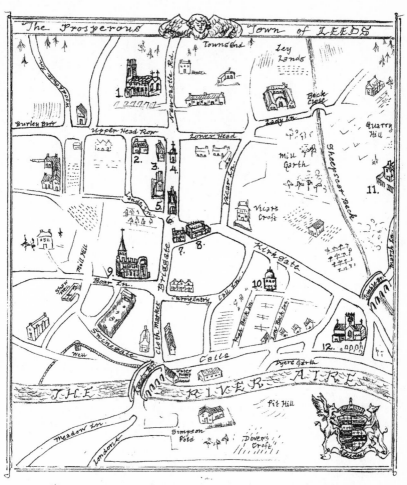

The Prosperous Town of LEEDS

1. St. John's Church
2. Garroway's Coffee House
3. The Rose & Crown
4. The Market Cross
5. The Talbot
6. The Moot Hall
7. The White Swan
8. The Gaol
9. Holy Trinity
10. White Cloth Hall
11. Nottingham's House
12. Leeds Parish Church

How can you go abroad fighting for
strangers?
Why don't you stay at home free from
all danger?

Our Captain Cried All Hands,
Traditional Folk Song

One

Sometimes he felt like a ghost in his own life. The past had become his country, so familiar that its lanes and its byways were imprinted on his heart. He remembered a time when he'd been too busy to consider all the things that had gone before. But he was young then, eager and reckless and dashing headlong towards the future. Now the years had found him. His body ached in the mornings, he moved more slowly; he was scarred inside and out. His hair was wispy and grey and whenever he noticed his face in the glass it was full of creases and folds, like the lines on a map. Sometimes he woke, not quite sure who he was now, or why. There was comfort in the past. There was love.

Richard Nottingham crossed Timble Bridge and started up Kirkgate, the cobbles slippery under his shoes. At the Parish Church he turned, following the path through the yard to the graves. Rose Waters, his older daughter, married and dead of fever before she could give birth. And next to her, Mary Nottingham, his wife, murdered because of his own arrogance; every day he missed her, missed both of them. He stooped and picked a leaf from the grass by her headstone. October already. Soon there would

1

be a flood of dead leaves as the year tumbled to a close.

Most of the people he cared about lay here. John Sedgwick, who'd been his deputy and his friend. Even Amos Worthy. The man had been a panderer, a killer, but they'd shared a curious relationship of hatred and friendship until cancer turned him into a husk and finally claimed him.

And now there were just two left alive. Richard and Emily Nottingham. Himself and his younger daughter. She ran a school for poor young girls and she had her man, Rob Lister, the deputy constable of Leeds these days. They were both young enough for life to wind out endlessly into the distance, its possibilities broad and open.

He stood for a minute then sighed as he straightened the clean stock around his neck and left the dead to their peace. As he passed the jail he glanced through the window. Empty, but that was no surprise. Lister and the men he commanded would be out, working. Rob had been in charge of everything since Simon Kirkstall, the constable, died a fortnight before. Fallen down stone dead in the White Swan as his heart suddenly stopped beating, the tankard still in his hand.

Nottingham turned on to Briggate. People nodded and said their hellos as he went by. The street was busy, clattering and booming with the sound of voices and the rumble of carts, the harsh mixture of smells – the iron tang of blood in the Shambles, horse dung, night soil left on the cobbles, a press of unwashed bodies.

At the steps to the Moot Hall, he glanced up at the statue of Queen Anne, then pushed open the

2

heavy wooden door. At the top of the stairs the corridor had rich, dark panelling and a thick Turkey carpet. A different, grander world from the one below.

The mayor's office stood at the far end. Nottingham brushed some faint dust from the shoulder of his good coat and glanced down at the polished metal buckles of his shoes. He knocked and waited until a weary voice said, 'Enter.'

John Brooke had become Mayor of Leeds only three weeks before, taking his year in office. He was a wool merchant, a man who'd been a member of the corporation for more than a decade. Successful, wealthy, busy, and now he was burdened with this position for the next twelve months.

'Richard,' he said with a welcoming smile as he rose, a curling grey wig falling onto his shoulders. He had his hand extended, two gold rings twinkling on his thick fingers. 'Thank you for coming. Sit down.'

Nottingham eased himself into the chair, feeling the creak in his knees.

'I wondered why you sent a message.' It had arrived the afternoon before, just an invitation with no reason or detail. A mystery he'd mentioned to no one.

Brooke took a breath.

'I'll get right to the point: of course, you know what happened to poor Simon. You must, everyone's heard by now.' He filled his clay pipe, lit a taper from the candle on his desk and brought it to the bowl. 'Leeds needs a new constable.'

It did, Nottingham knew that, and a better one than Kirkstall had been. He'd heard about the man every night from Rob. The way he always grasped the credit and did none of the work, rarely even dirtied his hands. The town deserved much more than that. Brooke knew it too, he could see it in his eyes.

'Yes, but what do you want from me?' Nottingham began. 'My opinion? Rob Lister knows the job. He has plenty of experience. He'd be a credit to us all.'

Brooke pushed his lips together. 'I've no doubt he would. He's an impressive lad, very quick, and he's clever.' He hesitated. 'There's only one problem.'

'What?' He didn't understand. He knew Rob. He shared his house with the lad and Emily, he saw him each day. There was nothing wrong with his character or his work. And Lister wanted the position.

'He's too young,' Brooke answered slowly. 'I've talked to the other aldermen. We're all agreed: we need someone older. Someone with more authority.'

Nottingham frowned. If the man didn't want his advice, why bother inviting him here? 'You should give him the chance. I know he'd do well.'

The mayor shook his head. 'No. We've decided against that.'

'Then make him constable until you find someone older for the job. Give him that, at least. The men respect him.'

Brooke sighed. 'Believe me, Richard, I don't doubt him. But the aldermen were unanimous.

What we want is to find someone who can live up to everything you did as constable.'

'Then why are you asking me? You don't want Rob and there's nobody else I can think of.'

'Yes, there is.' The mayor looked straight into his face. 'We want you to come back as Constable of Leeds – until we find someone.'

For a moment he was certain that his ears had deceived him, that he'd slipped into a ridiculous dream.

'Me?'

'You,' Brooke told him again. 'Until we find the right man for the job. You were the best we've ever had, Richard.'

Nottingham had to smile. It was unbelievable. How many enemies had he made among the corporation over the years? How many times had he sat in this office and argued with different mayors? Half the aldermen in town had rubbed their hands with glee when he retired, he knew that. And now they claimed he was the finest constable Leeds had ever known.

'It's been a long time,' he said.

'Not that long. Only two years.'

But it felt like a lifetime.

Along with Tom Williamson the merchant, Brooke had been one of his few true supporters among the aldermen. This was probably his idea, one he'd bullied through.

'And you all agreed?' he asked doubtfully.

'All of us,' Brooke confirmed.

'I'm older now.'

'Wiser, too, I hope.' The mayor smiled.

Maybe it would be a good thing, Nottingham

thought. Something to stir him. He knew he needed to stop hiding in the past. This would give him purpose, it would keep him solid. If he accepted the job he'd be forced to live in the here and now, to always be aware and alert. He remembered when he was young and without a home, sleeping behind bushes, living on what little he could earn or steal. Each morning had brought the task of surviving until night fell. The only thing that mattered was today. No future, only now.

He took a deep breath.

'I'll do it.'

Brooke was on his feet, beaming and shaking hands again.

'I hoped you'd agree. Thank you, Richard. I know you'll do an excellent job.'

'Only until you appoint someone, though,' he said. 'And you agree to consider Rob for the job.'

'Of course.' But Brooke's assurance was just gloss. The man would say anything at the moment. He'd make sure to hold the mayor to that promise when the time came.

The whole thing seemed impossible. He'd never imagined returning to the job, never dreamed of it. He'd been happy to walk away from it. Even now, after he'd agreed, a part of him wasn't certain this was the right thing to do. But it had happened, he'd made his decision. He was the Constable of Leeds once again.

The mayor reached into a drawer, brought out a bunch of keys on a heavy ring and pushed them across the desk.

'You'll be needing these.'

6

Nottingham weighed them in his hand, the metal cold against his palm. So familiar that he might never have put them down.

'I believe I will.'

Two

Nottingham turned the key in the lock and pushed open the door to the jail. The smell of the place – the fear, the old sweat, the dust that lay everywhere – brought memories flooding down through his mind. As he sat behind the desk, touching the old, worn wood, he felt as if the last two years had melted away and he'd never retired at all.

Piles of notes, documents, all needing attention. A battered quill tossed down, the sharpening knife beside it. The pot of ink with the top open so the liquid inside had dried. He breathed slowly, looking around the room, then walked through to the cells. He'd spent so much time in this place that it was part of his blood.

The sound of footsteps and a voice calling out brought him back. His heels rang out on the flagstones.

Rob stood, one hand ready on the hilt of his knife. He'd filled out from the lad Nottingham had first taken on as a constable's man and his eyes had the wariness of experience. He was dressed in his working clothes, an old, stained coat, thick breeches, woollen socks that Lucy the servant had darned again and again, and heavy boots. There was a small scar on his cheek and more that were hidden, but he'd earned every one of them on the job. Nottingham understood that; he had enough of his own.

'Richard. What are you doing here?' His mouth was open, eyes wide with astonishment. 'You're all dressed up, too.'

'The mayor wanted to see me.' He hesitated. There was no easy way to break the news. 'He's asked me to return as constable until they find someone permanent.' Nottingham opened his hand. 'I told him you should have the job, but the corporation want someone older. He asked me. For now, at least.'

'But—' He could see the resentment, plain and bright on the young man's face. God knew he deserved the position. And now it had been given to his lover's father. 'When you retired . . .'

'I know. I swore I'd never come back,' Nottingham agreed gently. 'I remember. And I haven't set foot in here since. This is John Brooke's request.'

Lister's body seemed to tighten, his face set so he'd give nothing away.

'What about me?'

'You're still the deputy. No, you're more than that,' he added, as if it might make a difference. 'I'm going to need your help.' He'd realized just how true that was as he walked down from the Moot Hall. His skills had rusted to nothing. He was older, not the same man the mayor remembered as Constable of Leeds. He'd lost touch with the town. Every day the place grew more

8

crowded. People arrived, hoping to find their fortune here. But prosperity only existed for the few. Most only managed to discover more desperation. So many of the faces he saw now belonged to strangers, people who'd arrived to hope, to live. He didn't know them or their crimes. 'I hope you can give it.'

Rob pushed a hand through his hair.

'I have to go and meet someone,' he said quickly and stalked out, slamming the door behind himself.

Nottingham sighed. It was going to be a difficult return.

Lister seethed as he walked away. His hands were bunched into fists, the knuckles white, his mouth clenched shut. He'd earned that job. For two years he carried Simon Kirkstall; the man had only been given the post because his wife was an alderman's cousin. Rob had done the work, all the dark, dirty tasks that came along. But it was Kirkstall who courted the corporation, who boasted to the *Mercury* and the aldermen about the arrests he made. He testified in court about events he'd never seen, and walked in processions with the proper gravity and sober expression and grand clothes.

All the constable's men knew the truth. Probably many others, too. The only ones to mourn Kirkstall would be his wife and children.

And now . . . now Richard Nottingham was back. He liked the man, loved him like a father. He lived in his house, Nottingham's daughter was his wife in everything but name. And he'd been an excellent constable. But his day was over. Two years was a long time. Leeds had swirled and changed beyond anything he knew.

He strode out and kicked angrily at the leaves that had blown across from the churchyard, sending up a spray of red and green. The Calls was noisy with men working on the river barges, women hawking this and that while their grimy children played games in the gutter.

He ducked through a doorway and twenty young girls turned to stare at him.

'Read your books for a minute,' Emily Nottingham told them. 'And do it quietly.'

She wore a plain brown woollen dress, old and frayed at the hem, the sleeves smudged white with chalk dust. Her hair was twisted up, out of the way, showing the curve of her neck. To him, she was the loveliest woman in the world.

He guided her outside, letting the carters and the porters make their way around them.

'What's wrong?' she asked quickly as she saw his expression. 'Has something happened?'

'They've asked your father to come back as constable,' Lister said, and he couldn't keep the bitterness from his voice.

'What?' Her voice rose, eyes widened in disbelief. 'But why?' She glanced through the window into the class room and made a sharp gesture as a girl stared at them.

'Just until they find someone else. That's what he told me. They say he has the age and experience.' He snorted.

'I didn't know they'd even talked to him. He

never said a word to me.' She reached for his hand and stroked it lightly. 'I'm sorry.'

'It sounds as if it just happened. He's never shown any sign of wanting to come back.' He needed to talk, to get it out. But she was torn, he could see it. She loved him. But she loved her father, too, and now here she was, caught between them. 'He seemed happy enough doing nothing.'

'Papa was withering away.' She rapped once on the glass and the murmur from the girls inside dropped to silence. 'You know that's true.'

It was; Richard had started to exist, not to live. He'd lost interest in things, as if he was withdrawing from life.

'He's going to need your help,' Emily said.

'That's exactly what he said.' He let out a slow breath. 'I'm sorry. I just needed to tell someone.'

She nodded, her mouth in a soft, sad smile.

'Papa's a good man. You know he is.' Emily looked at him pleadingly. 'Give him a chance, Rob. Please. He gave you one when he took you on, remember? You always admired him before.'

'Yes.' He kissed her cheek. 'You'd better go before there's a riot in there.'

A few yards down the street, he glanced over his shoulder. Emily had already vanished, but he felt heartened. It helped to tell someone who understood, who could see. The anger inside him had already shrunk. An old woman selling apples from a basket shouted her wares. He bought one, crunched down on the crisp sweetness and felt the fires subside.

* * *

11

Nottingham locked the door of the jail. The ring of keys weighed heavy in his pocket as he walked down Briggate towards the river.

Rob . . . he couldn't really blame the lad. He'd always been outstanding at his work, he'd earned his chance to shine, and now it had been pulled away from him. But there was nothing he could do about that. He was going to need Lister at his side. Pray God Rob would let his rage burn out and then come around. He didn't want work and home poisoned with an atmosphere of resentment.

He was close to the bridge when a voice hailed him and he turned to see Tom Williamson hurrying along the path from his warehouse on the river.

The rich chestnut periwig fell to his shoulders, and he was dressed in a black coat of fine wool with an embroidered yellow silk waistcoat as bright as a summer flower. The merchant had the grace to seem faintly embarrassed by his peacock appearance. He was growing portly, Nottingham decided, face flushed from moving quickly. But underneath the fancy clothing there was a very sharp mind.

'Brooke made you the offer, then?'

The constable smiled. Of course, Tom Williamson would know; he was an alderman.

'He did, and I accepted. But I told him Rob Lister should have the job.'

'No.' Williamson shook his head firmly. 'He's good, but he's not ready yet. We need some stability, Richard. You're the perfect man for that. I told them you were the best we've ever had in the post.'

12

Nottingham reddened a little at the praise. 'You look as if you're doing well yourself.'

The merchant brushed a hand over his coat. 'The business keeps growing, and my wife insists I dress the part.' He leaned forward and lowered his voice. 'Between you and me, I feel like a fool dressed this way. How can a man work in these clothes?' He pulled a watch from the waistcoat. 'I'm sorry, I have an appointment. We're thinking of a venture to export to more of those American colonies. Times change, eh?' He raised an eyebrow and chuckled. 'Good luck with the job. I'm glad to have you back.'

He bustled away up Briggate.

Nottingham placed his elbows on the bench.

'Tell me what's been going on. The things I ought to know.'

Rob rubbed his chin as he thought, sipping at a mug of ale. The White Swan was busy, men talking loudly and laughing, but they had the table to themselves; people always gave the law a berth. Lister had returned from wherever he'd gone half an hour before. To see Emily, the constable supposed; at least he'd come back calmer and ready to talk.

'It's been quiet lately. There's not much more than I've told you most evenings over supper.' He shrugged.

'That's for home,' Nottingham told him and Lister dipped his head in acknowledgement. 'I need to know for the job.'

'There's still very little to say. We haven't had any real trouble since early summer and that

13

killing up by Woodhouse.' He took another drink. 'Two pimps have disappeared in the last few weeks. But you know how it is. They come and go.'

'What about the girls who worked for them?'

'Still here with new protectors, I suppose.' He gave a bleak smile. 'I haven't looked. Cutpurses, of course. Fights and drownings. All the usual things. Oh,' he added, 'Matthew Bell sold the Talbot six months ago. But everyone knows about that.'

Nottingham had heard the news and forgotten it again. The Talbot Inn had been where half the criminals in town congregated. A cockpit in the back room, whores upstairs. And Bell himself, surly, quick with his fists. He was no loss to Leeds.

'What's the place like now?'

'The new owner still has the cock fighting on a Saturday night. It's popular. But he's spruced the place up. It's a pleasure to go there now.'

'Who bought it?'

'Someone named Harry Meadows. Not local, from up north, I think. Amiable enough.' Lister smiled and raised his mug. 'And he doesn't charge us for ale.'

Nottingham was listening carefully. He needed to learn so many things about his own town. But if there was little crime he'd have time to ease himself back into the job. And the Talbot becoming respectable after all these years? He'd have to see that for himself.

'I told you, I'm going to need to rely on you. We both understand that I don't know Leeds too

14

well any more.' Lister opened his mouth to speak but Nottingham stopped him. 'I know you think you should have had the job. So do I. But Brooke made it clear they wouldn't have appointed you, anyway. They think you're still too young. Perhaps we can change their minds.'

He watched the young man's face. Rob hadn't learned to control it yet; it was like reading a book. His expression gave away his thoughts, all the anger he'd tamped down.

'I'm with you,' he said after a moment. 'Boss.'

'Thank you.' The constable smiled. 'Now, tell me the rest.'

It was late; Nottingham knew that as the banging stirred him from a deep, dreamless sleep. By the time he reached the stairs, Rob was already at the door, listening as one of the men spoke quickly.

'What is it?' he called out.

'Body in the river, sir,' the man answered. He didn't recognize the face.

'A drunk?'

'That's what we thought at first, sir.' The man shifted uncomfortably from foot to foot. 'We got a hook and pulled him to the bank. Someone had cut his throat.'

'Where's the body?' Nottingham asked.

'Just past the bridge, sir.'

'We'll be there. Have you sent for Mr Brogden?'

'Who?' The man looked confused.

'Brogden. The coroner.'

'It's Hoggart now,' Lister corrected him softly. 'Brogden retired last year.'

Of course. Without thinking, he'd issued the order he'd given so often in the past.

'Then get Mr Hoggart there, please.'

'I already sent someone for him, sir.'

Leeds slept. No lights through the shutters, still far too early for smoke to start rising from the chimneys. Shadowed gables all along Kirkgate. The only sound was their boots on the cobbles, matching each other stride for stride. Nottingham glanced across as they passed the churchyard, the way he always did, then huddled deeper into his old greatcoat as a chill wind pawed at his face. They passed places so familiar that he didn't even need to see them: the old tithe barn, the mansions built by Pawson and Cookson and Barstow, Widow Clifton's house, Mr Dodshon's shop, the White Cloth Hall. Across from Vicar's Croft they turned down Call Lane, footsteps echoing sharply off the high stone wall that shielded the Dissenters' Meeting House and Mr Atkinson's large home with its grand Italian cupola.

Someone had thrown a cloth over the corpse, a ragged piece of old sailcloth that stank of tar. Three men stood close by, one holding up a lantern to light the scene. He didn't know a single one of them.

'Mr Hoggart,' Lister said, and the tallest of the men turned. He had the type of face that would always need a shave, stubble dark on his cheeks, a weak chin, and watery eyes.

'He's dead, no doubt about that.' A dark chuckle. His hands were thrust deep into the pockets of a

16

finely-woven coat and the gleaming leather of his boots caught the light.

'This is Richard Nottingham, the new constable.'

'A pleasure to meet you, sir. I just hope we don't see each other too often.' With that, he gave a nod, turned, and walked off into the darkness.

Nottingham pushed back his old bicorn hat and knelt slowly, feeling the ache in his knees and the dampness of the earth through his breeches.

In the lamplight the man's hair seemed to glisten long and black, slicked down against his skull, a few weeds clinging to his skin. The river had washed his wound clean, but the slash across his neck gaped like a smile. He heard the sharp intake of breath.

'Do you know him?'

'Robert Stanbridge,' Lister said coldly. 'He's a moneylender. I can't say I'm sorry to see him dead.'

'Who were his enforcers?' Slowly, Nottingham pushed himself upright. He needed to examine the corpse properly, somewhere with light, not out here in the wind and the chill.

'He only had one. Daniel Turner.'

'I want him at the jail.' He turned to the two waiting men. 'Bring the body, I'll look at him later.'

He set the fire with chips of wood under the coals and a few hanks of wool, lit it with sparks from the tinder box, and waited for some warmth to fill the room.

'Who'd want this Stanbridge dead, do you think?'

'It could be almost anyone.' Rob chewed his lip as he thought. 'He's only been in town for a year or so. Moneylending's become quite an industry here.' He paused for a moment. 'Maybe a competitor or someone who couldn't repay him and thought he'd cancel the debt forever.'

'Who would you go after first?'

'Toby Smith. He's the other one who lends money to the poor.'

'Why him?' Nottingham asked.

'Because I'm certain he's responsible for two killings, but I've never been able to prove it. People were too scared even to talk about it, let alone testify.'

'Drag him down here.' He thought for a moment. 'Leave it until later, when everyone can see. No one's going to be above the law here.'

Lister smiled. 'Yes, boss.'

By seven he'd marched home for his breakfast. Emily had already left for her school, and Lucy was pounding down the bread dough in the kitchen.

'Was it urgent?' she asked as she brought a bowl of porridge for him.

'Urgent enough,' he allowed. She'd grown into a stout, open-faced young woman, very different from the fearful little orphan he'd brought into the house. Now she ruled the home so thoroughly that it was impossible to imagine her not here.

She'd been delighted by the news that he was constable again, sponging down his old work

18

coat and carefully brushing it, ready for him to wear. Emily had hugged him, eyes bright. And Rob seemed to have come to terms with it all well enough; in the evening they'd sat by the fire and talked.

Two years and he hadn't realized quite how much Leeds had altered. The surface looked the same, but underneath the currents had all shifted. He needed to master them or drown.

At eight he was back on Briggate, watching the progress of the cloth market. That remained a constant, there long before he was born, its business conducted in whispers, thousands of pounds changing hands in just an hour. But it had grown, too, just like everything else; these days the trestles were tightly packed along both sides of the street from Leeds Bridge all the way up to Boar Lane, filled with merchants strutting in their grandeur and the hopeful weavers with heavy eyes and bent backs who'd made their way in from the surrounding villages.

Further up the street, men and women were setting up their stalls for the Tuesday market. All manner of things were for sale, from fruit and vegetables to chickens and butter, the tinkers with their mended pots and pans and the bustling trade in old clothes.

Nottingham walked from the bridge all the way to the market cross by the Head Row and slowly back. He'd done his duty. Now it was time for some real work.

Three

Stanbridge's body lay in the cold cell. Next door to him, Daniel Turner waited to be questioned, pulled from his lodging house in the middle of the night. He'd speak to the living in a few minutes; first Nottingham would see what the dead could tell him.

The river had taken one shoe. The other clung to Stanbridge's foot, the leather lumpen and wet. But the buckle looked like real silver. Finely woven hose, breeches that fitted well against his thighs. A few coins in the pockets and a handkerchief of best linen.

No cuts or tears on the fingernails. No bruises under the jacket and shirt; it didn't look as if he'd had chance to fight. The long gash across the front of his neck had probably been made from behind. The moneylender had been dead in an instant.

He found a notebook inside the coat pocket. The constable flipped through the pages but water had blurred the ink beyond reading.

Stanbridge's scalp was all stubble, cut close to be comfortable under a wig.

He walked around the slab, staring, hoping for some inspiration, any clue that might prod him along. But there was nothing here to help him find the murderer.

Time to talk to the man's enforcer.

Daniel Turner was a large man with dull eyes, a heavy body edging into fat. His belly bulged and there were jowls under his cheeks, although he couldn't have been more than twenty-five.

'Why did you kill him?'

'Kill?' He squinted. 'I en't killed nobody.'

'The man you work for is dead. Someone slit his throat,' Nottingham said.

'It wan't me.' He started to rise off the bunk in the cell then sat once more, eyes glinting. 'I were with a lass last night, anyway.'

'Who?'

'At Mrs Wyndham's.' He had a thick, empty voice. The stink of beer wafted on his breath. 'There until two. The clock were striking as I went home.' He stared resentfully. 'I'd just got to sleep when your men came.'

'What was the girl's name?'

'Don't remember.'

That didn't matter; it would be easy enough to check.

'Who saw you come back to your lodgings?'

'No one. All asleep, weren't they?'

They'd found no blood on his knife or his clothes, no evidence that he'd been the killer, and it was impossible to tell how long Stanbridge had been in the water before they found him. He took Turner back to his cell.

At the desk he scribbled a note to the brothel keeper:

Was someone called Turner there last night? Large, ugly fellow, quite young. If so, what time did he leave? He hesitated for a moment, then signed it *Nottingham* and folded the paper carefully.

21

Standing at the door, he called to a boy.

'Do you know Mrs Wyndham's on Vicar Lane?'

'Yes, sir.' He was ragged, hands and face filthy, legs bare and pimpled with cold below his breeches.

'Take this and wait for an answer. There's a farthing in it for you.'

The lad snatched the note and ran off. He'd know the truth soon enough. But that wasn't any guarantee of Turner's innocence. The murder would only have taken a second, then one more to tumble the body into the Aire.

He couldn't feel his direction in this yet. He felt like a man fumbling his way around a maze in the darkness.

The door opened and Lister pushed a small man into the room before taking him by the collar and sitting him on the chair.

'Toby Smith,' he announced. 'A moneylender and maybe a murderer. Who knows?'

The man turned and showed a set of sharp, discoloured teeth. He had a feral look, eyes wild, his hair unkempt and dark.

'Why would I want to kill Stanbridge?' Smith shouted. 'He wasn't even competition to me.'

'He's certainly not now, is he?'

Nottingham gave a small nod to Rob; he'd dealt with the man before, he could question him. Let the lad see he trusted his instincts. And there was someone who might be able to give him some helpful information . . .

Tom Finer was in his usual seat at the window of Garroway's Coffee House, holding a bowl to his mouth. He looked shrunken now, an old

22

man's body growing more compact each year. But his eyes were clear, shining with a darting, sly intelligence.

'Richard Nottingham.' He smiled. 'And the Constable of Leeds again, I hear. Congratulations to you.'

'Thank you.' He lowered himself on to the bench. Outside, the world went by, carts rumbling and the steady, even clop of horses' hooves, men and women passing on foot. Inside, the window was covered in condensation and the heavy aroma of coffee cloyed in the air.

'A dish of tea? Coffee?'

Nottingham shook his head. He'd never acquired the taste for either.

'What do you know about moneylending here?'

Finer raised a bushy eyebrow. He'd started out as a crook in Leeds before running off to London a few decades earlier. He'd made himself rich there and returned a little more than two years ago. Since then he'd earned himself another small fortune in property as the town boomed.

'Straight to the point.' He sat back. 'But I'm curious – why would you think I'd know anything about that?'

'Do you?' Nottingham countered with a smile.

Finer raised the bowl of coffee again and drank, hiding his face.

'I suppose I might have heard a few things,' he admitted after a while. 'One of the moneylenders is dead.'

'I already know that. I was just examining his body. That's hardly news.'

'The rumour is that three pimps have vanished, too.'

'Three?' He couldn't hide his surprise. 'I knew about two.'

'Three,' Finer said with certainty.

'What are you trying to say? They're connected?'

The old man shrugged his bony shoulders and spread his hands on the table.

'I'm not saying anything, Mr Nottingham. That's your job. I'm just observing. But perhaps it's a thought worth considering.'

Three pimps? Was that true? And why would Finer know, but not Rob? He frowned.

'It's an idea, I suppose.' He didn't believe it. One of the man's misdirections, perhaps. That had always been his way. 'Who'd be behind something like that?'

Finer stared down at his fingers. The knuckles were knotted, twisted with time.

'Maybe nobody. I suppose it could all be coincidence,' he said slowly, and smiled. 'But tell me: when have you ever believed in coincidence?'

Nottingham shook his head. 'No. I don't see why they'd be connected.' Pimps stuck to their trade, moneylenders to theirs. The only man he could recall in Leeds who'd done both was Amos Worthy, and he'd been under the sod for four years. 'I can't see it.'

Finer smiled and shrugged again. 'That's your choice. You asked for ideas; I gave you one.'

'True.' But it was one that went nowhere. 'How's business?' he asked.

* * *

24

Rob was sitting behind the desk when he returned to the jail. There was no sign of Smith.

'You let him go?' Nottingham asked.

'He was at the Old King's Arms till late,' Lister replied with a sigh. 'The landlord remembers him. Then he was playing hazard until daybreak. Two of those with him were merchants,' he added.

'He could have paid someone to kill.'

Rob shook his head. 'Not him. He enjoys doing the rough work himself.' He pushed a piece of paper across the desk. 'A boy brought this. Said you promised him a farthing.'

Nottingham unfolded the note.

I made him leave. The clock struck two as I closed the door. He was so drunk he could hardly walk. Does that help, sir?

Mrs W.

'Turner,' he said, handing Rob the letter.

'That leaves us with nobody.'

'For the moment.' He paced around the room. 'Didn't you mention other moneylenders?'

'There's only one more and he's been in York since Friday. I checked. He lends to businesses, anyway. All above board and very respectable. Sorry, boss.'

'Stanbridge had a notebook in his pocket. Most of the ink had run but we might find something when the pages dry. In the meantime, let's find out where he went last night. Was he married?'

'Him?' Rob laughed. 'No woman's that daft. He lodged on the Head Row, just up from Rockley Court.'

'Any servants?'

25

'A man, I think.'

'I'll start there, have a look around and see where it takes me. What about the people who owed him money? Any of them could have done it.'

'I'll talk to Turner before I let him go. He'll give me some names,' Lister said with a thin smile.

'Get some of the men on it. How many are worthwhile?'

'There are three I'd trust.'

'That's better than it used to be,' Nottingham told him with a chuckle. 'I remember when it was just you and John Sedgwick who were worth your salt.'

People greeted him as he walked through the market. A few familiar faces, some he believed he knew, others he could swear he'd never seen before. At the house by Rockley Court he introduced himself to the landlady.

'Upstairs,' she told him. 'He has the top floor. Paid until the end of the year, too.'

'Did he have many visitors?'

'One or two.' She pursed her mouth. She was a respectable woman, plainly dressed in a muslin gown with a patterned shawl draped over her shoulders. He could read her story on her drawn face. A husband who'd died and left her the house but little else, forcing her to let out rooms to make ends meet.

The wooden stairs glowed with polish, and as soon as he knocked on the door a man opened it as if he'd been standing there, waiting.

'I'm Richard Nottingham, Constable of Leeds.' The words felt unfamiliar and awkward in his mouth. 'I'm sure you've heard about your employer by now.'

'I have.' The man looked him directly in the eye. He was young, probably not even twenty yet, with thick, fair hair and a curiously grave bearing, as if he was trying to appear older.

'What's your name?'

'Joshua.'

'How long have you worked for Mr Stanbridge?'

'Three months.' His answers were brisk and crisp. Polite enough, but no respect behind the words.

'You know what he did?'

'I do.'

'I need to see his desk.'

No more than a moment's hesitation before he led the way to a large drawing room that looked out over the street. Well-furnished, with a desk pushed against the wall. Nottingham began to glance through the papers.

'Where did he go last night?'

'He had dinner at the Rose and Crown,' Joshua said. 'Mr Stanbridge left here just after six.'

'Did he return?'

'No, sir.'

There was nothing about Stanbridge's business in the desk. Nothing he could spot elsewhere as he searched through the rooms. Maybe everything was in his notebook. Or perhaps he kept the details in his head. At the door he turned to face the young man. There was something in the set of his mouth that stirred a faint memory.

27

'Was your father named Michael?'

'Yes.' Surprise filled the lad's eyes.

Michael Lawton. A thief, a fighter, a drunk, an unhappy, violent man. Someone who believed the world owed him a living and tried to claim it with his fists. He'd tumbled into the river during a flood, drunk. His body was never found.

'And you're working for a criminal. It seems you didn't learn much growing up.'

The young man straightened his back. 'I'm not my father. I do honest work.'

'I hope that's true,' the constable said, then added, 'and if you have any ideas about taking over Stanbridge's business, Mr Lawton, you'd do well to forget them.'

'Oh aye, he was here,' John Reynolds said at the Rose and Crown. 'Dinner for three in a private parlour.'

'Who were the other guests?' He sipped at a mug of small beer the landlord had filled for him.

'We were that busy, I didn't see. You'll need to ask the serving girl.' He vanished through a door for a moment and called a name. 'She'll only be a moment.' He grinned. 'Here, I'll tell you what, Mr Nottingham. We have someone you might recall bedding down in the stable.'

'Who's that?'

'Old Jem. Remember him? He showed up yesterday.'

Jem had always seemed old, with his long white beard and stringy grey hair. Nottingham had been

28

a boy when he'd first seen him and he'd looked ancient even then. Jem walked around the county, telling his stories in the marketplace for coins, finding bed and a hot meal with folk who'd take him in for a night or two. He'd stayed at the house on Marsh Lane a few times when the girls were small, rolling out his blanket near the hearth, exchanging a tale or two for warmth and a bowl of stew. But he'd heard nothing of the man in ten years or more.

'It's been so long I thought he must be dead.'

'Aye, well, he doesn't look as if he'll last another winter if he stays on the tramp,' Reynolds said with a sigh. 'I told him he was welcome to the room where Hercules used to live. Stay as long as he likes, until spring if he wants. You know how he is, though. Itchy feet.'

He'd just finished speaking when a young woman appeared, tucking her dark hair under a cap.

'I was just cleaning that pantry,' she said with an impish grin. 'What have they been doing in there? It's a tip.'

Reynolds smiled indulgently.

'My daughter,' he explained. 'You were working in the top parlour last night, Molly. Who was up there with Mr Stanbridge?'

'Let's see.' She narrowed her eyes. 'There was Mark Ferguson, getting himself drunk and spilling his food all over himself, same as ever. And Tom Warren. You know what he's like, he looked down his nose the whole time.'

'No one else came? How long were they here?' Nottingham asked.

'It was just them. They must have stayed about

three hours, I suppose.' Her face cleared. 'Yes, it must have been. Lily was just finishing as I cleared the plates and she leaves at nine.'

'Did you hear where they were going?'

She shook her head. 'I never pay attention to what customers say unless they're talking to me.' She gave a quick smile. 'Better that way. And I bat their hands away, of course.'

'Thank you.' He turned to leave and Reynolds said, 'If you want to see Jem he's probably down by the Moot Hall now.'

Four

Jem was exactly where the landlord had promised, sitting atop his pack on the Moot Hall steps and entertaining a small audience with his tale. Market days always meant a good crowd of people to entertain.

He looked as old as Methuselah now, with his long beard wispy and pale as the first snow, hardly any hair left on his head. He still wore the same old coat, although it was little more than tatters on his back. The constable waited until he'd finished the story, one or two coins dropped into his hat, then approached.

'It's been a long time, Jem.'

The man looked up. His eyes were clouded and Nottingham noticed the stout hawthorn stick at his side.

'I know you,' he said. 'I know your voice.'

'Richard Nottingham.'

The man broke into a grin, showing a mouth that was more gums than teeth.

'Aye, that's it. With the wife and two girls and the warm fire.'

'Only one girl now.' He tried to keep the sorrow out of his voice. 'My wife's gone, and one of my daughters. The other's all grown up.'

'I'm right sorry. She was a kind woman, your missus.' He moved his head around. 'It's grown, this place, hasn't it?'

'Bigger every single day. Where have you been?'

Jem struggled to his feet, reaching for the stick to steady himself.

'I've mostly been on the coast these last few years. Scarborough, Whitby, all the way up to Newcastle.' He wheezed a little as he stood. 'Grand folk up there. But I had the urge to come back here again. You were constable, weren't you,' he said as if he'd suddenly recalled it.

'I am. For the second time.' He laughed. 'It's a long story and not worth the telling.'

He remembered the way Rose and Emily were always entranced by Jem's stories, reluctant to go to their beds until they'd heard just one more, then another. Maybe the girls at Emily's school would be, too. And maybe the tales would take his daughter back to a time when they were all together.

'How would you like to make a little money?' he asked. Mark Ferguson and Tom Warren could wait a few minutes. He'd need to talk to Rob, anyway; he didn't know either of the men.

* * *

31

It had been a waste of a morning, Lister thought. First Smith, then working his way through the names of those who owed Stanbridge money. All he'd seen on their faces was relief to learn he was dead and their debts cancelled. A tradesman, a minor merchant, a mechanic with a house in Turk's Head Yard. But not a sniff of a killer about any of them.

Nothing. All they had were wisps of smoke that vanished as soon as he reached for them.

He was striding over Leeds Bridge when he caught a glance of Nottingham escorting an old man who moved slowly and leaned on a stick. What was he doing? For the love of God, they were supposed to be working, finding a murderer, not aiding the infirm. He shook his head. The boss had been good once but bringing him back was a mistake.

Nottingham waved through the window to draw Emily outside. She had a distracted air, mouth twitching in annoyance at being interrupted, but to him that barely mattered; she'd always be his girl, smart, beautiful and brave.

'What is it, Papa?' Her voice was sharp as she stared at Jem, curious, not sure why he was here.

'Don't you remember him?'

'No,' she answered with irritation and sighed. 'I'm sorry, Papa, but I'm in the middle of a lesson.' She wiped a strand of hair off her face. 'I need to get back.'

'When you were little he used to stay with us sometimes and he'd tell you stories.'

Emily looked at Jem again and Nottingham

could see the memories start to flood back into her eyes.

'Yes, of course.' She reached out and took the old man's hand. 'I'm sorry. I should have known.'

'Nowt to worry about, lass,' Jem told her. 'You weren't no more than a bairn then. You da says you run this school and you've got a man of your own now.'

She blushed, the first time Nottingham had seen that in years.

'I thought your girls might like to hear some of Jem's stories,' he said. 'You too, perhaps.'

'Oh, they'd love it.' She laughed. 'It'll give them a break from all that learning. And from me.'

The constable took a few coins from his breeches and placed them in Jem's hand.

'Thank you, sir. Now, young, lady, if tha'll just lead me in.'

Nottingham winked at Emily and walked away.

Lister was waiting at the jail, sipping on a mug of ale.

'Any luck?' Nottingham asked as he entered.

'No.' He slammed down the mug on the desk. 'Stanbridge had dinner with Mark Ferguson and Tom Warren last night. Do you know them?'

'We've met,' he said shortly and snorted. 'They're quite a pair. Ferguson likes to try and talk widows out of their savings when he's in bed with them and Warren's very clever with figures. Too clever for his own good; he almost ended up transported to the Indies last year.'

'They dined together at the Rose and Crown.'
Nottingham hesitated. 'Didn't you tell me yesterday
that two pimps have left Leeds?'

'That's right,' Lister replied. 'Why?'

'Someone said it was three, that's all.'

'No. Only two that I know of.' He cocked his
head. 'Who was the old man I saw you with?'

'Him?' He laughed. 'That's Jem. He used to
come through here quite often, years back. I
thought the girls at school might enjoy his stories.
Emily always did.'

'We need to attend to this murder,' Lister
reminded him.

'We will,' Nottingham said calmly. He heard
the rebuke in Rob's tone and ignored it. 'Which
of the pair do you want?'

'I'll take Ferguson. I'd like to wipe the smirk
off his face. He's too slippery and charming.
About time he got his comeuppance.'

'Where will I find Warren?'

'Try the Talbot, he usually has his dinner there.
You can't miss him, the man must have the
longest nose in England.'

'Tell me what you know about him.'

Lister thought for a moment. 'If I remember
rightly, he must have come here just after you
retired. Doesn't speak much. A very dour face,
thin lips, always looks like he disapproves of
everything. He's a bookkeeper. From some of
the talk, he might do a little forging, but I've
never had cause to look. I think he takes care of
the accounts for that old man you know, the one
who keeps buying land.'

'Tom Finer?'

'That's the one. And a few more who keep right on the edge of the law. We had him in court June of last year for altering some ledgers. Swore he didn't do it and managed to get off.'

Interesting that Finer's name would crop up, Nottingham thought as he strolled up Briggate, hardly sensing the clamour and call of voices that surrounded him.

The Talbot was busy with the market crowd. The floor was swept and windows sparkled to let in the light. They were only small changes but they made the place much brighter and airier than he'd ever seen it. It felt welcoming. A tall man stood behind the bar, heavy belly hidden behind a leather apron, a piece of linen thrown over his shoulder and a broad, honest smile on his face.

'Good day to you, sir.'

A serving girl brushed by, cheery-faced, in a clean gown. He recalled the way the inn had been during all the years Matthew Bell owned it. Grimy and greasy, with everyone surly and on the border of anger.

'I'm Richard Nottingham, the Constable here. You must be Mr Meadows.'

'At your service, sir.' He ducked his head slightly. 'I heard they'd asked you back to replace poor Simon Kirkstall. Terrible thing, terrible.' He waved his hand around. 'Do you think the place has improved?'

'It has. Beyond belief.' As he glanced around he couldn't see any of the old, familiar faces. But he did spot Warren in the corner, a bowl pushed away across the bench. He held a mug, head down as he read the *Mercury*. Rob had been right; the man's nose was something anyone would remember, long, thin, and straight. 'Definitely much better.'

'You'll have a drink on me, I hope, sir,' Meadows continued, as he filled a mug from the barrel. 'I'm trying to run a good house here. It's building slow but steady.'

'Thank you. What made you come to Leeds?'

'Opportunity. Pure and simple.' His smile was open and infectious. He looked to be a little past thirty, a full head of curly hair and warm eyes. 'I had a place up in Settle, but there's only so much a man can do there.' He leaned forward conspiratorially. 'It's too small, you see. I have ambitions.'

'And what might they be, Mr Meadows?'

'Call me Harry, everyone does. I want to own the best inn in England. So I came down here with my wife and daughter and two sons. Brought my staff with me.' He laughed.

'And you think this place could be it?' Nottingham asked doubtfully. He knew the reputation the Talbot had enjoyed for far too many years.

Meadows laughed. 'A new broom, sir. It's not easy, but in time, people will flock here. You mark my words.' He turned to serve another customer and the constable wandered away. Harry Meadows was jovial, everything a land-lord should be, and he'd certainly done this place the power of good. But with the heavy weight of the past it carried, he'd need plenty of luck.

Warren scarcely raised his head as Nottingham sat on the other side of the bench. His long fingers were heavily stained with ink and his shoulders were stooped; too long spent bent over a desk.

'I believe you're a bookkeeper.'

That made the man pay attention. He looked up, eyes widening a little but showing nothing.

'What if I am?' He had a deep bass voice that seemed to rise from somewhere deep in his chest. 'What does it matter to you?'

'You ate with Robert Stanbridge last night.'

Warren put down the newspaper and leaned back against the wall.

'And if I did?'

'I'm the Constable of Leeds. I'm looking into his murder.'

The word didn't bring a tremor to the man's face.

'It's a sad business. But it's nothing to do with me.'

'Where did you go after you left the Rose and Crown?'

'Home,' Warren replied. 'On my own.'

He was offering nothing but miserly answers, as if every word cost him money.

'And where might that be?'

'I have a room on Water Lane.'

'What about Mr Stanbridge? Where did he and Mr Ferguson go?'

'I've no idea.'

'He didn't talk about his plans?'

'Not to me. Maybe to Mr Ferguson.'

'Was there anywhere he went regularly at night?'

'I wouldn't know, Mr . . .'

'Nottingham.'

'I dined with the man occasionally. That's all. I know nothing about the rest of his life. Or his death,' he added pointedly.

'Where do you have your office?'

'Above Ogle's bookshop on Kirkgate.' Warren allowed himself a thin smile. 'Quite close to your jail.'

'I believe Tom Finer is one of your clients.'

'That would be for him to say.'

'What about Mark Ferguson? How well do you know him?'

'I don't,' the man answered. 'He was one of Stanbridge's friends.'

Nottingham drained the mug and stood. 'Then I thank you for the information.' He left with a wave for Meadows.

He had no doubt Warren was a bookkeeper of sorts, maybe even a good one. But there were other things that he was keeping hidden; he could feel it. He was someone to watch and see again. But next time it would be where he had his office.

Ferguson sat uncomfortably on the hard chair. He was fashionably dressed, fastidious in his gleaming white hose, breeches as tight as decency allowed, and the stock tied just so at his neck. But his good clothes looked too elegant and out of place in the dirt of the jail. Lister watched him quietly, letting the man stew and sweat a little before he began with his questions.

A snore came from one of the cells, a weaver who'd celebrated too much after the cloth market, dead drunk and stung for half his money by a whore. They knew her name; she'd be behind bars soon enough.

Lister knew he'd had good teachers in this job. John Sedgwick, so natural in his post as deputy until he was killed. He could charm anyone and have them opening up before they even realized it. And the boss, back when he was sharp. His questions circled slowly around the heart of the matter until the time was right to pounce.

But Rob could never be like them. He didn't have that skill. He could listen but he never quite heard the way they had. Instead, he'd developed his own method. Not as subtle, not as flowing. Not always as successful. But it was what he had.

He paced around behind Ferguson, watching as the man kept shifting on the chair. Finally he leaned forward until his mouth was close to the man's ear and said, 'Tell me about Robert Stanbridge.'

Ferguson seemed relieved to talk and break the awkward, pressing silence. The story spilled out in a torrent. He liked women and they liked him. Widows in particular; they were grateful for some attention and happy to lavish him with gifts. He'd come to know Stanbridge not long after a woman near York had been very generous to him. The man had suggested investing a little money with him to use in his business, and he promised a good return.

'Did you receive it?'

39

'At first,' Ferguson replied, craning his head to try and see Lister. 'But lately it's been less and less. He said that business was in a bad patch, that's all.'

'But you still had dinner with him last night.'

'We dined together once a month. He invited someone else last night. I didn't know him. Never met him before. A bookkeeper,' he added with distaste.

'Where did you go afterwards?'

'I went to my rooms.' He tried to turn his head again, but Lister moved to the other side.

'What about the others?'

'I don't know.'

'Did Stanbridge say anything about his plans?'

'No. I was shocked when I heard about him this morning.'

'If you weren't getting a return on your investment, you had good reason to want him dead.'

'What?' He began to rise. 'No!'

'Sit down, Mr Ferguson,' Lister ordered quietly, waiting as the man settled back on the chair. 'Right now you're the best person I have for this murder. You said it yourself, you had a reason.'

'But—' the man began.

Lister rode over his words. 'Cutting a man's throat and dropping him in the river is easy enough to do. Even for someone like you.'

'I was with a lady last night,' Ferguson said reluctantly.

'Who?'

'Mrs Hardisty. Her coach brought her at ten and collected her at two.'

He gave her up readily enough, Rob thought. Not an ounce of gallantry when it came to saving his neck.

'And what did you do together?'

'We . . . sported.' He blushed a little.

'Will the lady confirm all this if I ask her?'

'You can't.'

'I can. This is murder, Mr Ferguson. Do you really believe I'm going to take your word for it? Where does she live? Or should I start shouting her name around town until I find her?'

The man slumped a little, defeated. 'She lives at Town End. Her husband died last year.'

Rob knew her now. The widow of Hardisty the merchant. About thirty, wealthy, attended all the balls and concerts. Every eligible man in Leeds paid court to her. Why in God's name would she choose someone like Ferguson?

He had a fair build, and his black hair and sallow skin gave him the look of a changeling. Maybe that appealed to her. But he had no money of his own, very little of anything to attract women of substance. His prowess must lie elsewhere.

'I'll ask her,' Lister warned. 'And if she says she was never with you, I'll have you in the cells. Do you understand?'

The man was innocent; he was convinced of that by the time he watched Ferguson leave. He could happily strip widows of their fortunes but he'd never be able to kill a man. There wasn't enough will about him. Still, he'd send Mrs Hardisty a note and ask her discreetly. At least it would mark the end of that association, he thought with satisfaction.

As they walked home in the evening gloom they were no further along in the case. A breeze shimmered the leaves and a few floated down into the water of Timble Beck, carried along to the river.

Nottingham felt weary to his bones. He hadn't missed all those times of being woken in the middle of the night and then working all day. But he felt something beginning to stir in his core. A sense of returning, of desire.

'How did the girls like Jem?' he asked Emily as they ate.

'It was the only thing they could talk about for the rest of the day.' Her face glowed in the light from the hearth. 'I'd forgotten half the stories he told them. It was a wonderful idea, Papa.'

'I wish I'd known,' Lucy said as she carried through a loaf of bread from the kitchen. 'Most of the tellers I've heard couldn't hold a tale in a sack.'

'He's coming back next week,' Emily told her. 'You can sit with us.'

'Is he really going to stay in Leeds?' Nottingham asked in surprise. He knew the offer was there, but Jem had always moved on after a few days.

'All winter, he says. He claims he's too old for the snow on the roads now.'

'Then you'll have plenty of chances to hear him,' Nottingham told Lucy.

* * *

Full, he sat by the fire for a few minutes. Emily was busy correcting exercises and preparing lessons. In the kitchen, Lucy was scouring the pots. Rob was reading the *Mercury*.

He felt his eyes beginning to close. Time to sleep, he told himself. It had been a long day. But every day would be like this until the job ended and a new constable was appointed. Before he could leave the room, Lister coughed and said, 'I meant to tell you earlier. One of the men said this afternoon that Brandon the pimp hasn't been seen for two days.' He raised his eyebrows. 'That's three of them. It looks as if the information you had was right. Your man couldn't have had anything to do with it, could he?'

The constable shook his head. In the old days it wouldn't have been beyond Finer; he'd revelled in deceit and destruction. But not now; he'd become a respectable businessman.

Five

'We need to know where Stanbridge went after he left the Rose and Crown,' Nottingham said. It was still full dark, frost sharp in the air, as they marched across Timble Bridge and into Leeds. The cocks had barely crowed and the dawn chorus was a cacophony of song from the branches. He dug his hands deeper into his greatcoat pockets to keep them warm.

'I told the night men to go around asking,' Lister answered. 'They might have something for us.'

'See if you can follow his path.'

'Yes, boss.'

Exhausted as he was, the constable had lain awake long into the night, thinking and trying to make sense of the death. He felt like he was treading over ice, not sure whether it would hold his weight, scared of moving the wrong way.

Smoke was starting to rise from the chimneys along Kirkgate as servants set the morning fires. The town was beginning to come alive, breathing in the day. He unlocked the jail and stirred the coals left to bank on the fire, releasing the warmth.

The night man's report lay on the desk. He glanced through it, then passed it to Lister. Two drunks in the cells, another man brought in for fighting.

They'd found two places where Stanbridge had been seen: at the Pack Horse on Briggate, then an inn just south of the river where he'd played cards in a back parlour until midnight.

'He was probably killed on his way home,' Lister suggested. 'Knifed and then thrown off the bridge. That would be easy enough to do.'

'Very likely.' There'd been hardly any money on the corpse. If he'd won, someone could have followed and robbed him. 'I'll go over there. You take the Pack Horse.' He didn't need to say more; Rob knew what to do.

* * *

Nottingham walked past the inn. The door was closed, shutters up in the windows. But there was somewhere else he wanted to go first. Early still, but the streets were already bustling, men and carts on the move, women and servants with their baskets gossiping together as they walked off for their errands.

He stopped at a gleaming door on a small street and knocked three times. It was a full half minute before he heard footsteps inside, then someone drew back the bolt. He stared at a black face that slowly creased into a smile. Older now, the curls of hair turning white. But they were all ageing, uncomfortable with the pains of living and starting to make their peace with death.

'Mr Nottingham. I heard you were back. You look well.'

'No need to lie, Henry. I look like someone who'd be better off put out to pasture and we both know it. Is he up?'

'Just finishing his breakfast. Come on, I'll tell him you're here. He'll be right pleased.'

Henry had been Joe Buck's servant for years, his molly boy, his friend, his bodyguard. He could never think of one without the other. The man opened a door and stood to one side with a wink.

Buck was sumptuously dressed. An impeccably cut coat, stock as dazzling as snow, and a long waistcoat of turquoise silk embroidered with some elaborate design. But he'd always been vain with his clothes, spending money on them like it was water. He'd never been short of brass, though; for many years he'd been one of the biggest, subtlest fences in Leeds, always two steps ahead of justice. Crook that he was, with his easy, merry laugh, it was impossible not to like the man.

'Well, well, well.' He put down a piece of bread and wiped his hands on a linen napkin. 'Turning up like a bad penny. I told Henry it wouldn't be long before we saw you.' He stood and gestured to a pair of chairs in front of a roaring fire. 'Settling back into the job yet, Mr Nottingham?'

'It would be easier if I wasn't starting with a murder.' From nowhere, Henry appeared with a mug of ale for him.

'A certain moneylender, from what I hear.' Buck lit a clay pipe from a taper and blew a thin stream of smoke.

'I don't suppose you were out playing cards the night before last?' He knew Buck's passion for gaming.

'Perhaps I was.' He gave a slow smile. 'A few of us play every week. It's more a way to pass a dreary Monday night than anything. The stakes are never especially high. The gentleman we're talking about has joined us a few times. A confident sort, very cocky.' He sighed. 'It's a curious thing. Somehow he always managed to lose. You'd think he was old enough to know better after several lessons. We were never going to let him win. Of course,' he added with a wink, 'a little bird might have seen him as a mark and tipped him off there was a game to be had. It's his own fault if he lacks skill at cards. And he's a fool if he keeps coming back in hope.'

'How much did he lose?'

'Everything he'd brought. We cleaned him out, poor soul, and sent him on his way at midnight.'

'How was he when he left?'

'Downcast. I don't know what he was like in business, but he was reckless at the table.'

'Was he drunk?'

Buck shook his head. 'No. It's not that sort of evening.'

'Could someone from the place have followed him? Anyone there you didn't know, Joe?'

'Mr Nottingham, there are more and more people around Leeds that I don't know,' he answered with a chuckle. 'I'm not even sure I recognize the town any more. But no, there was nothing I saw. We all went home ourselves soon after.'

'I'll go to the inn and see if they can tell anything else.'

'Take Henry with you. The people there can have poor memories. They know him, they'll talk more freely, if you get my meaning.'

'I do.' He nodded. 'And thank you. Is business good?'

'Business is business.' He drew on the pipe. 'That's changing, too. About time to let it go, I think.'

'You were saying that long before I retired,' Nottingham reminded him.

'Was I?' The ready grin returned. 'Then perhaps I'll do it one of these days.'

The inn must have been a house once. A crudely painted sign over the door showed an attempt at a bishop's hat and the words *The Mitre*. Nottingham hammered on the door, waiting until a man appeared with a cudgel in his hand and a weary, angry look on his face. Before he could say a word, Henry stood tall and said, 'Mr Buck would like you to help this gentleman, Billy. He's the constable.'

Grudgingly, the landlord let them in. He answered gruffly, still trying to pull himself awake. Yes, Stanbridge had been there three or four times. Always on a Monday. He played cards with the other gentlemen in the back room. Left somewhere near midnight.

'Did anyone else follow him out?' Nottingham asked. 'Were there any strangers in here?'

The man's laugh was like an ugly bark.

'It's hard enough to get folk in here when they've just been paid. On a Monday, when they've hardly got a farthing to their names? You must be joking. No. Nobody I didn't know.'

One more road that led nowhere, the constable thought as he walked back into town. He stopped on the bridge. Barges and boats were loading cloth from the warehouses that lined the river-bank. More buildings than ever now, as the wool trade kept growing and the men at the top grew richer and richer.

Could Stanbridge have been killed right here and bundled over the parapet into the water? It would have been so simple, exactly as Rob said: a cut and a push, then the quiet splash as he entered the river in the darkness. Deep in the night, would anyone have even noticed? No lights burned here. It seemed as likely an explanation as they were ever likely to find.

At ten in the morning the White Swan was still quiet, a few older men gathered in a corner, talking and eking out their ale.

'A serving girl at the Pack Horse remembered Stanbridge,' Lister said. 'She said he tipped her well. But she didn't notice him leave. The landlord never even saw him. He must have gone over the river after that.'

'Then we're back to the beginning.' He watched Nottingham frown as he toyed with his bread and cheese.

'We've traced him to midnight. That's something.'

'It doesn't bring us closer to the killer, does it?'

'I know,' Lister agreed quietly. 'Just remember, boss, Stanbridge is no loss.'

But he understood the constable's frustration. He needed to prove himself. In part to the mayor and the corporation, but above all to Richard Nottingham, to show he was the man he used to be, that he was still master of the job.

'I'm sure he's not, but we still have to find whoever killed him.' The constable's face softened. 'How would you do it?'

'The same way you have,' Rob admitted after a moment, and he was pleased to see the man give a brief grin. 'We've followed his trail, we know where he went. We've talked to his main competitor and the ones we know who owe him money.'

'How many more moneylenders are there?' Nottingham asked.

'Apart from Toby Smith? Just that one who was away from town. And a couple of very small fish on top of that.'

'Even small fish can put up a fight.'

'Not these two. I've talked to them. I'd swear they had nothing to do with it.' He finished the last of his meat and potato pie and asked the question that had been nagging at him. 'Who was it who told you about that third missing pimp?'

'Someone I've known a long time.'

'Do you trust him?'

Nottingham's chuckle surprised him. 'Not as far as I can throw him. But I told you: he wouldn't be responsible for anything like that.'

'It worries me when people know things before we do.'

'It's always been that way.' The constable shrugged. 'If we're lucky, they tell us. Just be grateful when they do. I learned long ago that you can't know everything.'

'We can try,' Lister said.

'For whatever it's worth,' the constable agreed with a shrug. 'But it was impossible twenty years ago, and the place was smaller then.' He looked around. 'What chance do we have now? I'm happy if any secrets manage to slip out at all. Why, do you think we should be concerned about these disappearances?'

Lister shook his head. 'I'd be glad if they all vanished. It would make our lives easier.' Fewer cuttings, he thought, and fewer beatings.

'We're always going to have pimps to deal

with. Anyway, what about Stanbridge? Any other ideas?'

'Just ask people we know.' It felt strange, wrong, to be giving him advice. But Nottingham listened and nodded. 'Stanbridge mostly lent to people who own small shops and are having a bad time,' Rob continued. 'You know how it works – the interest keeps mounting so they can never repay it all.' He leaned forward, elbows on the bench. 'And they have to keep going to moneylenders because there's nowhere else to turn.'

The constable rubbed his chin. 'Do you remember Amos Worthy?'

'Yes,' Lister answered, surprised by the question. He'd never known Worthy; he died not long after Rob became a constable's man. But there were enough stories about him and the boss and some strange connection that bound them. He knew that Worthy had left money to Emily, enough to start her school and keep it going. Some said that was his revenge on Nottingham, his laughter from beyond the grave. But they'd never talked about it, leaving it all buried in the past.

'He lent money, too. But his went to the merchants and the aldermen. He let them use his whores, as well. It gave him a hold over them. Stanbridge was much smaller than that.'

'Worthy caused plenty of misery, didn't he?' Rob said

'Too much,' Nottingham agreed. 'We don't want a return to those days.'

Six

'Papa?'

He looked up, taking his gaze from the flames. 'What?'

'You were miles away,' Emily told him. She was sitting at the table, where she seemed to spend every evening, taking care of work for her school. A candle lit her face and for a moment she looked exactly the way Mary had when she was young.

He saw it in her sometimes, some trick of the light, the way she held her head, and it always made him catch his breath, like a memory he couldn't quite touch.

'Sorry. I was thinking about this killing,' he said.

'Rob seems certain the two of you will catch the murderer.'

'Let's hope he's right.' After a few hours talking to shop owners he wasn't so confident. One or two had been customers of Stanbridge, he could tell it in the way they talked and shuffled from foot to foot, but none would admit it. Nowhere, yet again. 'Where is he, anyway? It's not like him to miss a meal.'

'He's meeting some of his friends at the Turk's Head.' She giggled and for a moment she was a girl again. 'You'd better expect him to have a sore head in the morning.'

Lucy came from the kitchen, a broom in her

52

hand, and started to sweep up invisible crumbs. This house was her kingdom and she was determined to keep it spotless; Nottingham winked at his daughter.

'I saw the coalman's lad when I was on my way home, Lucy. He said he'd like to come calling for you.'

She stopped and glared. 'I hope you told him not to waste his breath, then. What do I want with someone all covered in dust and muck?' Her arms stopped moving and she stared at him. 'You're having me on, aren't you?'

'Maybe a little.' There were plenty of young men sweet on her, he'd seen them flirting at the market. But she was wedded to this place.

'You're lucky I don't take this besom to you,' she warned. 'Making fun of a poor lass like that.' But she was grinning and shaking her head. 'I'll tell you something. This job is doing you a power of good. You've already got your sense of fun back. I thought it had done a flit.' She swept a little more. 'Anyway, if he was sweet on me, he should have said something when he brought our coal from Middleton.'

'Too shy.' They both laughed.

'Honestly, you two,' Emily said. 'I'm trying to work.'

Lucy put a finger to her lips and finished the floor in silence.

'I'm away to my bed,' Nottingham said.

'Goodnight, Papa.' Emily stood and kissed the top of his head.

* * *

53

'Did you enjoy yourself?' Nottingham asked. As he spoke, his breath clouded the air. Frost showed white in the late moonlight and he could feel the cold on his cheeks. Off in a fallow field he could make out the faint shape of a woodpile. Each day it grew until it would be a bonfire for Gunpowder Treason Night. Another year slipping away too quickly.

Rob grimaced. 'My head feels like a horse galloped through it.' He groaned and yawned. 'But it was worth it. We had a good night.'

Crandall, in charge of the night men, was pacing up and down in the jail as they arrived. Kirkstall had appointed him, some relative of his wife, a man with a permanently worried, confused expression and a periwig that refused to sit properly on his head.

'I was about to send someone for you,' he said.

'Why?' Nottingham asked. 'Has something happened?'

'They pulled a body from the water just past Fearn's Island. One of the men recognized it. He says it's Toby Smith. I thought you'd want to know, what with . . .' He let the words tail away, as if he was unsure how to finish the sentence.

'Good work.' The constable looked at Rob. His face was alert, the colour back in his cheeks, lips pursed. 'Has anyone told the coroner?'

'He's already on his way.'

They strode out side by side along the riverbank. Past the warehouses and along the track that led to the fulling mill with its stench of stale piss and to Fearn's Island. Not an island at all, it jutted into the river close to the old dam.

'What do you think?' Nottingham asked.

'Two moneylenders dead in a few days?' He shook his head. 'Smith wasn't the type to get drunk and fall into the water. Anyway, he lived at the other end of Leeds, out past Town End.'

Workers from the mill were standing in the cold and watching a group gathered around the body on the shore. Hoggart the coroner had arrived, and was giving an order to two of the constable's men to turn the corpse.

The evidence was right there: a jagged cut across the man's throat. Not as neat as Stanbridge's wound, two awkward slashes this time, but Smith was just as dead. The silt and slime of the river clung to his clothes and his hair.

'Another one,' the coroner said wearily as he rose to his feet. 'It looks as if you have your work cut out for you, Mr Nottingham.'

'Where was he found?' the constable asked.

'Right there, sir.' One of the men pointed. 'His coat had snagged on one of the posts by that jetty. If it hadn't, he'd be halfway to Hull by now.' He gave a toothless smirk at his own joke. 'One of them reporting for work at the mill noticed him.'

Rob was squatting, his hands going through the dead man's pockets and emptying everything on to the dirt. A sodden notebook, coins, linen handkerchief. The water had taken Smith's shoes and muddied his hose and breeches. They'd find nothing to help them here.

'Take him to the jail,' the constable ordered.

* * *

55

'Exactly the same way as Stanbridge,' Lister said as they walked back towards the town.

'Go and search his rooms,' Nottingham ordered. 'And let's hope we have more luck this time. The usual – you know what to do.'

'Yes, boss. Stanbridge was no loss but this one's death is a blessing.'

'You really suspected him of murder?'

'Two of them,' Rob said. He turned his head and spat. 'He terrified people. Stanbridge was a lapdog next to him.'

For a moment Nottingham didn't reply, considering once again the idea Tom Finer had planted in his mind.

'Two moneylenders dead, three pimps vanished, all close together. The numbers keep rising.'

Lister shook his head. 'You're the only one who's suggested a connection. The moneylenders, yes. But the rest doesn't make any sense.'

Nottingham was silent for a moment. 'Those pimps, did they have many girls?'

'Not really, perhaps two each. I think the last of them only had one. Why?'

'What were the pimps' names?'

'Heaton and Goldsmith were the first two. Brandon's the most recent.'

'What happened to their girls?'

'I've no idea, I told you. Gone, or found someone else to look after them. Does it matter?' There was an edge to his voice. 'We've got two murders to think about.'

It was full, grey light, a day of heavy clouds, the time just after dawn when the cold nipped hardest. Smoke was rising from chimneys all across Leeds, curling up into the sky as the town stirred. Men on their way to work gave them cautious glances as they passed.

At the jail, Nottingham said, 'You go on and start looking into Smith. I doubt his body has much to tell us.'

'Where are you going, boss?'

'To see a man,' he answered with a smile.

Rob watched the constable walk away, then poured himself a glass of ale, downing it in a single gulp. He was thirsty and his head hurt whenever he moved it. His own fault, but that didn't matter; they'd had a grand time, going from inn to inn, merrier in each one.

He sighed, started to pour another mug and stopped. One was ample. He needed his wits clear. He'd relished seeing Toby Smith dead. It was the best thing that could have happened to the man. He'd preyed on too many.

And now the boss had wandered off somewhere and left him to do the work. He was right about one thing, though: they wouldn't learn anything from Smith's body. Perhaps his house would reveal some secrets.

It was a small cottage about a quarter of a mile along the Newcastle road. Carts and carriages trundled slowly past him as he walked, an endless procession of goods and people in and out of Leeds, but he barely noticed them.

The boss was better than Simon Kirkstall had ever been, but Rob was starting to worry about him. This strange idea about a connection

57

between the disappearance of the pimps and the murder of the moneylenders. Going off on his errands with barely a word. Long silences when he seemed to vanish into that curious world that had occupied him for most of the last two years. It wasn't right. It wasn't normal.

And Rob knew he couldn't say anything to Emily about it. He couldn't leave her caught between him and her father. She'd been so happy to see him as constable again, with a purpose once more. And Lucy would take Richard's part every time; there wasn't a grain of sense in telling her about his reservations.

All he could do was keep it inside and do his job.

The door was locked but that barely hindered him; John Sedgwick had schooled him well when he started out as a constable's man. Inside, the house had the clean scent of beeswax polish. He pulled the shutters wide.

Everything was tidy, the table cleared, wood shining. There was little furniture, a chair, a desk, that was all. No sense of comfort or home. The bedroom was clean, clothes hanging from pegs on the wall, two jackets, breeches, hose rolled into a ball on the table by a looking glass. In the kitchen the pots were all in their places.

It was a man's house, bare and purposeful. Probably the only woman ever allowed in here was the one who cleaned and cooked for him.

He broke the lock on the desk and began sorting through the papers. Smith had been careless. There was plenty about his business: notes, a thick ledger detailing payments made and punishments meted out to who couldn't stump up money when he came calling. He leafed back through the pages, checking names until he found the two he was seeking. *Account closed!* was marked by each. He'd been right. Smith had been a killer himself.

He'd just started to glance through the letters when the door opened wide and a woman marched in. She had an old bonnet on her head, a thick shawl over a plain gown and a clean apron. Small, almost as round as she was tall, her chins wobbled as she glowered at him.

'What do you think you're doing here?'

He stood, towering over her.

'I'm Robert Lister, the deputy constable.'

'Happen you are.' She put her hands defiantly on her hips. 'But this place belongs to Mr Smith.'

'Not any more,' he told her. 'We pulled him out of the river this morning.'

Rob watched the colour drain from her face, mouth open as she gulped at the air.

'He's dead?'

'He is.' He didn't have time to waste on sympathy; the man deserved to be in hell. 'Do you know where he went last night?'

'No.' She sat, one hand clutching the table as if it could steady her. 'I never saw him after dinner time and he told me not to leave a meal for him.'

He'd need to look elsewhere for that. No matter; he'd pulled enough gold from the desk.

'You might as well go home,' he said. 'There's no job for you here any more.'

She nodded slowly and after a minute composed herself enough to stand. At the door she turned.

'I know what he did and it weren't right. But he was allus fair to me. Paid me decent.' With that, she was gone. It was an odd obituary, he thought. Half praise, half damnation.

At least his head had stopped hammering.

Leeds might be changing, but some things would always remain the same, Nottingham thought. Day or night there would be whores on Briggate touting for business. They stood at the dark little ginnels that led through from the street to the yards where people lived crammed together. A handy place for business, deep in the shadows.

Only two or three were out so early, looking weary and footsore. They smiled hopefully at every man who passed, as if his coins could bring salvation.

Annie was the first, nestled away from the wind that blew out of the north. She looked at him suspiciously as he took off his bicorn hat.

'I'm looking for any girl that worked for Heaton, Goldsmith or Brandon.'

'Why?' Her hand moved to her pocket. If she had any sense, she'd carry a knife there. He held up his hands.

'They've disappeared. I'm the constable here. I'm trying to find out what happened. Don't worry, I don't want to cause you any trouble.'

He took a ha'penny from his breeches and held it out to her. Annie snatched at it then stepped back a pace. He didn't move.

'There was a lass,' she said. 'Barbara. Not seen

her in a week nor more. She was with Heaton. I heard he'd gone.'

'Do you know where she went?'

She shook her head, dark, untidy ringlets waving.

'Please,' he said to her. 'If you hear anything, I need to know.'

In a sudden movement she brushed by him, out to Briggate. But as she passed, she whispered, 'Find Charlotte.'

Then she was gone, hurrying down the street, not looking back. Whatever she was afraid of, he didn't want to make it worse. He lingered for a moment, listening to the noise of the carts and the voices, then moved on.

Neither of the other whores knew the pimps. One thought she'd heard of a Charlotte, but she wasn't certain. He gave them each a farthing for their time and walked back to the jail. He'd try later, when more were around.

Rob sat at the desk, a heavy ledger open in front of him. He was scribbling notes as he went through the pages.

'From Smith's house?' Nottingham asked.

'All his business dealings,' Lister replied with satisfaction. 'The murderer's name might be in here.'

'Let's hope so.' He washed away the dirt of the town with a swig of ale. 'Any important clients?'

'None that I've found. Smith preferred people he could intimidate.'

'Give me some of the names. I'll talk to them.'

Lister tore off part of the sheet. 'They're just ordinary folk,' he said.

Nottingham read through the list; he knew

perhaps half of them. Working men, a few who were older. Honest people. But anyone could kill if they were desperate enough.

'See if that book shows any who were far behind on their payments. Start by questioning them.'

'Yes, boss.' Rob grinned; that had been his plan, anyway.

The day brought no joy. Lister had three who were late with what they owed to Smith. One of them turned away to hide his black eye and the bruises on his face. Another wore a broken little finger strapped up, and the third hobbled carefully around. They were all thankful to hear the news. One of them cried for joy. But none of them was a killer; their faces made that plain. They were only cowed, frightened men.

He made the rounds of his informers, from the Head Row over to Holbeck, but none of them could help. Whoever murdered Stanbridge and Smith was holding his tongue. It was possible that someone was looking to take over the money-lending business in Leeds. But there was no whisper of it. Nobody was mentioning any names. That was odd; usually gossip and rumour flowed like a river.

It wasn't Thompson, the third moneylender, he felt certain of that; the man was still in York, and he was a businessman, everything spelled out in contracts, above board and legal.

He returned to the jail as the light was beginning to fade. Already there was a nip of frost, his breath clouding in the air.

The boss was talking to Mr Shipley, the prim little draper with a shop near the top of Briggate. The man's face was red with outrage.

Nottingham looked at Rob and gave a small nod.

'The girl stepped in front of me and asked if I could help her,' Shipley said. 'She was crying, so of course I stopped. As soon as I was close enough, she pushed me. While I was off balance, the boy came out of nowhere and cut my purse strings. Then they were running off before I knew what had happened.'

'How much money was in the purse?' the constable asked.

'Very nearly a guinea,' Shipley replied.

'What did they look like?'

'She had long fair hair. Very pretty. A shawl over her shoulders. Threadbare, and an old dress that was too big for her. Thin as you like. I didn't really catch a glimpse of the boy. I think he was about the same size as her. Dark hair, I do remember that.'

'How old would you say they were?'

'I don't know. Thirteen or so,' the man answered. 'Twelve, perhaps.'

'We'll look for them,' Nottingham promised.

'Will I get my money back?'

'We'll do our best, sir.' He put down the quill and stared at Shipley until he left.

'We had another just like that last week,' Rob said as he settled into the empty chair and poured some ale. 'The description was more or less the same, worked the same way. Happened down by Holy Trinity Church.'

'This was on Vicar Lane.'

63

Lister shrugged. 'I've had the men looking, but . . .' It was a needle buried deep in a haystack.

'I know. Keep them on it.' He shook his head. 'Fair hair and dark hair. A girl and a boy. It's nothing to go on. A guinea could keep them for a long time.'

Feral children, trying to live by their wits. Rob saw plenty of them every day. They haunted the market, snatching at anything left over at the end of the day. Most of them died after a few weeks. He'd been called out to look at their bodies often enough, in old buildings, in the woods, trying to find shelter on the tenter fields down by the river, and he'd sent them off to be buried with no name. Abandoned, run away, sold into labour and escaped; the same stories came over and over. Lucy, their servant, had been one until the boss rescued her.

The tale was that Nottingham had been one himself. His father was a merchant who threw his wife and son from the house after he discovered her affair. She'd become a prostitute and he'd worked, stolen, done whatever they needed. She died when he was twelve and he'd continued his half-life until old Arkwright had made a constable's man of him.

'Did you find any suspects from that list?' he asked.

'Not one,' Nottingham replied. 'Plenty of folk happy to hear he's dead, though. What about you?'

'The same.'

'Are you positive this other moneylender isn't involved?' the constable asked.

Lister shook his head in irritation. 'I told you,

he keeps it all legal. Lends to merchants and businesses, everything in writing. He wouldn't be stupid enough to risk that.'

'Then there's something here we don't understand.'

'We need to keep our ears open for any new moneylender in town. I've put the word out.'

The constable gave a dark smile. 'It won't be today or tomorrow. But soon enough. And we'll come down hard on him.' He glanced out of the window. Candles were burning in the windows on the other side of Kirkgate. 'Come on, let's go home.'

'A fair girl and a dark-headed boy aged twelve or thirteen?' Emily pursed her lips and narrowed her eyes. Across the table, Nottingham watched her. She was already working when they arrived, scouring through her books to find something, then smiling in triumph when she discovered it.

He was proud of all his daughter had achieved with the school. Some had opposed it at the beginning but she'd never given in. Quietly, conscientiously, she'd kept going. The families of the poor girls she taught paid what they could; usually nothing. Tom Williamson and his wife had persuaded a few of the merchants to donate money to help. Between that and her legacy, it all limped along. All sorts appeared at her door, young and older, all eager to learn. She might have seen the pair.

'No,' she answered finally, running a piece of bread around her plate to sop up the last of the gravy. 'They're too old for school.'

'If we catch them a judge will hang them,' Rob said. He picked up his mug and drank. 'Transportation to the Americas if they're very lucky.'

Nottingham stayed silent. He knew both sides. Years before, he'd cut the occasional purse when he was desperate. When survival became a crime, the laws were wrong. He'd learned that the hard way. And he'd been lucky never to be caught.

Seven

'Do you know a prostitute called Charlotte?' Nottingham asked.

Lister gave him a sharp look. Cold weather had moved in overnight, leaving the grass rimed with frost, the leaves snapping under their boots as they walked into Leeds.

'No,' he answered. 'Should I?'

'No reason. Maybe it doesn't matter.'

Nottingham had gone out again in the late evening, wandering quietly up and down Briggate and talking to the whores. One or two of the older women remembered him, but most were younger faces that were ageing quickly and growing hard. If he wasn't a customer they didn't have the time for him; they could be earning money. A few were happy to be called Charlotte if that was what he wanted. He smiled and walked on.

Finally he found Four-Finger Jane. Once she'd been the queen of Briggate, spending her evenings at the top of the street, up by the market cross where trade was brisk. But that had been years before. Now she had a spot down by the river, scratching for business. She always wore a glove to hide the missing finger a pimp had cut off in anger. The rumour was she'd killed him in revenge. No body was ever recovered. She'd never been charged.

'Hello, Jane.' He stood close to her. Across the road, the door opened at the tavern and in the brief wedge of light spilled out he could see the ravages of the French pox on her face.

'I heard you were back, Mr Nottingham.' She smiled, showing a mouth with half the teeth missing.

'I'm looking for someone. A girl named Charlotte.'

'Never for poor Jane, though.'

He took a coin from his breeches and placed it in her hand, watching as it vanished into the pocket of her dress.

'I'll take it but you're wasting your money,' she said. 'I've seen more Charlottes and Emilys and Emmas than I can count over the years.'

'I'm interested in the last few weeks.'

She shook her head. 'They come and go so quickly, they might as well not bother with names. And none of them talk to me the way they once did.'

'Someone told me to look for Charlotte.'

'I can ask, if you like, but I don't know any.' She began to cough; it lasted fully half a minute before she could speak again. 'Winter again. It always comes around too soon. Why do you want her, anyway?'

'I'm looking into those pimps that have vanished. Three of them.'

'If there's a God they'll all be rotting in hell.' There was fire behind her voice.

'Do you know anything about that?'

'No. I mind my own business. They let me be, I'm not going to make them money.'

'If you hear anything . . . especially about Charlotte . . .'

'I'll send word,' she promised.

'Where do we look today, boss?' Lister asked.

'Let's start turning over rocks and see what's underneath. I want you to talk to that other moneylender. I know—' he raised a hand to stop the protest '—he's a proper businessman. But they have their secrets, too. And if someone's trying to force their way in, they'll have their eye on him, too. When is he due back from York?'

'He should have returned last night.'

'Then go and see him this morning.' Nottingham began to look through the papers on the desk, tearing away the wax seal of a note. 'It looks as if I'm going to have to spend some time with the mayor.'

'Two killings, Richard. Two.' Brooke didn't raise his voice. He didn't need to. Instead he drew quietly on the clay pipe. 'It's not the best way to start, is it?'

Beyond the window the day was grey, with

68

thick, heavy clouds and a bleak, sober light. A fire burned in the grate and he was grateful for the warmth.

'We've been looking into it since the first body was pulled from the river,' Nottingham answered.

'Any idea who's behind it?' The mayor's sharp eyes were watching him.

'Not yet.' He wasn't going to dissemble. 'If you want my guess, someone is looking to take over that business. He'll show his hand soon enough and then we'll have him.'

'Soon isn't now,' Brooke reminded him quietly. 'Some of the members of the Corporation have been muttering.'

Already? he thought. So much for having their confidence. 'They always will.'

'I fought hard to convince them to have you back.'

'You're the one who said they all wanted me,' he reminded Brooke.

'They did – after I persuaded them. And you really were the best we've had. But they're after results. They want to know there's law here.' His gaze hardened. 'So do I.'

'You'll have it.' Inside, he could feel the anger beginning to bubble. 'Once we have someone to arrest.'

'Make it soon, Richard. Please. I know you can do that.'

Edward Thompson's house on Briggate was modest, two doors away from the office of the *Leeds Mercury*. As Lister passed the newspaper's building, he glanced through the window. His father was already at work inside, head bent over the desk, quill scratching rapidly. Good luck to him, he thought.

A servant showed him through to Thompson's parlour, everything neat, the furniture all the best quality. But the man could easily afford it. He hadn't been in Leeds too long, but he'd done well for himself. He loaned to merchants to see them through the times when cash was short. And as the wool trade kept growing, his business increased.

Rob had met him a few times. Thompson was a family man, with a wife and three daughters. Somewhere near forty by the look of him, flesh beginning to turn jowly from expansive living, but always well turned-out.

He bustled through the door five minutes later, wearing a dark, heavy jacket and a white silk waistcoat.

'I'm sorry you had to wait,' he said. 'It's about these deaths, I suppose? Sophie told me about them when I came back last night. My wife,' he explained with a quick smile.

'Has anyone threatened you?' Lister asked.

'Me?' Thompson said in disbelief. 'Why would they do that?'

'Because you're a moneylender. There were three of you in Leeds. Now there's only one.'

'No. They haven't.' He pursed his lips, eyes hard. 'And if there's another sense to your question, I don't like it.'

'I wouldn't be doing my job if I didn't ask, Mr Thompson.'

'If you did your job properly you'd know I'm

not like Smith and Stanbridge.' He glared. 'They were leeches. I conduct business. We don't have a bank up here. I'm as close to it as you'll find in Leeds.'

'And it's paid you handsomely.'

'Why shouldn't it?' He had an edge to his voice. 'I just told you, this is business. I provide a service the merchants need and they use it. Now, if you've finished, I think this is over, don't you?'

'As you wish.' Lister picked his tricorn hat off the table. 'But watch out for yourself, please. Keep on guard.'

Thompson looked as if he was about to speak, then gave a quick nod and left the room. The servant let Rob out into the cold.

Maybe Brooke made a mistake in persuading the Corporation, Nottingham thought. Perhaps he wasn't the right man to do this job now. He'd spent two years away from crime and murder, living in the small world he'd allowed himself. Coming back to this was like plunging into icy water, so cold he could barely breathe, let alone swim.

But he'd accepted the offer, he'd made the bargain. He had to find his way. And underneath it all, he was angry that the mayor had doubted him so quickly. If he deserved the man's trust, he deserved all of it.

'No luck with Thompson?'

'He more or less threw me out of his house,' Rob answered with a smile. 'He's respectable.

His clients are merchants. That's true. I warned him to keep looking over his shoulder.'

'Probably best,' Nottingham agreed. 'And I told the mayor we're not going to find the murderer today or tomorrow.'

'What did he say?'

'He wasn't happy, probably best to leave it at that. But I can't remember when it was any different. With me, and old Arkwright before that. They expect us to work miracles for them, and when we can't, we're not worth what they pay us.'

'Where do we go from here, boss?'

'We keep asking questions,' the constable told him. 'And we keep our eyes and ears open. I don't see much else we can do.'

Lister had gone off somewhere. Nottingham was banking the fire for the night when he heard the timid knock on the door.

It was a small boy shuffling around in men's shoes that were far too big for his feet, his breeches holed at the knees, thin shirt through at the elbows. His face was ruddy from the cold.

'Are you Mr Nottingham, sir?' The lad looked up at him. Dirt was ingrained in his cheeks and his hair was matted.

'I am.'

'Jane says can you come and see her, sir.'

'Thank you.' He started to take out a farthing, then selected a penny. At least the boy could put something warm in his belly against the bitter night.

The lad looked at the coin wonderingly then

72

darted off, scared the constable might change his mind.

The same entrance to the same court, with the sound of the river a few yards away and the creak of boats moored for loading. A mist was rising, softening the edges of the world.

As he approached, a man came up to Jane. A few words and they vanished down the passage-way. The woman had a living to earn, after all. He could wait. The constable walked to the bridge and stood with his elbows resting on the stone parapet.

Shreds of fog drifted in the night air. There was no breeze, only the clinging dampness he could feel deep in his chest. He was growing old, noticing his aches and pains more and more each day and relishing the heat of a good fire to warm his bones.

A man shouted from somewhere and a voice answered before the pair of them began to laugh. A lone cart rumbled over the bridge, irons wheels rattling over the cobbles. Finally Nottingham moved. He'd given her enough time.

Jane wasn't waiting at the entrance to the court. Another customer already? From her appearance the night before she needed all she could get. He was about to go to the White Swan for a drink and try later when he heard a groan. Not pleasure; this was pure pain. He called out her name but there was no answer.

The passage was black. No light reached this far. He had to feel his way along, heart thumping, eyes trying to pick out something, anything.

His feet found her first, touching the soft lump on the ground. He knelt, fingertips searching until he found her head, then feeling for a pulse in the neck. Jane's flesh was still warm, but her life had gone. The man he saw must have been her killer.

There was blood on the front of her dress, wet and sticky under his fingertips. Barely dead.

He had to leave her. He needed some of the men to help. As fast as he could, he ran up to the jail, legs hurting with every stride. The night watch was just arriving. He sent one for the coroner, two more with the old door to transport the body, and another with a light to guard the scene.

His mouth was dry. Nottingham gulped at a drink of ale and saw he'd left a bloody print on the mug. It was all over him – his greatcoat, his hands. He began to clean himself but stopped – what was the point? The blood would be back as soon as he began to examine her.

'Find Mr Lister and have him meet me there,' he ordered as he left.

The men were waiting for him. They stood, silently watching him, all of them with dour, brutal faces. But that was who you needed to keep law in the darkness. The lantern flame flickered, enough for him to see Jane lying there. She'd drawn up her knees and thrown out her arms before she died. He must have heard her final sound.

Whores were killed. There were men who considered them fair sport. But this, just after she'd sent him her message? This wasn't anger. This was deliberate. He could feel it.

In his mind, Nottingham tried to picture the figure he'd seen disappear down this passageway with Jane. Tall, perhaps? A hat of some kind. But it was no more than a suggestion, a faint outline in the night and the mist.

There was no peace on the woman's dead face. Nothing more than agony, lips back in a rictus smile, eyes wide. He reached down and lowered the lids; it was the one thing he could do for her at this moment.

Hoggart came bustling through, wearing a heavy coat that reached down to his calves, the gold buckles of his shoes glittering in the light. He sighed, told the man to hold the lantern higher and squatted by the body.

'She hasn't been dead long, Mr Nottingham.'

'I know. Only a few minutes.'

'Well, there's nothing anyone on this earth can do for her now.' He stood, looked down at the corpse and shook her head. 'You might as well take her away.'

She was on the slab of the cold room in the jail when Lister arrived. The candles burning in each corner of the room made it nearly as bright as day.

He had her naked, the tattered old gown cut away so he could examine the wound. In the stomach. It must have taken her a few minutes to die, and she'd done so in horrible pain. If he'd come back sooner . . . but what could he have done? He couldn't have saved her. Nobody could, the knife had gone too deep. But he might have caught her killer.

'Boss?'

The word pulled him back from his thoughts.

'I saw the man who did it.' He explained it all, from the message to the finding.

Rob was looking at the body.

'I used to see her sometimes when I was doing my rounds,' Lister said. 'What did the man look like?'

Like everyone and nobody, Nottingham thought.

'Just a shape,' he said and raised his head. 'She had some information for me and then someone murdered her.' He breathed for a moment or two. 'There's something going on here, I'm certain of it.'

'Boss, you remember what it's like. We have four or five whores murdered every year. Often more.'

He knew. Sometimes they found the killer; usually there was nothing to set them on the trail. Nottingham held up Jane's hand with its little finger missing.

'She lasted out there for more than twenty years. This happened when she was young and she had her revenge on the man who did it. She was careful. She made sure she was never caught out.' He picked her knife from the shelf where it sat with the few other things she'd carried. The edge was sharp as a razor. 'She had some- thing to defend herself.'

'Maybe she let down her guard. He might have taken her by surprise. I don't know.'

But Nottingham had no doubts. The man had come to kill her. And he'd given him the chance, thinking Jane could earn a few pennies before they talked.

Charlotte. What had Jane discovered about her?

'I want the night men asking the prostitutes about someone called Charlotte.'

'Boss . . .'

'Give them the order.'

'It's terrible that she's dead,' Lister said patiently. 'But I think you're reading too much into it.'

'Then we disagree,' the constable answered calmly. 'Have them ask and then you might as well go home. We'll see what happens.'

'Yes, boss.'

He lingered for a few minutes, making his quiet farewells to her, then pulled a sheet over the body. He'd never known Jane well, but she'd seemed like a fixture in the town. Always a pleasant word, few complaints about her life.

He locked the door of the jail, but instead of turning down Kirkgate, the constable made his way through the streets to Lands Lane and knocked on a door. He could hear the voices inside, a woman hushing her children. A bolt was pulled back, the click of a latch and light spilling out, an eye staring.

'Mr Nottingham,' she said in astonishment.

'May I come in, Lizzie?'

A warm fire was burning and a young girl peered out shyly from her mother's skirts. At the table a boy looked up from his books.

Lizzie had been John Sedgwick's woman. She'd moved in, looked after his son James after Sedgwick's wife ran off with a soldier, and she was the mother of the other child left behind when he was killed. Before any of that, though, she'd been a prostitute, one who'd been a friend to Jane.

It must be six months since he'd visited, Nottingham thought, glancing around the room. All that had changed here were the children. They were growing so quickly. Isabell was three, already tall for her age, with the unkempt, open look of her father. James was still at the bluecoat school. He'd become a serious boy in the last two years, not speaking much, keeping his thoughts locked in his head. The town paid his fees. The constable had insisted on it, one of the things they could do for Sedgwick, along with the rent on this house and a pension for Lizzie.

She put a cup of ale in his hand. 'You've been a stranger.'

'I didn't think I had much to say.'

'Why would that matter?' she asked him. 'You know you're always welcome here. From everything I hear, I ought to congratulate you.'

'You might not think so in a minute. I'm afraid I have some bad news.'

But Lizzie had survived a life filled with that. One more thing might hurt, but it wouldn't crush her.

'What is it?' she asked with a steady gaze.

'Four-Finger Jane. Someone killed her tonight.' He saw Lizzie tighten her mouth. She'd cry, but later, when the children couldn't see her. 'I asked her to look for someone. She sent me a message. When I found her . . .'

'Poor lass.'

'I thought it might be better if you heard from me.'

'Thank you.' She gave a small nod. 'John always had a soft spot for her, too.'

They shared the pain of loss, her man, his wife, grief still hard as splintered glass. But while he'd chosen to disappear into himself, she had to carry on, to look after the children.

'I'll make sure you know about the funeral.'

'You said you'd asked her to look for someone. Who?'

'A woman named Charlotte.' To explain, he had to tell her the whole story. Lizzie listened attentively, saying nothing until he finished.

'I still know one or two of them. I could ask,' she said.

He weighed the offer and looked at her children. He needed help, he knew that. But she had too much to lose.

'It's kind, but safer if you didn't. I didn't come here for that. Just to let you know.'

'Of course.' She had a calm smile. 'Thank you. But visit more often, please.'

'I promise.' But they both knew he wouldn't.

Eight

He trudged home, shoulders bowed under the weight only he could feel. If he hadn't asked Jane to find out about Charlotte, she might still have been at the entrance to her passageway trying to earn the pennies and ha'pennies to last another day.

His mood was still sour and defeated when he entered the house on Marsh Lane. But the fire was warm and the candles gave a welcoming light. Someone was sitting in his place at the table as the others leaned forward, listening raptly. Even Lucy, a hand under her chin, was caught in the words, her eyes as wide as a child. They'd barely heard Nottingham arrive. He hung up his coat and stood close to the fire as Old Jem continued his tale.

It was one the constable had heard many times before, always a favourite with the girls whenever Jem had stayed here. Hearing it again, he felt he could conjure up his wife's ghost, then Rose's, to listen beside him.

Then it was over. Silence hung for a moment as the mood slowly dissolved, then Lucy hurried into the kitchen, returning with a plate.

'I kept it warm for you,' she said.

As he ate, Rob gave him a questioning look and Nottingham answered with a shake of his head. At the other end of the table, Emily and Jem were talking. When she raised her head she said, 'I saw Jem in town and asked him to spend the night. It'll be warmer than that stable. You don't mind, do you, Papa?'

'Of course not.' He smiled at the storyteller. 'We'll always be glad to have you here.'

'That's right kind,' the old man answered and pushed his mug towards Lucy. 'If you'll just wet my whistle, young lady, I might be able to think of another tale or two.'

The constable listened, as attentive as the rest, taken out of himself for an hour. That was what he needed tonight. Simply to forget, to be some-where better.

In the morning Nottingham left while Jem still dozed in front of the fire. He could hear Rob moving around, but he was ready to go. To think. It was still full darkness as he opened the door and headed towards Timble Bridge. A dry, crisp morning, chilly enough to catch in his chest.

Jane was waiting in the cold cell, but he couldn't face her again. He'd already given her his apologies; he'd attend her funeral. The constable glanced through the night report. No mention of any of the men finding information about Charlotte. But he knew there was a fair chance they hadn't even asked.

He wrote his own report for the mayor, a note for the undertaker, and walked around the town. Leeds was waking slowly, men on their way to work. The butchers in the Shambles under the Moot Hall lowered their shutters and opened their shops, the hard, bloody smell spilling into the street.

Garroway's had a brisk early trade of busi-nessmen who used the time to make their deals here. Tom Finer was there, one of the first customers, sitting alone in the corner and sipping his bowl of coffee as he listened carefully to all the conversations around him.

'You're up with the lark,' he said as Nottingham took the seat across the table. 'Something to drink?'

'Just questions. That's all.'

Finer eyed him carefully. 'Ask what you like.

I won't guarantee you answers, though.' In a heavy greatcoat and muffler, gloves resting by his cup, Finer was dressed for deep winter. But he was an old man, he felt the cold all the way to his marrow.

'How did you know a third pimp had gone?'

'Someone told me.'

'Who?'

'I don't recall.' Finer kept his gaze steady. He remembered full well, but he wasn't about to say.

'There's something else,' the constable said. 'Why did you hint that the killings of the money-lenders and the disappearance of the pimps were connected?'

'Because it makes sense.' He sipped his coffee and ran his tongue across his lips. 'Can't you see it?'

'Not when you said it.'

'And now?' the old man asked sharply.

'I'm still not convinced. It's too flimsy. But I'm beginning to wonder.'

Finer raised a bushy eyebrow. 'A little bird told me that a prostitute was murdered last night.'

'Your birds sing loud.'

'They should.' True enough, the constable thought; he probably paid them enough.

'If there is a connection, who's behind it?'

'That I don't know. And if it's true . . .' Finer picked his way carefully through the words, 'these could be dangerous times for anyone to start asking questions.'

He was right. Four-Finger Jane was the proof.

'Tell me anything you hear.'

'Perhaps I will,' the man promised as he stared out of the window. 'It's funny, but I've developed an affection for this town since I returned.'

There was one more place to go: Jane's room. He'd taken the key from her possessions and now he turned it in the lock. The house, hidden away from the sun in one of the courts that ran off Vicar Lane, seemed filled with the foetid stench of overcooked cabbage, piss and hopelessness. Night soil turned hard as rocks on the ground outside.

The window was cracked but clean, the bed tidily made, a blanket draped over it. There was a single hard-backed chair and a table with a bowl and pitcher of water. Jane must have salvaged an old rag rug from somewhere, faded reds and yellows on the floor trying to brighten the place.

A broken comb sat by the bowl, with a small shard of mirror propped against the wall next to it. A dress of good wool hung from a nail, probably the only thing of any value Jane owned. He held it up. It was made for a woman smaller than she had been. A keepsake, a memory from when she was young? He'd never know now; all Jane's truth was lost.

No books, no paper, but he knew she'd never learned to read or write. Nothing hidden in the bed. A stub of a candle in a holder on the floor.

He searched more, finding a leather purse hidden under a loose floorboard. She'd saved almost two pounds in coins. It was no fortune, not for all her years of work, but there would be no more hard times for her now. He slid it into his pocket and locked the door as he left. Soon enough someone else would be living there; an empty room was like gold.

Nottingham was lost in his thoughts. At first he didn't notice the fair-haired girl trying to keep pace with him. Then she darted in front, turned and stopped.

'Please sir,' she began. Before she could say another word, he'd grabbed her wrist and moved so his back was against the wall.

The boy with long black hair was taken by surprise. He had his penknife out, ready to cut purse strings. For a moment he stood still, unsure what to do. The girl began to scream and lash out with her hand and feet and the boy slid forward.

Nottingham held up his arm. The blade sliced into his palm. He let go of the girl and she pulled away from him.

'Bastard!' she shouted and spat in his face. A heartbeat and she was running after the boy.

The constable took out his handkerchief and pressed it into his hand to try and staunch the bleeding. It wasn't a deep cut, but it stung like the devil.

He was breathing as if he'd run a mile. The pair were nowhere to be seen, vanished into the network of courts and ginnels; it was pointless to even start searching. They'd show up again, he was certain of that.

They'd taken him for a defenceless old man. Not quite, he thought. Not yet. But a few years before he'd have been quick enough to take the pair of them.

The apothecary poured something on the wound that made him wince and bound it with a clean bandage. He felt chastened; a constable who couldn't even catch a couple of young thieves.

Lister was at the jail, raising an eyebrow when he saw Nottingham's hand.

'I met our cutpurses.'

He'd seen them long enough to give a good description, but he kept one thing to himself: the look of pure viciousness and satisfaction on the boy's face as his small knife cut into the constable's skin.

'Anything more on the moneylenders?' he asked.

'If anybody knows, they're keeping very quiet.'

'Stay on it. You seem to know the right people to talk to. And I want all the men alert for that boy and girl. We need to arrest them before someone is seriously hurt.'

'Yes, boss.'

'I told you I was going to rely on you,' the constable said. 'I'm going to find whoever murdered Jane.' But all he had was the faint outline of a man, half-hidden in the mist.

Keep working on the deaths of the money-lenders. Easier said than done, Lister thought. Every way he turned he found himself staring at nothing. No whispers, not even a rumour tossed about on the breeze. Only silence.

Usually there was someone ready to talk, eager to trade information for money or a favour. But this time they might as well have all been mute. He hadn't even been able to pick up a hint. The murderer was keeping his mouth closed. That had to mean one man, working alone. Any more than that and some secret was bound to spill. Someone would drink and his tongue would loosen.

Maybe the boss was right and they'd have to wait for the arrival of a new moneylender. Still, that shouldn't take too long, not when business was there. He sighed and finished the dregs of his ale. Time to go out and make himself hoarse by asking the same questions over and over.

Nottingham walked up and down Briggate, searching for the prostitute who'd whispered that he should look for Charlotte. But there was no sign of her. He talked to the few who were out, about Jane, adding the other name almost casually. All he received were blank looks or shakes of the head. Either they didn't know or they were too frightened to talk.

A new whore had already taken Jane's old post in the passageway close to the river. She was young and scared, smiling nervously at all the men who passed. She'd probably only been in Leeds for a few days, still dressed in her country clothes, the rough homespun dress, with a cap over her hair and worn clogs on her feet.

'Who told you to try this spot?' he asked kindly.

She blushed before she answered. 'A man, sir. He said the girl who worked here had gone.'

'What man was this?'

'He helped me find a room, sir, and bought

86

me some food.' She lowered her gaze. 'I haven't been able to find a job here, you see.'

He'd heard the story so often over the years he could have recited it to her. Now here she was, desperate, selling her body to repay someone. Yet there was something about her, some hint in the dark hair and wide eyes, that reminded him of Rose, his dead daughter.

'What's his name?'

'Peter, sir. Peter Kidd. He said he'd take me out to eat in one of the inns tonight if I do well.'

Nottingham took two pennies from his pocket. 'Where can I find him?'

'He has a room, sir. On Lady Lane.'

'Which house?'

'It has a black door, sir. That's all I know.'

That was enough; he'd be able to find the man. The constable pressed the coins into her palm.

Two more girls had appeared on Briggate. One looked baffled at the mention of Charlotte. The other shook her head hard, but in her eyes he wondered if she knew something but was too terrified to ever say.

Lady Lane had changed in the last two years. One side was filled with new houses. Nothing grand, hardly the merchants' mansions of Town End. These had gone up hastily, never intended to last. Built by Tom Finer, and all of them money in his pocket.

The other side remained old and battered, a jumbled collection of buildings that looked as if it had been tossed together and stayed upright in some strange reprieve of ruin. The house with the peeling black door was easy to find. This visit was stupid, he knew. It was pointless. But he had the urge to try to protect that girl.

Kidd's room stood at the top of the place, a cold garret under the eaves. As he climbed the stairs, the constable eased his old cudgel from his coat, wrapping the leather thong around his wrist. Kidd appeared, a self-satisfied expression on his face, after Nottingham hammered on the wood.

'Peter Kidd?'

'Yes.' His eyes narrowed 'What—'

He didn't have the chance to finish. The constable pushed him back into the room and slammed the door.

'What?' Kidd began again, eyes shifting round, searching for a weapon.

'Do you know who I am?'

'No. Should I?' Kidd gave a small, nervous laugh.

'I'm the Constable of Leeds. You have a girl where Four-Finger Jane used to be.'

'Yes. But—'

Nottingham took a step closer and let the cudgel swing. 'Someone murdered Jane. That wouldn't have been you, would it?'

He already knew the answer. Kidd was short and round, nothing like the faint figure he'd seen enter the passageway. But he felt the need to put the fear of God into the man.

'No! I just heard she was dead and I had this girl . . .'

'That's right. You *had* a girl. You don't any more.'

88

'Wait—' The man's eyes were wide.

'There's nothing to wait for. I'm offering you a choice. Either you leave Leeds immediately, on your own, or I arrest you for pandering.'

Kidd stared for a moment, then nodded in defeat.

'What about the girl?' he asked.

'She's old enough to make her own choices. You don't speak to her before you go, and if you hurt her, believe me I'll make sure you pay.' His voice was steady and controlled. He knew the irony: three pimps vanished and now he was sending another one packing. But he'd get rid of every last one of them if he could.

'Where do I go?' Kidd asked helplessly.

'That's up to you. But don't come back here.'

It didn't feel like a victory; it didn't feel like anything. Nottingham knew it didn't help solve Jane's murder. There was still a killer and a pair of cutpurses out there. But perhaps he'd improved the town a little.

Nine

'I've been thinking,' Rob began. He sat by the fire, gazing into the flames. In the kitchen, Lucy was washing the pots from supper. Emily had a meeting with the Williamsons about money for the school: they wanted to hold a dance at the Cloth Hall to raise more funds.

'What about?' Nottingham asked. He was in the other chair, holding a mug of ale and savouring the warmth of the blaze. It had been another day filled with frustration. Kidd had been the only success, but he wasn't going to talk about his reasons; he wasn't even sure they'd make sense to anyone.

'This idea of yours about someone moving in to control things. Getting rid of the pimps and killing the moneylenders.'

The constable turned his head to look at the younger man.

'Are you starting to believe it?'

Rob rubbed a hand across his lips and shook his head.

'I really can't see it. Tell me, Amos Worthy ran most things here when he was alive, didn't he?'

'For quite a few years,' Nottingham agreed.

'That's how Leeds was back then. But things have changed. It's . . .' he searched for the right words. 'Imagine a glass that's shattered. Everything in small pieces now.'

'Someone with a small piece can become greedy for more,' Nottingham said.

'Then they fight it out among themselves.' Lister shrugged. 'It makes our lives easier. Nobody grows too powerful.'

'You don't believe it can happen, do you?'

'Honestly, no, I don't,' Rob admitted with a sigh. He knew what he wanted to say but somehow he couldn't make the words come out as he wished. 'What I'm trying to tell you is that things have altered since you left.'

'Then how do you explain Stanbridge and Smith being murdered?'

Rob leaned forward, elbows resting on his knees.

'I'm willing to believe that someone wants to take over the moneylending business. I can understand that. But it's harder to picture someone killing to take charge of most of the crime here. Leeds is just too big.' His voice was earnest. 'You know Kirkstall did nothing, don't you?' He waited until Nottingham nodded his agreement. 'I was the one who handled everything. Don't you think I'd be aware if something like that was going on?'

'We all see the things we want to see,' Nottingham answered quietly. 'I'm guilty of it; I've been blind often enough. I'm not doubting you. You're good at your job. Very good,' he added with a quick smile. 'You know Leeds. If you want the truth, I can't be certain that anything's connected. I'm aware there's no evidence. But it's a possibility, and we have to consider it.'

Lister nodded. It was fine as one small thing to keep at the back of his mind. Someone had planted this seed in the boss's mind and it had sprouted. The real fact was that most criminals were too stupid to plan an hour ahead, let alone conjure up a scheme as grand as this. The man had been away too long. Rob understood what things were like in Leeds *now*. The past was dead and buried with Worthy in the churchyard.

Nottingham hadn't slept well. A bad dream woke him, creeping back into his head again and again until he gave up on rest. He was dancing with his dead wife. As they moved around with the

91

music, the flesh slid off her bones until he was left holding her skeleton.

Now, well before first light, he stopped at Timble Bridge, gratefully listening to the soft burble of water for a minute to calm his mind.

The Parish Church was no more than a smudged outline against the night as he made his way up Kirkgate. The houses were silent. Somewhere in the distance he heard footsteps, the echoes falling away slowly.

Rob was probably right. Perhaps he was looking at Leeds through the prism of the past, trying to see things that weren't there. On the surface the town seemed familiar enough, but once you dug down . . .

At the jail he sifted through the reports. Four drunks sleeping in the cells; even with the door closed he could smell their stink. No word on any woman named Charlotte but he never expected to be so lucky.

Some scribblings on a note made him stop and frown, then he set it aside for Lister. The rest was the wasted time that came with the job. He pushed a poker into the fire, then fed most of the paper into the flames. Might as well gain a moment's heat from them.

By the time Rob arrived, his thoughts had led him nowhere. It was full light, all the noises of the town outside, but he hadn't moved from his chair.

'Take a look at this,' Nottingham said and pushed the letter towards him.

'What?' Lister laughed in disbelief. 'Who sent this?'

'It was waiting this morning.'

'This is wrong,' he said. 'It has to be.'

'But it's possible.'

Rob let the note fall to the desk. 'No. Why would Thompson arrange to have Stanbridge and Smith killed? He's making good money lending to merchants and he knows they'll pay him back.'

The paper was unsigned, denouncing Thompson as the person behind the murders. He knew it was unlikely, just someone with a poisoned mind, but . . .

'You need to look into it.'

'We won't find any proof, boss.'

'I daresay we won't,' he agreed. 'But this way, if the mayor gets wind of it, we can say we've checked.' He heard the church bell ring the hour. 'I've a funeral to attend.'

Nottingham stood by the graveside as the curate rushed through the service. It was the desolate part of the graveyard where no headstones stood to mark the dead. In her best gown and hat, Lizzie was next to him, Isabell at her side, her young face frowning and serious. Two women, older prostitutes, stayed a few yards behind.

Nottingham wore his good jacket and breeches, shoes polished. He owed Jane that, at least, bowing his head as the cheap coffin was lowered into the ground. If he hadn't asked her to find out about Charlotte . . . He gazed around. Apart from the few in the churchyard, nobody paid the burial any mind. No men watching from a distance. The killer hadn't come to watch.

It was over quickly, the parson hurrying away to the warmth of the vestry, as the gravediggers bent their backs and the hollow sound of sod falling on wood filled the air.

Lizzie put a hand on his arm. 'Don't blame yourself, Mr Nottingham.'

He sighed. 'That's easier said than done.'

'Jane knew the risks in everything. You don't understand what it's like out there.'

'No,' he agreed. 'But I can guess.'

She shook her head. 'Believe me, you can't. Just think well of her and remember her. That's all we can do.' Her voice dropped. 'I asked a few of the girls I used to know about Charlotte. One of them remembered her.'

'Who?' he said, but Lizzie didn't answer his question.

'All she could say was that Charlotte vanished. Not even a word. Her pimp was frantic, didn't want to lose the income. He didn't know what had happened.' She paused and stared at him. 'Then he disappeared, too. She didn't tell me his name.'

They followed the flagstones to the lych gate. His eyes checked again. No one was giving them a second glance.

'How long ago was this?'

'I'm not sure. It sounded quite recent. Does that help at all?'

'Yes.' He smiled at her. 'John would be proud.'

Lizzie grinned and gave a tight, tired laugh. 'That's the best praise I've had all year.' She turned to her daughter. The girl still hadn't said a word. 'Come on you, we'd better go and buy some wool to darn your stockings.'

'Thank you.' He took out a farthing and presented it to Isabell. 'Treat yourself.'

Her eyes widened as she reached out to take it. Then the girl remembered her manners.

'Thank you, sir,' she told him in a high voice.

'You shouldn't spoil her,' Lizzie chided.

'It's only a farthing. A few more years and she'll be going to Emily's school.'

'I hope so.' She took a firmer hold of the girl's hand. 'Say goodbye to Mr Nottingham.'

'Goodbye, sir.' She glanced back over her shoulder as they walked away and for a quick moment her sober expression dissolved into an eager grin.

He stood by the jail and watched until they were out of sight. People pressed around, carts trundled up and down the road. But no one appeared to be following them.

Lizzie shouldn't have started asking questions; it was dangerous. At the same time, she'd brought him something useful.

At the jail, a note in Lister's hand waited on the desk: *Lady Lane, house with black door. Come as soon as you can.*

He knew what he was going to find as he climbed the stairs to the garret. He could hear footsteps moving around and the rough murmur of men's voices.

The body lay face down on the floor, blood soaked dark into the boards around it. Lister turned around. Hoggart the coroner was picking up his bag, ready to leave. He nodded as he passed.

95

'Peter Kidd,' the constable said.

'You knew him?' Rob asked in surprise.

'I was here yesterday morning. He was a pimp. I told him to leave Leeds. How long has he been dead?'

'Since last night.' Lister gestured at a small bundle on the bed. 'It looks like he took your order seriously.'

'Who discovered him?'

'The people downstairs. They woke this morning and found blood had dripped through the ceiling.'

He grimaced; that was a gruesome way to start a day.

'Let's get him to the jail and see what killed him.'

'No need to look, boss. His throat was cut.' He gave a small, apologetic cough. 'Just like the moneylenders.'

'Take him down there, anyway,' the constable said. 'Talk to the people downstairs. What time did they go to sleep, did they hear anything . . . you know what to do.'

'Where are you going?'

'I have to see someone who might know more.' At least he hoped to God she would.

Nottingham marched quickly down Briggate, dodging through the crowds on the street, until he could smell the rotted stink of the river. But there was no girl who looked like Rose standing at the entrance to the passageway. This time he wasn't going to wait and see if someone emerged. He entered, squinting against the dimness.

Nobody waited in the shadows and the yard beyond was empty. The constable came back out, looking around for anywhere she might be. A woman watched from across the street, leaning idly against the opening of another passage.

'The girl who was there yesterday,' he began.

'What about her?' As she turned her head to speak he could smell the gin on her breath and see the dullness in her eyes.

'Have you seen her today?'

He watched as she tried to focus on him then turned her head away again.

'Young, was she, luv?'

'Yes. With dark hair.'

The woman shook her head. She had to put out a hand to steady herself against the wall. He moved away; she'd already forgotten he'd even been there, lost in her own dreams.

There was only one more prostitute out, close to the corner of Boar Lane. But she knew nothing, eyes darting worriedly as he asked his questions.

He'd return later. Maybe the girl would be there. He realized he'd never even asked her name.

Lister walked around the body. Peter Kidd, the boss had said, although the man carried nothing to identify himself. But he had precious little of anything. A few coins in his pocket and some spare, tattered clothes in the bundle he'd packed.

The landlady said that Kidd had taken the room just a fortnight before; he was already late with his rent.

Any whore he ran had to be very new or very stupid.

'Have you found anything?' Nottingham asked as he entered the cell.

'There's nothing to find,' Rob told him. 'Nothing at all. If you didn't have his name we'd never have known who he was.'

'He was someone who made a bad choice.'

'Well, he won't be making any more,' Lister said. 'Before you say it, there's no proof this is connected to anything else. He might have owed money, there could have been an argument—'

'What about the people downstairs?'

'From the look of them they probably wouldn't have heard the last trumpet.' Rob snorted. 'Drunks, the pair of them. We don't have any proof of anything.' He pointed at the corpse. 'Chances are we'll never know the truth.'

'That girl I mentioned, Charlotte?'

'Yes.'

'I've heard that she vanished a little while before her pimp. He had no idea what happened to her.'

'Boss,' Lister said with a sigh, 'do you remember what you told me not long after I began on the job?'

'What was that?'

'The simplest explanation is usually the right one.'

He saw Nottingham smile.

'Very likely I did. But usually doesn't mean always. This,' he said, looking down at Kidd's body, 'is connected to the other murders. I can feel it.'

'Is that what you're going to tell the mayor?' Lister kept his voice at an urgent hiss. 'Do you think he'll want to hear that? You know we don't have any evidence to back it up. Believe it if you really have to, but for God's sake, keep it between the two of us.'

He could see the doubt in the constable's eyes. Then he nodded.

'Between us,' he agreed. 'For now.'

'Good.' That was something.

Ten

The day brought no luck. By the time darkness arrived, Nottingham felt drained. But there was still work to do. Lister would go around the inns once more, asking more questions and trying to pry small nuggets of truth out of the lies.

He pulled on his old greatcoat, buttoning it to the neck, and slipped his cudgel into the large pocket. Men filled the taverns, finding relief in drink after a day of work. The whores were on Briggate, shivering in the cold and trying to look enticing as they set out to draw a few pennies from the night. But the dark-haired girl who'd taken Jane's spot was nowhere to be seen. No one waited by the passageway.

He went from one woman to the next, but only two could remember her. No one knew her name, none had spoken to her. The most anyone recalled was that she'd stayed long into the evening, looking lost. There one minute and gone the next time they looked.

His face was chapped by the wind, he was weary and aching, but he wasn't ready to give up and go home yet. Instead he stopped at the White Swan to lose himself in the chatter and the warmth for a few minutes. Michael the landlord poured him a mug of the special twice-brewed and he took a long sip. A fire burned in the grate and the air was thick with the smoke from a dozen clay pipes and the rank smell of bodies.

Nottingham sat and listened. Across the years he'd heard interesting things in the taverns and inns around Leeds. People dropped hints of this and that without thinking. Once someone in his cups had sat beside him and confessed to a killing.

Now all the talk was of the dead pimp and the moneylenders. People loved a good murder, the gorier the better. He heard imaginations roam, wild suggestions. But nothing to set him thinking.

The constable finished the drink and pondered another before pushing the mug away and leaving. Outside, he shivered. The sky was clear, the air sharp and bitter.

A lantern was burning in the jail. He turned the door handle. Crandall, the night man, was sitting at the table, a quill in his hand, looking anxious as he tried to write.

'Is something wrong?'

'Not really, sir.' The man bit his lip, then he sighed and said, 'We've found another body in the river. Pretty young thing, that's all. It's sad.'

He breathed in, feeling the fear rising up his spine. He hadn't even seen the corpse but he was certain he'd know her face.

'I'll take a look at her.'

Nottingham lit a candle and walked back to the cold cell. The flame flickered and dimmed, then suddenly burned brighter so he could see her stretched out on the slab.

She looked even younger now, so much like Rose that it took his breath for a moment. Her skin was a startling white in the soft light, dark hair sodden, almost black, the same cheap gown he'd seen her wear the day before pressed wetly against her body There were tiny cuts on her hands, little red lines, and her nails were torn. A heavy bruise on her cheek and marks on her neck. He'd seen enough drownings in his time: this was no accident. Someone had hit her and forced her head under the water until she was dead. Then she'd been tipped into the Aire. She'd fought hard for her life and lost.

He bunched his fist, digging his nails into his palm until he could feel the pain. For a long time he stood, simply staring at her. Memories of his daughter surfaced and he could feel the hopelessness all over again. He hadn't been able to help Rose when the fever took her and her unborn child. And he hadn't been able to stop this one from dying.

'I don't suppose you found anything with her?' he asked as he returned to the office.

'No, sir.'

Dead without a name, all her past slipped away.

'Call her Rose if you like.' He blew out the candle. 'I'll wish you goodnight.'

Rob listened, watching the constable's face. He looked drawn and serious as he sat in front of the fire with his shoulders slumped. The man had lost weight; it started once he retired. His wrists had become bony and his face was gaunt. Before too long he'd appear older than his years.

'Are you still going to tell me it's coincidence?' Nottingham asked.

'I don't know.' He wasn't sure what to think. There seemed to be something the boss wasn't saying, some undercurrent of anger or despair he couldn't penetrate. 'Let's think about it in the morning.'

Emily was lost in the book she was reading, away in the world of *Gulliver's Travels*. She probably hadn't heard a word. Maybe that was just as well.

'The cutpurses struck again,' Lister said. 'A couple came in just before I left. This time took a woman's reticule and cut her arm. It was the Underwoods.'

Nottingham grimaced. Underwood was a wool merchant, not on the corporation yet, but aiming for election. He'd be loud in his complaints about law and order.

'How badly hurt was she?'

'Nothing really, only a scratch. But we need to catch them, boss. They're becoming dangerous.'

'We will.' He looked up. 'We certainly will.'

Another night of broken sleep. The dead girl's face kept rising in his mind as if she was

102

surfacing through the water. He'd wake for a minute, just long enough for her image to disappear, then drift back to his rest.

Lucy had the oven warm, and he breathed in the comforting smell of baking bread. Nottingham took the heel of the old loaf and some cheese before pouring a mug of ale.

'Those cutpurses I heard you and Master Rob talk about last night,' she began.

'What about them?' he asked as he ate.

'I think I've seen them a few times when I've been buying things from the market.'

The constable cocked his head. 'Go on.'

'They're careful. Sly. I watched them follow a man for a few minutes. As soon as he met someone else they melted away.'

Lucy had spent long enough living wild when she was younger. She had the eye to notice something like that.

'I don't suppose you'd like to spend some time in town, would you?'

'Keep my eyes open, you mean?' She was grinning widely.

'And tell one of my men if you spot anything.'

'I suppose I could, if you're asking. It's market day, you can bet the pair of them will be around.'

Every Saturday and Tuesday, before the market came the cloth market. It had been that way for more years than anyone could remember, probably before there were even records. The constable made his circuit, watching as the weavers set out their cloth then vanished into the inns for their hot Brigg-end shot breakfast.

They'd certainly need something warm this morning; frost had turned the ground white again as he walked into Leeds, leaving the cobbles shiny and slick.

The girl he'd called Rose was waiting at the jail. Her body was stiff now, bitterly cold to the touch. Seeing her in daylight he had no doubt: she'd been murdered. Hit with something to subdue her, then drowned.

She'd clung hard to life; her hands and nails showed that. Her killer would be marked. He leaned against the wall, studying her, turning as the door opened and Rob walked in.

'No age at all, was she?'

'She probably came here thinking she'd make her fortune,' the constable said bleakly.

The deputy walked around the corpse, examining her from all angles.

'Why?' he wondered.

'I've been asking myself the same thing,' Nottingham answered. 'I don't know. But Jane, her, Kidd.'

'I still can't see any link to the moneylenders.'

The constable pushed himself upright and shook his head

'I'm not sure what I know any longer. Come on, we have work to do.'

Nottingham left, but Rob lingered, staring again into the young, dead face. She was probably only a year or two older than Lucy, all the cares and trials stripped from her face now. He slammed the palm of his hand against the stone wall, letting the smack echo, and walked out.

He'd lain awake in bed, tossing and turning under the blanket. Finally Emily couldn't take it any longer.

'You might as well tell me,' she whispered. 'We're not going to get any sleep until you do.'

Rob stared up into the darkness and put his arm around her shoulder. He didn't want to do it, but he knew he had to let it out. His put his mouth close to her ear and whispered.

'It's your father.'

With a sudden movement she pulled away, resting on one elbow.

'What? What is it? Tell me.'

He did, and it felt like sacred relief to finally say it, to talk about the man's strange idea that one person could be behind the spate of murders in Leeds.

'Well?' Emily asked when he finished. 'Could he be right?'

'No.' For a moment, moonlight leaked through the shutters and he could see her outline next to him. 'He's not. Don't you think I'd know if there was anything like that? I keep trying to tell him, but someone put this idea in his head and he won't let it go.'

'Papa's not a fool.'

'I know he's not.' He exhaled slowly, trying to trace a path to the right words. 'It's as if he believes there's another Amos Worthy waiting and planning. But there isn't. There can't be.'

'Give him time, Rob. He's coming back to the job.' She stroked his hair and settled herself against his shoulder. 'Please.'

And now, as he closed the door of the cold cell,

for one tiny moment he wondered if he wasn't the one who'd been wrong.

The constable was already issuing a crisp series of orders to the men.

'Waterhouse and Dyer, I want you to go to every house on Lady Lane. Ask if anyone remembers a woman there yesterday evening. Young, dark hair, homespun dress. She'd probably have been wearing a cap and looking very nervous and cold.'

They left. At least the boss had picked two with brains for that job, Lister thought approvingly.

'Carter, Naylor, I want you at the market,' the constable continued. He described the two young cutpurses. 'I have someone there looking, so be ready if you hear a shout. And if you see them yourselves, arrest them. The boy has a penknife, though: be careful.' He held up his bandaged hands. 'He'll use it, too.'

'If he pulls that on me I'll make him wish he'd never been born,' Naylor snorted.

'Don't be so cocky. He's quick and he's vicious,' Nottingham warned.

That left two to patrol the town. Once they'd gone, Lister said, 'What about us, boss?'

'We start thinking.' He leaned back in the chair and steepled his hands under his chin. 'How many pimps do you know?'

'Five,' Rob answered after a few moments.

'Do you talk with any of them?'

'Only one.' Joshua Bartlett. A stained, messy

bull of a man. But he'd passed on plenty of good information in the past.

'Find out if anyone's been threatening him.'

Lister grinned at the idea. 'He'd beat the brains out of anyone who tried.'

'Ask him, anyway. He might have heard things. Let's see what we can discover, shall we?'

'What are you going to do?'

'See if there's anyone from the old days who might know a few things.'

Another visit to Joe Buck brought only two names. Dinner time had arrived before the constable tracked down John Wood at the Turk's Head, settled on a bench in the far corner where he could watch people come and go.

He seemed to have shrivelled. Wood had never been a large man, but now he looked to have sunk in on himself. In his time he'd tried plenty of things – run girls, broken into houses – and failed at every one of them. But Buck said Wood knew some of the pimps.

The constable carried a cup of ale across and placed it in front of the man. Wood's eyes darted around.

'I don't want anyone seeing me with you.' His voice was quiet and urgent. 'I don't want anyone thinking I'm in trouble with the law.'

'Then you're too late.' He took a sip from his own mug. 'I'm already here.'

'I've got an honest job these days.'

'Work?' He raised an eyebrow. 'That must have come as a shock to you.'

'I'm employed by Mr Warren now.'

Warren? He knew that name. Then he placed it. The bookkeeper who'd dined with Stanbridge the night he died. Interesting.

'What do you do for him?'

'Turns out I've got a mind for numbers.' Wood grinned, showing a set of brown teeth. 'Hadn't expected that, had you, Mr Nottingham?'

'No,' he admitted. But he wouldn't have expected anything at all from the man.

'Goes to show, doesn't it?'

'What do you hear, when you're not adding columns of figures?'

'Me?' Wood blinked with surprise. 'I told you, I'm an honest man. Got a woman and everything.'

It was hard to believe that anyone could find Wood attractive, with his bulging frog eyes and thick nose. But the world was a strange place.

'And no ear to the ground? Hear anything about pimps these days?'

'Not any more. Left it all behind.' There was the ring of truth in his words. The constable changed tack.

'Tell me something, John. How honest is Mr Warren's work?'

'Look at it yourself if you like.' There was a note of offence in his voice.

'Maybe I will.' Nottingham pushed himself up, knees aching. 'I wish you well of life.'

The market was still busy, people crowding around the stalls at the top of Briggate. Men and women hawked their wares, voices competing. Everyone had the best goods, the best prices.

The constable stopped for a minute, eyes searching for Lucy, for his men somewhere in the press of people, and for the boy and girl who were becoming too dangerous.

He didn't spot any of them and moved on, glancing through the clean windows of the Talbot as he passed: there was barely room to stand. In the old days only a bloody cock fight would have drawn so many. It looked as if Harry Meadows had made the right decision in changing the place.

The man he wanted wasn't in any tavern. A few more yards and he could make out the sound over the noise and bustle. The scrape of a bow over catgut floated from the market cross at the head of the street. Con the blind fiddler playing his tunes. A jig to set feet moving faster, an air so gentle it could pull softly at the heart. A battered old hat lay between his feet, the coins inside glittering; a market meant good money for any man who played so beautifully.

He waited as Con let the last note fade before he approached. The man turned his head just as if he could see and smiled.

'That sounds like Mr Nottingham.'

His voice was cracked and rasping, but full of good humour. Con always had a sweet smile and a ready laugh. He'd arrived in Leeds not long after Nottingham first became constable, and somehow decided to stay. He had to be sixty now, still thin as a sapling, fingers every bit as nimble as a young man's. He'd been spry with his tunes back then but over time he seemed to discover a deeper quality in his music. It moved directly from his soul to his fingers.

The constable laughed. 'Well met, Con. You haven't lost your hearing.'

'Everyone's tread is different. I've told you that before.' He put up the instrument, lightly plucking a string with his thumb. 'With you in charge again and old Jem back in town it's starting to feel like better times.'

'I wish that was true,' Nottingham said.

'I know.' Con nodded his head. 'We all lose the best things, don't we?'

He'd never seen Con with a woman, never even heard of one. For a few years a boy led him around. But he disappeared and since then the man had managed alone.

'Times change.'

'And yet we're still here, Mr Nottingham. The Good Lord has his own ways of working.'

'Do you still hear bits of this and that?'

People seemed to think that if Con was blind, he must be deaf to their words, too. They gossiped, they garbled their secrets where he could hear them and he passed them along.

'Not so much these days,' Con replied. 'People have become—'

The scream cut him off and Nottingham started to run. From the far side of the market, he thought. People had stopped as if they were frozen, heads craning round. He pushed through them, shouldering them aside, the cudgel already gripped tight in his hand.

Eleven

A space had opened up around the man on the ground as people pulled back, horrified. He was awake, groaning, face ghostly pale as one hand tried to cover the wound in his side. Blood had leaked, staining the silk waistcoat. His wig had slipped on to the cobbles. The woman kneeling at his side picked it up and pushed it under his head as a pillow.

George Armistead. The manager of a cropping mill where they cut the nap off the wool to finish the cloth.

The constable squatted and stared down at the man.

'We'll help you,' he said, gazing up at the crowd. Where in God's name were his men?

'It was a boy and a girl,' the woman with Armistead began, and he already knew the rest of the tale. Then someone else was next to him, plump fingers taking charge of everything.

'It's not deep,' Lucy said as she examined him, then gave a reassuring smile. 'And it's in your side, nothing too dangerous. Don't you worry. We need someone to help him home.'

One of the stallholders found an old door and laid it next to Armistead. Very gently, a pair of men lifted him on to it.

'Send for the physician. I'll come and talk to

you later,' the constable said to the woman as they carried the man away.

'I never saw them,' Lucy told him as she watched them leave. Like a wave, people flowed back into the empty hole, chattering loudly. 'I'm sorry.'

'It's hardly your fault. It's impossible to see anything here. Will he survive?'

'Him? He'll be fine. It's only a gash, and that's mostly in the fat.' She pursed her lips. 'He has plenty of padding. He could probably walk home if he'd a mind to.'

'His wife said it was a boy and a girl.'

Lucy looked at him sharply.

'That's not his wife. Her name's Sophie Marsden. Acts like Lady Muck.' Her mouth twitched into a grin. 'He's going to have an interesting time explaining her to his missus.'

'It won't help us find the pair who did this.' He could feel the sting of the boy's knife on his palm. This was the third time he'd used the blade. If they weren't caught soon, the lad would kill someone.

By the time Carter and Naylor arrived, Lucy had gone, basket over her arm. The constable talked to a few who'd witnessed the attack. The girl had stopped the couple while the boy started to cut the man's purse. Armistead tried to stop him and the lad had lashed out with his penknife before the pair darted away.

'Sorry, boss,' Naylor said. 'We were on the other side of the market.'

As soon as the man opened his mouth, Nottingham could smell it. He turned to Carter.

112

'Say something.'

'What?' He looked confused. 'He's telling the truth, boss. We couldn't get through the people.'

'You're dismissed. Both of you.'

They looked at him, not believing his words.

'I told you to patrol here,' the constable said. 'Not spend your time drinking. Any questions?'

The men glanced at each other. Naylor reddened and looked down at the ground.

'It won't happen again,' he said.

'No,' Nottingham agreed. 'You're damned right it won't. You don't work for me any more. Mr Lister will pay you what you're owed. Now get out of here.'

'But—'

'Go.' For a second he wondered if they'd defy him, then Carter's shoulders slumped and he turned away. With a glare, Naylor followed. If they'd been doing their job, the boy and girl could have been in jail now.

Lister could hear the girl sobbing softly upstairs. But Joshua Bartlett didn't even seem to notice. He sat in front of the roaring fire in his dirty shirt and breeches with a mug of ale clamped in his large hand.

'You've had no threats? None of your girls, either?'

He snorted. 'Not unless someone has a death wish.'

Bartlett was a large man, with a barrel chest and a blacksmith's muscles. Long dark hair covered his neck, a mat of it on his chest, and a pale scar stood out on his chin. He did well enough to afford a small house by Mill Hill, out on the western edge of Leeds. Plates covered with scraps of food sat on the table. A mouse scurried quickly across the far corner of the room.

'Did you hear about the murder last night?'

The man raised his tankard, staring into the blaze. 'What about it?'

'A pimp. That's on top of three who've vanished in the last few weeks.'

Bartlett snorted. He was a man who relished violence; it was his answer to everything. But he was clever enough with it not to be caught. And people knew better than to complain to the constable about him.

He was a man with his tiny empire, three girls who either earned him money each day or wore their bruises. Once their bloom had faded, he found others to take their place. But he wasn't ambitious – all he wanted was not to have to work, to keep a little money in his pocket and some ale in his belly.

The sobbing upstairs grew quieter.

'Anyone tries it with me or my lasses, they'll be the ones who vanish,' he warned. 'And you can take that as a promise.' He tipped the mug up and drained it. 'Was that it?'

'Yes.'

He was glad to get away from the house, with its perfume of rotting food and the woman's crying. After that, the stink and the noise of Leeds swept over him like pure relief.

Bartlett thought with his fists. No one was going to cow him or send him packing. And if he was telling the truth, no one had tried. Maybe there was something else behind Kidd's death.

Rob had a hard job even finding the other pimps. It was late afternoon by the time he'd seen them all, pathetic men content to make their living off a woman's body. But none of them had been threatened; their denials were real enough.

'How do you feel, Mr Armistead?'

The man was in his bed, a servant dancing attendance. The doctor had been and gone, prescribing a poultice to draw out any sickness from the wound. Armistead was wealthy enough to have a hearth in the bedroom, and the servants had the fire blazing merrily.

'I'll be fine. That's what they say,' he answered gruffly. But he looked shaken. Without his wig and fine clothes, Armistead looked older, more frail, with a worn, padded body. His face was pale, and he kept sipping from the glass of brandy at the bedside. His expression turned hard as he looked at the constable. 'But it's no thanks to you, is it?'

'I'm sorry,' Nottingham answered. 'I had men there. But we couldn't catch them.' It was a lie, but he wasn't about to give him the truth.

'Then you'd damned well better try harder! I'll be sending John Brooke a letter about it. I was lucky. Happen the next one won't be.'

The constable nodded. With one hand on the doorknob he turned and said, 'I take it you'd prefer I said nothing to Mrs Armistead about Miss Marsden's presence at the market.'

That changed the man's tone. But he was right.

The boy and girl needed to be found very soon. Five more minutes and he left, passing the icy, disapproving stare of the man's wife and hearing the long-clock in the hall ominously ticking away the seconds.

'Carter and Naylor were waiting for me,' Rob said. 'They had some story that you'd dismissed them.'

'I have. We need to find a pair who won't spend their duty drinking. They could have had those cutpurses.'

They talked about it all as they walked out to Marsh Lane. The night hung cold and foggy around them. How did you catch a pair who were small and nimble? The constable's men couldn't be everywhere in town to stop them.

'Tomorrow we'll start going through Leeds. Everywhere they might sleep.'

'They'll simply disappear for a while and go back as soon as we've left,' Lister said.

'I know,' Nottingham agreed wearily. 'Maybe we'll be lucky.' But he didn't believe his own words. 'What else can we do?'

'Two wounded,' Brooke exploded. 'One of them a woman.'

'Three,' Nottingham said as he held up his bandaged hand. Not long after seven o'clock and still pitch dark outside. Candles burned bright in the mayor's office. The anger came off him in waves. Brooke picked up Armistead's letter then tossed it down again.

Damn the man, he'd written anyway, the

116

constable thought. He'd hoped the mention of Miss Marsden might keep pen from paper.

'Why haven't you caught them yet? I asked you back because you were good, Richard. Now we have all this.'

'We have five murders—'

'Moneylenders, a pimp and a pair of whores!' He slammed down a fist. 'Do you really think decent folk give a damn about them? They want to feel safe when they walk down Briggate. That's what's important.'

'We're going through all the places they could be.'

'Then catch them. I want them in the jail, Richard. That's an order.' He picked up the dish of coffee going cold on his desk. 'Well? What are you waiting for?'

'You don't look happy,' Rob said.

'I've just been flayed alive by the mayor,' Nottingham said. He poured a mug of ale and downed it in a single gulp. 'For now, we go after the cutpurses and ignore everything else.' He paused. 'That's what he wants.'

Lister hadn't expected anything else. If people didn't feel secure, they'd complain. To the aldermen, to the *Mercury*. That embarrassed the corporation. Simon Kirkstall had been good at keeping them all sweet; it had been his sole talent. But he'd never had to deal with anything like this pair.

'Waterhouse and Dyer are already out. They're starting by the old manor house. I sent the other two down past Fearn's Island. They'll work their way back from there.'

'We'll begin by the grammar school,' Nottingham decided.

They'd barely crossed the Head Row when Lister heard someone calling his name. He turned and saw the sexton of St John's church, a large, sweating man with a halo of wild white hair around his head, puffing his way out of the lych gate.

'What is it, Mr Castle?' he shouted. 'We're busy.'

'At the church,' the sexton said. 'Please, sir.'

Rob looked at the constable. Nottingham nodded. A minute or two would make no difference. They followed as the sexton waddled along the flagstones and into the porch of the church.

There, wrapped in a bundle of rags, lay a baby.

'I just came in and I saw it,' Castle explained. 'I was going to fetch me wife.'

'Get the poor thing inside,' the constable said. 'It's bitter out here.' He picked up the child. 'Skin's cold. It only looks a few hours old. In the vestry. Start a fire before it freezes to death.'

The baby hadn't woken. Rob wasn't sure it ever would.

'We can't take it,' Castle protested. 'We've had six and my wife won't stand for another.'

So much for Christian charity, Lister thought.

'What about Mrs Brett?' Nottingham asked. 'She used to take care of foundlings.'

'She died last year, boss.'

'Who do we have, then?'

'No one,' Rob admitted. He watched as the constable held the child close inside his greatcoat, trying to keep it warm and alive.

'A girl,' Nottingham said after a moment and looked at Castle. 'Your wife's going to have to look after her until you can find a wet nurse.'

'But—' the older man began.

'She was left here,' the constable reminded him quietly. 'The church will want to do its share, I'm sure.' He put the child in Castle's unwilling arms. 'Suffer the little children to come unto me, isn't that the verse?'

'What about the mother?' Lister asked as they walked through the churchyard.

'We can't do anything about her,' Nottingham replied bleakly. 'Except hope.'

Nottingham remembered some of the places they searched, a few from his childhood, others from all the years of work. Rob knew more spots. But by the time they arrived, most of the children had scattered. The ones who remained were ill or simply too tired to run off.

The constable saw their faces, grim, defiant as they stared up at him. They couldn't know he'd once been exactly like them. He'd waste his breath if he tried to explain. He was authority, he was the enemy.

'Those are all the camps I know,' Rob said by late afternoon. It was already dark, with a chill that ate through their clothes. They hadn't found the pair, but Nottingham had never truly expected they would.

'More children than there used to be,' the constable said as he settled into his chair at the jail, grateful for the warmth of the fire.

'Sign of the times, boss,' Lister told him,

pouring a mug of ale. 'People keep coming here. You must have seen that.'

'It's been that way as long as I can remember.' He had the scrawled reports from the other searchers. Nothing, of course. He pushed them across the desk for Rob. 'So how are we going to catch them?'

'Unless we have a stroke of luck, we probably won't,' Lister answered.

It was the bleak truth and Nottingham knew it. He sighed and nodded.

'You might as well go home. There's nothing more we can do here.'

'What about you?'

'I have a few people to see first.'

Never mind what the mayor said. Nottingham wasn't going to ignore the murders. Brooke could issue all the commands he liked but those deaths wouldn't vanish.

For two hours he walked up and down Briggate, trying to talk to the whores about the dead girl, about Charlotte, about pimps and moneylenders. He wasn't about to give up. He ducked into the inns and taverns, talking to the few old faces he recognized.

It was futile, he decided as he walked back down Kirkgate. But it confirmed what he suspected. Only one man, working alone, could stop any word from spreading. The knowledge didn't help him find the killer, but at least that offered some faint direction.

He tried not to think about the children he'd seen earlier. They'd freeze on a night like this, gathered tightly together to try and stay warm. He knew them better than they could ever imagine, and there was nothing he could do to help them.

Rob didn't go home immediately. Five minutes after leaving the jail he was knocking on Sexton Castle's door, a tiny stone cottage tucked behind Harrison's almshouses on the edge of St John's churchyard.

'Have you found her?' the man asked. 'The mother.'

'No.' There was no sense in saying they had too many things to do; he'd never understand. 'I was wondering if you'd found somewhere for the baby.'

The image of the tiny girl had stayed in his mind throughout the day. Not just her, but the way Nottingham held her and gazed at the child. It had stirred something. He couldn't even put a name to it, just a sense of unease, and a little fear. Emily wanted a child, but no matter how they tried, she never caught. Her miscarriage two years before seemed to have changed something inside.

'Mrs Webb is suckling,' Castle told him. 'She has milk for one more.'

'Will the girl survive?'

'That's in God's hands now. Mrs Castle said she was very sickly. Maybe it would be better for her if she passed.'

Rob stared at him, shocked. 'Why do you say that?' How could any death be good?

'Why?' The sexton seemed surprised by the question. 'The poor girl's come into the world with no one to want her. It would be a blessing.' Reproach crept into his voice. 'But we'll do what we can for her while she's here, sir.'

'The poor little thing,' Emily said when he told her. She didn't need to ask how anyone could abandon a baby. Emily spent her days with the poor and the desperate; she understood their hold on life was precarious.

'She might not live.' He sat by the fire with his boots off, toying with a cup of ale as he soaked in the warmth.

'Too many don't.' She looked at him and arched an eyebrow. 'What are you trying to say?'

'I don't know.' The only thing certain was the way the thought of the girl's face and tiny, helpless body had stayed with him. 'I . . .' He shook his head.

Twelve

A chill mist laced the dawn, leaving everything hazy and blurred. No wind, a clear sky, and dark smoke slowly spiralling up from the chimneys. Nottingham pulled the greatcoat closer around his neck.

It was cold enough to keep most people off the streets. But he was hoping that two children who'd found the taste for theft and wounding would be out. He'd primed the men, spreading them around the town. Rob had brought in two new recruits from somewhere, a pair he swore could think and who'd do the job soberly; he'd see how they liked a day of being out in this.

The constable tried to stay out of sight. They knew his face, and he had the wound to prove it. It was healing now, the skin on his palm itching, a reminder to stay alert and keep his own knife close to hand.

By dinner his feet were numb with cold. A pale sun shone but it offered no warmth. He had to keep walking, to keep watching, but he'd seen not the slightest trace of the pair. He felt as if his body knew every inch of Briggate and the Head Row. Too cold for Con to play his fiddle or for Jem to sit and tell his tales. Even the butchers in the Shambles only shouted their wares listlessly, wrapped in their heavy coats and mufflers.

He was close to the Talbot and his belly was rumbling. He'd see if Harry Meadows's improvements extended to the food.

'Mr Nottingham.' The man had the same broad smile, rubbing his hands together. 'What can I do for you?'

'Ale and some stew, Mr Meadows.' He began to reach for some coins, but Meadows stopped him.

'You and your men never pay here. You have a hard enough job as it is.'

The food was good, a far cry from the spiced, rancid beef Matthew Bell used to serve. Warmed inside, he sat by the fire, letting the heat fill him as he ate and drank. The place was doing a fair trade; word must have spread.

Then it was back to the cold, until he returned to the jail as dusk fell. Rob was already there, poking the fire to stir the blaze. He shook his head.

'I checked with the men. No one's seen them. No reports of cutpurses, though. Maybe we've scared them away.'

Nottingham shook his head. 'You don't really believe that, do you?'

'No.' He exhaled slowly. 'But we can hope.'

'Go home. You look perished.'

'What about you?'

'I still have things to do.' When Rob looked at him curiously, he simply smiled. 'Go and spend some time with that daughter of mine.'

Lister walked by Emily's school; the shutters were closed and the door locked. But she wasn't at Marsh Lane.

'Not seen her since this morning,' Lucy told him. 'You two haven't been rowing, have you?'

'You'd have heard if we had.'

'True enough.' She put her hands on her hips and stared at him. 'Then I daresay she'll be back when she's ready, unless she's run off with a tinker.' Lucy grinned.

Once Emily arrived, she hung her long, heavy cloak on a nail and hurried up the stairs without even glancing at him.

'What is it?' he asked. She was sitting on their bed, hands over her face. He put his arms around her. 'What's wrong?'

'I went to see that baby.' She sniffled and tried to smile as she wiped the tears from her cheeks. 'She's just so helpless.'

He didn't know how to reply; he'd never seen her like this. Emily was always so certain about things, ploughing ahead and expecting everyone else to follow. This was a side of her he didn't know, fragile and unsure. He held her close.

'We could take her,' she said tentatively after a long silence.

'Us?' Rob couldn't believe it. She had her school, he worked all hours . . . he didn't even know how long before the baby would be weaned.

'In time. When she's ready.' She moved, resting her head against his chest. 'I've thought about it. Lucy's here all the time. Papa's only going to be constable until they find someone else; you said that yourself.'

'I know, but—'

'And we don't seem to be able to have our own children.' That was the nub.

'Maybe we will.'

'We need to face the truth. There's no point in hoping, is there? She's going to need a home. We could call her Mary, after Mama.'

He'd been wrong. Emily wasn't unsure at all. She'd already come to her decision and made her plans.

'Are you certain?' It was the only thing he could ask.

'Yes,' she replied after the slightest hesitation. 'I am.'

'Perhaps I suppose I should start calling you Mama, then.'

Suddenly she had her arms around his neck, kissing him deeply.

'Don't tell anyone yet,' Emily warned. 'Nobody.

Not until I have everything arranged.' She hesitated. 'And we know she'll live.'

At least he was out of the weather. With darkness, a light rain had begun to fall, quickly turning to sleet so sharp that it seemed to burn his cheeks. Nottingham moved from one inn to the next. Con was playing in one corner of the Pack Horse, his old hat set out for coins, a cup of ale on the table next to him.

The constable searched for all the faces he'd once relied on once for information. Only a few were still around, two in the New King's Arms, one in the Rose and Crown. What had happened to them all, he wondered? But none of them had anything to offer him on the killings.

'Nowt,' Ned Carr said. 'I haven't been asking, but there's no one saying a word, and that's not like folk. Nobody knows what's going on.'

'What do you think?'

'Ee, don't ask me.' He lit a taper from the fire and put it to his pipe. 'I listen, and there's nothing to hear.' His eyes narrowed. 'I'll tell you summat odd, though. Do you remember Walter Dunkley?'

He had a faint memory of the man. Big, rowdy, liked to drink.

'What about him?'

'He's been slinking around the last few weeks. Not been out taking a drink. Hardly seen him anywhere,' he added. 'Not like him at all.'

The constable laid two coins on the table. 'Where does he live?'

* * *

126

A cellar room, and pitch black on the stairs. Nottingham felt his way down carefully, one hand against the wall, testing each of the wooden steps before he put his weight on it. At the bottom he groped his way to a door and knocked hard.

He remembered Walter as soon as he saw him, illuminated by the weak glow from a lantern. But the man had changed. His cheeks were hollow and the clothes sagged on his body. This wasn't a killer; this was someone who barely had a hold on life. Come spring he'd be no more than a husk, if he was still here.

'What do you want?' There was no menace in his voice.

'People are wondering where you've been.'

'None of their business.'

The constable could see past him. There was no fire in the room, only a brown patch of slow, trickling damp on the wall.

'Maybe it's not,' he agreed. 'But they worry.'

Dunkley snorted and spat on the ground.

'You know who I am, don't you?' Nottingham asked.

'Right enough.'

'What do you know about the recent murders?'

The man started to laugh. Before he could catch his breath it turned into a bout of coughing that doubled him over. Dunkley groped for a small bottle on the table and managed to take a swig.

'Me? Know anything?' He wiped his eyes and gulped down air. 'What would I know about killings? Got me work cut out trying to last till evening. I don't have time for any of that now.'

'Then who might?' Nottingham asked. The man was dying, but there was nothing he could do about that. Nothing anyone could do; Dunkley wouldn't let them.

'Have you tried John Wood?' The cough began again. Another nip from the bottle stopped it.

John Wood. Interesting that his name should come up again.

'He claims he's working for Mr Warren these days. A bookkeeper.'

'If you believe that, happen you should have stayed retired.' Dunkley turned his head and spat. 'Now go on, get out of here.'

John Wood. It would be a good place to start in the morning.

Ogle's bookshop was no more than a hundred yards along Kirkgate from the jail. He'd rarely been inside, but the manager knew him, wishing him a pleasant good morning. The musty smell of mildew and old paper followed him up the stairs.

Warren's office was a jumble of papers, but there was no sign of the man himself. Wood was alone, bent over his desk, a quill in his hand. He looked up with a start as Nottingham entered, trying to pull papers over his work.

Too late, though. The constable picked up the document and the one beside it.

'I thought you said you had a talent for numbers.'

'I do,' Wood answered. His face was red and his hand began to shake. 'I'm just copying that for a gentleman. We do it if they ask.'

'Copying?' He read through one paper, then the other. 'You're not doing a good job of it, then. Look, you've changed a few words. Here and here and here. If I didn't know better, I'd think that Mr Joseph Middleton owned a certain property in Holbeck instead of Mr Martin.' The constable shook his head. 'That's very poor work. Should I tell your employer?'

'Don't, please. He dun't know.' His eyes were pleading. 'The gentleman offered me a guinea to do it and mek it look official. I've got a woman now, Mr Nottingham.' He reached out a hand for the papers but the constable rolled them and put them in his jacket pocket.

'What else am I going to find in here, John?' He leaned forward, hands on the desk, his face close enough to Wood's to smell the sour, frightened breath. 'Something like that could see you transported for seven years. Not too many last long enough to come home from there.'

'What do you want?' He lowered his head.

'I want to know about the killings that have been going on. Moneylenders. A pimp. Two whores. I need to find out who's behind it.'

'I can't—'

Nottingham cut him off. 'I don't think you heard me properly.' His voice was cold. 'I'm not offering you a choice. I don't care how you find out. And if you try to lie to me, you'll be up before a judge before you know it. Maybe that woman of yours will even miss you.'

Back on Kirkgate he smiled to himself. He knew he could have searched the office and found plenty to damn Warren. But he didn't care about that for now. It could wait for another day. He wanted the killer.

Something was growing. He could feel it, as certain as the fact that day would break tomorrow. Something was festering under the surface. And he needed to lance it before it took over.

Lister slid on to the bench beside the constable. All around them, the White Swan was filled with people. A group of merchants huddled in one corner discussing business. Working men warmed themselves by the fire before an afternoon in the cold.

'Dyer caught a glimpse of the cutpurses this morning,' he said. 'He went after them but they'd already gone. Into thin air, he said.'

Nottingham put the pie back on the plate.

'Where did it happen?'

'Mill Hill. Out near the tenter fields. He said the Parish Church had just rung eight o'clock.'

Nottingham gulped down the last of his ale and stood. 'Let's take a look.'

'I was going to eat.'

The constable grinned. 'Then you should have arrived earlier. Come on.'

The thin wind down by the river seemed to slice at his skin. Rob pulled the high collar closer around his ears. His legs felt heavy with the cold, like moving lead. Not a soul to be seen on the grass. No cloth hung out to stretch on the tenter posts in this weather.

Where was the boss going? He was striding out ahead, never pausing or glancing around until Leeds lay half a mile behind them, only grass

130

and woods ahead. The air might be fresh here, but it was bitter.

Near the top of a rise, Nottingham stopped and pointed.

'Do you see that? Smoke.'

He was right; a wispy spiral rose through the trees, almost invisible in the pale light.

'What now, boss?' Rob asked.

'We go in as quietly as we can. We'll do it together. No one's going to be watching in this weather. They'll all be huddled round the fire.'

Lister followed. Once they were in the trees, the constable stopped for a moment, finding his bearings, then eased through the tall grass, trying to be silent. Soon enough Rob could smell the fire and the scent of cooking. Nottingham halted again and whispered 'We'll just walk straight in. You're faster than me, you go after the boy if he's there. I'll point him out.'

Without another word he plunged into the small clearing. Rob barely had chance to take in the rough shelters made of branches before the children were up and scattering like a flock of birds, darting off hither and yon through the trees.

'There!' He pointed towards a scrawny lad with black hair, already vanishing deeper into the woods. Lister followed, running hard. He had surprise on his side, quickly gaining on the boy. He passed the other children, barely noticing them, intent on the figure ahead.

He was no more than ten yards away when the boy suddenly swerved and grabbed a girl who was trying to hide between a tree. The penknife was in his fist, the blade at the child's throat.

131

'You don't want to do that.' Rob was panting hard, keeping his distance. He put his hands out, showing they were empty. The little girl looked terrified, too frightened to move. But the boy's face showed nothing. No emotion of any kind. Just dark, calculating eyes.

'Let her go. You can run. I won't follow if you don't harm her.' He moved a step closer. The boy pulled the girl's hair, exposing her throat and pushing the blade against the skin.

'I promise,' Rob said, a desperate edge in his voice. 'Just go, leave her.'

The boy stayed silent. Then, in one swift move, he slid the knife across the girl's neck and let her drop. Without a backward glance, he skittered away, jumping over a fallen log and disappearing.

Lister was on his knees, cradling the girl's head. She'd fainted. He took off his greatcoat, wrapping it around her. The wound was bleeding, but it wasn't deep or dangerous. And definitely not fatal.

The boy was already out of sight. Sweet Christ, he thought, how could anyone do that? The girl was beginning to stir, crying, screaming. Rob stroked her hair and tried to soothe her. The blood was already starting to dry on her neck. He pulled out a dirty handkerchief, spat on it and tried to wipe the wound clean.

'You're going to be fine,' he told her softly, repeating it until she looked at him with wide eyes and began to nod. The tears still came, trailing down her cheeks, and she was shivering hard.

Carefully, he picked her up and began to walk to the camp, talking softly. She was no weight at all in his arms, nothing more than skin and bone.

The constable was already there. 'What happened?'

It only took three quick sentences to recount the tale. Nottingham looked down at the girl.

'Don't worry,' he told her. 'We'll look after you now.'

There was something in his tone: she believed him and gave a timid smile. Rob could imagine how Nottingham had been as a father. He'd shown it just now, and with the baby in the church porch. The tenderness, the gentleness.

'What are we going to do with her, boss?'

'Take her home to Lucy. She'll know what to do.'

'But—'

'Look at her. She needs a good meal, some clean clothes, and somewhere warm. We'll think about the rest after that. Would you like to sleep inside, by the fire?' he asked the girl, and she nodded her reply. 'What's your name?'

She hesitated for a moment, as if she needed to remember it. 'Annie.'

'That's a pretty name. There's a lady called Lucy who'll take care of you. Mr Lister will take you there.'

'What happened with the girl?' Rob asked.

He grimaced. 'She was too quick for me. Gone before I even started.' He rubbed the bristles on his chin. 'I want that lad.' He clapped his hands together. 'You look after Annie here, then come back to the jail.'

* * *

Lucy examined the girl while he recounted it all. From the moment he came through the door she'd taken charge, carefully shepherding Annie into the kitchen and settling her down on a stool.

'Don't you worry, we'll have you warm and clean in no time,' she said as she ladled soup into a bowl. 'Go on, get that inside you. Your skin's like ice.' He watched, knowing there was no more he could do. 'You did right, bringing her here,' Lucy said as he turned to leave.

'It was the boss's idea.'

'Doesn't matter whose it was,' she said. 'It was still good.'

Thirteen

He'd never had a hope of catching the girl. As soon as she saw his face she was darting away, surefooted through the trees. Nottingham had started to give chase but gave up quickly. She was too fast for him, she knew these woods too well. He'd often slept out here when he was young, but that was years before. The young man he'd been back then had long since vanished.

The boy was going to kill. It felt inevitable. As they walked into town, Rob had described his expression. No feeling, no fear. He'd had a taste of blood and he liked it. How were they going to stop him?

He paced around the jail, trying to find a plan.

* * *

134

'They're going to be even more careful now,' the constable said.

Evening now, sitting at home with hot food in their bellies. The day had sparked no new schemes, just thoughts that trickled nowhere.

'At least we know who they are,' Rob said.

'That's not worth much.'

Nick and Kate. Those were the names Annie had given when Lucy talked to her. They'd arrived just a fortnight before, she said, the two of them together, and taken over the group of homeless children.

'From what she says, they're a right evil pair,' Lucy told him. 'He beats anyone who steps out of line or questions him. Keeps all the money they steal for themselves.'

'How's Annie?' Nottingham asked.

'Asleep in my bed. It's probably the first warm night she's had in an age. Her mam died a year back and she's never had a da that she's ever seen. Doesn't know what happened to her little brother.'

It was no different from so many histories the constable had heard through the years. Life was rarely soft and gentle. 'What about her wound?'

'She won't even have a scar,' Lucy replied. 'It's just a scratch. Bled a bit, but that's the worst of it. A week and you won't know it was ever there.'

'I'll need to talk to her.'

'When she wakes, Papa,' Emily said quietly. 'Let her rest.'

He nodded. The girl deserved her sleep, at the very least.

'What are we going to do with her?' Rob asked.

Nottingham could feel their eyes on him. He didn't know the answer; he hadn't even thought that far ahead when he told Rob to bring her here. Find a family to take Annie in? Let her stay? But where would she sleep? What would she do?

'I could ask the Williamsons,' Emily suggested. 'They might know of someone. Oh.' She frowned, annoyed at herself. 'With everything else, I forgot: Mr Williamson stopped at the school this afternoon. They're holding the dance to benefit the school on November the fifth at the Cloth Hall. Isn't that wonderful?'

Nottingham glanced at Lister. Any other day in the year and that would be excellent news. But November the fifth was Gunpowder Treason Night. Bonfires burning all over Leeds and men shooting off their guns to celebrate. The apprentices would be out drinking and ready to riot. There'd be no rest for the constable and his men until the early hours.

'That's very good, indeed,' he told her. From the head of the table he could see Rob and Emily exchanging looks. No matter; if there was something they wanted him to know, they'd tell him in time. 'I'm off to my bed.'

'Annie was still asleep when I left,' Nottingham said. He'd put fresh coal on the fire in the jail to take off the dawn chill. 'Lucy's going to try and find out more about this Nick and Kate from her.'

'They'll have their eyes open for us now.' Rob poured a mug of ale.

'Good. I want them looking over their shoulder the whole time. That way they'll make mistakes. Keep the men out around town again.'

'Yes, boss.' He hesitated. 'You know that Emily will expect us to go to that dance.'

'I daresay she will,' the constable agreed with a smile. 'Women always do. You can go, I'll take care of everything. I'm not sure who'll have the more troublesome job.'

The note had been pushed under the door of the jail during the night. John Wood had taken the threats seriously. *Talk to Oliver Nelson*, it said.

The constable had a hazy recollection of the man. Lanky, too thin for his clothes, the type who nibbled at the edge of the law but was scared to go too far on the other side. Someone who would once have spent his evenings at the Talbot. But where would he drink now?

Nottingham walked with no sense of where he was wandering. Nelson had worked, he seemed to remember that, but for the life of him, he didn't know at what. He stood at the top of Briggate, gazing back down the street towards the river. His breath bloomed in the air. At least the sun was shining to hearten everyone. And it was only the shank end of October; the cold had come too early this year.

Off in the distance he heard a fiddle begin to play a lively tune, the sounds rising above the rumble of cartwheels on the cobbles. Warm music for a frosty morning. He followed the sound down to Vicar Lane.

Blind Con was standing with his back against the wall, lost in the melody and keeping time with his foot. He'd cut the fingers off a pair of gloves, and his left hand danced swiftly over the strings. Nottingham watched the people who passed, seeing them start to smile, one or two of them dropping small coins in the hat. He waited until the final note then dropped in a farthing of his own.

'Well met, Mr Nottingham. I heard you arrive.' He always knew.

'Keep playing like that and you'll have spring here before we know it.'

'People like something cheerful on a day like this. And it stops my fingers from freezing. This weather's too bitter for an old man.'

'Tell me, Con, do you know someone called Oliver Nelson?'

'Tall fellow, a very light tread,' Con replied after a moment. 'Likes to talk when he's had a few drinks.'

That sounded like Nelson. 'Do you know where I'd find him?'

'Last I heard, he was working for Cooper the wheelwright.' He stared at the constable as if his blind eyes could see. 'What's he done?'

'Nothing that I know of. Why?'

'He's always kept low company, that's all.' He shrugged and raised the fiddle to his shoulder, drawing the bow over the strings slowly, as if deciding on a melody before starting on another lively piece.

Cooper had his business in a cramped yard off Swinegate, making the wheels for carts and

138

carriages. Two apprentices sweated to join the curved pieces as he supervised, cursing them until he was satisfied with their work. He wore a heavy leather apron that hid a big, broad chest, long hair tied back in a sailor's queue.

'Help you, sir?'

'I'm Richard Nottingham—'

'I know who you are,' Cooper cut him off. 'What do you want?'

'Oliver Nelson.'

'Steaming shed.' He gestured to the rear of the yard, then barked out, 'Olly!'

A few heartbeats later a door opened in a wreath of steam and Nelson emerged, wiping the damp from his face with a dirty rag. As soon as he saw the constable, he stopped, panic rising.

Nottingham took a step, but the other man was faster. In one quick movement he hauled himself on to the roof of the shed and was away over the wall behind, gone from sight in two blinks of an eye.

'Where does he live?' the constable asked. But Cooper was still staring, not believing what he'd seen. 'I said where?'

'Queen's Court,' one of the apprentices answered.

He pushed past the people on the street. A herder was driving his cattle up Briggate. Nottingham dodged between the animals, hearing them low and smelling their sweet breath, then ran through the tiny entrance to the court.

Houses were jammed one against the other, only a thin path threading through to another ginnel at the end that led through to Call Lane. Nottingham could feel his heart beating hard in his chest as he looked around for the smallest sign of movement.

Finally he caught something from the corner of his eye, there and gone as fast as a kingfisher. A shadow behind a dirty window, three houses along, up on the second storey. He pulled the loop of his cudgel around his wrist.

The front door gave easily as soon as he pushed against it. The stairs groaned as he climbed. His mouth was dry, the taste of metal on his tongue. The constable took each step carefully, watching and listening.

Nobody was waiting upstairs. There was only a single door in front of him, warped in its frame. He could hear a child whimpering on the other side. Nottingham turned the knob and forced his shoulder against the wood.

Nelson was there, standing in the middle of the room with a knife in his hand and terror on his face. A woman cowered in the corner, her shawl pulled over the infant in her arms.

The constable didn't hesitate. As Nelson raised his weapon, arm shaking, he brought the tip of the cudgel down on his wrist. The man's fingers opened and the blade clattered to the boards.

This was the time: bustle him out of there before the shock wore off. Nelson came easily, not even turning to look back at his family as Nottingham led him away.

'You've broken my wrist.' He had his teeth gritted against the pain.

'You shouldn't have been holding a knife.'

Nelson sat placidly in the cell, head bowed, gently rocking to and fro. A few hours of cold and pain would soften him up, Nottingham thought as he turned the key in the lock.

Lister marched out along Boar Lane, then over the tenter fields that ran down to the river. In the distance, the woods were silent, only the caw of a single crow breaking the stillness.

The camp had gone. Just a few branches strewn on the ground and the cold remains of a fire hinted it had ever existed. The children had moved on. He hadn't hoped for much, but he needed to check.

None of the men had spotted the cutpurses. But it was easy enough to stay out of sight in Leeds. Still, if they'd only been here a fortnight, Nick and Kate wouldn't really know the town yet. Yet that didn't seem to help catch the little bastards. Angrily, he kicked at a stone and watched it skitter across the grass.

Emily had visited the baby again after school, she told him as they lay in bed the night before; that was why she'd been late coming home. She'd held the girl, changed her, watched as she fed. He heard the wonder in her voice, the pleasure of it all. Mrs Webb was happy to suckle the child, especially if Emily gave her a few pennies every week. When the time was right they'd bring Mary home to Marsh Lane.

He hadn't said a word. He knew how much she wanted this. A part of him felt the same way, filled with the idea of a child that was theirs. But then he thought again and the whole thing terrified him, being responsible for something so tiny and fragile. He'd be scared to touch her,

141

let alone hold her in his arms. How could he look after someone so small? How could he teach her? How could he love her the way a father should when she wasn't his own flesh and blood?

And there was Annie. What were they going to do with her? The boss didn't appear worried, and Lucy was happy to have someone else around the house. But she couldn't say there forever. They'd have to find someone to take her in.

Back on Boar Lane, among the press of unwashed bodies, the thoughts fled. Nick and Kate, that was his business.

The apothecary set the wrist. A sharp tug made Nelson cry out, then the man held on to the splints and wrapped them with a grubby bandage. Richard Nottingham stood and watched, sipping from a mug of ale. Finally they were alone.

'I ent done nowt wrong.'

But his defiance was as thin as air.

'No?' The constable leaned against the wall. 'Of course you haven't. Innocent men always run from the law then pull knives.' He sighed. 'This time you can tell me the truth.'

'I were feart.'

'Maybe you were. After all, you know about a murder or two.'

Nelson brought his head up sharply, eyes wide. He opened his mouth, but no words came.

'I dun't know owt,' he said finally.

'Yes, you do,' Nottingham said. 'And you're going to tell me.'

Five minutes of prying and threats and he had it. Nelson had been walking back late from Hunslet, caught in the foggy night. He'd stopped as soon as he saw the figures on the bridge. Two men, struggling.

'Then I saw one mek a slash, like, and heave t' other over the parapet. Felt like forever afore I heard t' splash in watter. Then the man on the bridge, he picked summat up and tossed it over t' side 'fore he walked off.'

'Which direction did he take?'

'Into town. He'd have seen me elsewise.'

'What did you do?'

'I stayed there.' His eyes glared. Good, a little of the man's spark was returning. 'What do you think? I'm not daft.'

'What did the man look like?'

'Nobbut a shape in the fog. Big lad, mebbe. Strong, too, by t' look of him.' He shrugged. 'I don't rightly know. Don't want to, neither.'

'Did you see his face?'

Nelson shook his head. Silence filled the cell. It had been foggy the night Smith was killed, Nottingham thought, and always thickest by the river.

'What else?'

'Nowt.' He spat the answer. But it came too quickly and he looked away as he spoke.

'Don't lie to me.'

Still he said nothing. Then, 'I've heard what's been going on. Them killings. The way he just turned and walked off like it were nowt . . . if he knew I'd seen it I reckon he'd do for me, too.' There was a plea under his words.

The chase, the broken wrist. Nelson was terrified for his life.

'Go home,' he said.

'You won't say owt?'

'No.' People would hear that the man had been in the jail, but they wouldn't know why. He hadn't even had much to say, just an image as ghostly as the one the constable had seen. Big and broad. It could have been the same man. Or one of many in Leeds.

He was still sitting at the desk when Lister returned.

'Not a peep out of the cutpurses.' He sat with a long, weary sigh and stretched out his legs. 'Maybe yesterday made them decide to leave. I feel like I've been round the town ten times today hunting for them.'

'We'll find out in time if they've gone.' Nottingham raised an eyebrow. 'I want the men on the same duty for the moment. Let's keep the mayor happy.'

'Yes, boss.'

The constable smiled. 'Do you think you've got the strength to walk home?'

It was dark, but the chill of the day had eased. Thin cloud covered the sky, hiding the stars.

'What about this dance at the Cloth Hall?' Nottingham asked after he'd told Lister about Oliver Nelson. 'Looking forward to it?'

Rob grinned and laughed. 'You've never seen me dance, have you?'

'I'll wager you can't be any worse than me. Mary used to love going to the balls,' he began, then closed his mouth into a tight line and went quiet.

Annie was waiting in the house, wearing an

144

old house dress of Emily's that Lucy had cut down. The girl was bathed and clean, hair shining from the brush, but still nervous as she gazed up at all the adult eyes. Still, she was warm, she was fed. The cut on her neck was still a harsh red line, but it would heal well.

She helped to serve the meal, balancing each plate very carefully and walking slowly from the kitchen.

'I talked to her after I came home,' Emily said after she'd gone. 'Annie's a bright girl, Papa. Very sweet.'

'You sound like you have something in mind.' Nottingham's eyes were twinkling.

'Well,' she began slowly, 'I talked to Mrs Williamson today. They've just taken on a girl. But Lucy could use some help. And she could come to the school every morning.'

'She lasted out there for a year,' he reminded his daughter. 'That's a hard life. She might be a handful.'

'Lucy did that, too,' Emily reminded him. 'And you wouldn't want to be rid of her now.'

Was that what life was going to be like in the years ahead, he wondered? Taking in strays and giving them a home? Still, the girl needed somewhere, that was true enough.

'She can stay until we find her a place somewhere else,' he agreed. As Emily began to speak, he held up a finger. 'But she goes to school part of each day.'

'Yes, Papa,' she agreed, but she was smiling. He noticed her glance uncertainly at Rob. He gave a small nod. 'There's something else.'

'Go on.'

'The baby that was left at St John's.' He watched as she reached across and took Lister's hand and everything tumbled into place. 'We'd like to give her a home, too.'

'What about your teaching?' Nottingham asked.

'Lucy will look after her during the day. I've talked to her about it.' She blushed. 'That's why another servant here might help.'

'You're sure about this?' He looked from one of them to the other. Emily was glowing, Rob uncertain; but he'd do whatever she wanted.

'Yes,' she answered, 'I am. As soon as she doesn't need the breast any more. It's your house, though, Papa.'

Maybe it was, but she'd outmanoeuvred him and sprung her small ambush perfectly. He knew what his wife would have said. She had had a generous heart. And perhaps it was time to hear a baby crying here again, to bring some new life into the place and wake it up.

'You don't need to ask. She'll be welcome here.'

Emily beamed, her eyes brimming, on the edge of tears.

'There's one more thing, Papa: if you're willing, we'd like to call her Mary.'

Rob listened as the constable questioned Annie about the cutpurses, amazed by the soft way he approached her. Nottingham settled himself awkwardly on a low stool, looking her in the eye, smiled and started by telling the girl she had a home here if she wanted it.

He was used to seeing the boss question men, but here he was entirely different, gently nudging the girl in one direction or another with his words. The young children quickly learned to keep their distance from the older ones, she told him. But she'd kept her eyes open and remembered a few things. Nick was quick to anger and use his fists. He seemed to relish his temper and his violence. Kate looked as if she adored him for it.

'Why?' Annie asked. 'Why would she do that, sir?'

'Some people are made that way,' the constable told her quietly. 'They think power is important.'

He never talked down to the girl, he answered her questions seriously and thoughtfully. More than that, Rob thought, he made her feel welcome, a part of the family. Lucy hovered close the whole time like a mother hen, but she kept her mouth closed. Finally he thanked Annie and stood, pushing himself upright with a frown of pain.

'What do you make of that?' Nottingham said as they sat by the fire.

'I think we'd better hope they've left Leeds.'

'We can hope, but I doubt they have,' he said after a moment. 'Too much opportunity for them here. And it's easy to hide.'

'Then I don't think this Nick will let himself be taken.'

'No.' The constable sighed. 'Neither do I.'

Fourteen

There was a dampness in the air that leeched through his skin and made his joints ache as he walked into town. Mist lingered over the water and clung around the trestles set up on Briggate for the cloth market.

Nottingham walked up and down the street after the bell sounded to start trading, then past the small ginnel where Jane and the girl who looked like Rose had tried to make their living. Out on the bridge the fog hung more thickly, muffling all the sounds until they might have been coming from a different world.

All he had was a couple of blurred glimpses of a killer. But it was the same man, he knew that inside, even if he couldn't make sense of the why or how behind it. Slowly, he strolled back, alert for anything untoward. Near Kirkgate he spotted Tom Williamson. The man was smiling broadly; the morning must have brought some good bargains.

'A fine market today, Richard. Very fine.'

'Made some money?'

'I've spent enough.' He laughed. 'But never mind. I'll turn a good profit on it.' He rubbed at a sliver of dirt on his tricorn hat. 'You're coming to the dance, of course?'

'Bonfire Night. Someone has to keep an eye

on the town. I'll leave the dancing to Emily and Mr Lister.'

'Oh, come on, Richard. I remember you used to cut a fine figure.'

'A very reluctant one.'

'It's for a good cause. Your daughter's school.' Williamson grinned. 'I'm sure I could find a few widows who'd love to take a turn with you.'

Nottingham laughed. 'That's very kind of you. But we'd both be better off if I'm working. You know there's always trouble on Gunpowder Treason Night.'

'From what I hear, you already have enough of that. Armistead's been complaining to everyone who'll listen. He's saying it's too dangerous to walk on the streets of Leeds these days.'

'A pair of cutpurses have been giving us a problem,' he admitted and held up his bandaged hand as proof. 'Don't worry, we'll catch them. Still, between us, watch yourself.'

'I shall, don't you worry.' He glanced around the cloth market as if he was trying to spot something else worth his time. 'I'd better get to the warehouse before those weavers arrive.' His voice was merry. 'A pity, though, you'll miss an excellent dance.'

The constable had a man on the market at the top of Briggate, and walked through the crowds until he saw him in position.

Nottingham stayed by the Moot Hall steps, half listening to Jem entertain with his tales. But his eyes kept roaming across the faces. Maybe Rob was right; maybe Nick and Kate had been

149

frightened away. But in his heart he doubted it; they weren't done with Leeds yet.

The pair didn't appear at the market, though, or anywhere else in town. All along the inns on Briggate, the weavers were celebrating selling their cloth and the whores were doing good business, every one of them out for a market day, teasing and touting for business.

There were plenty of faces he'd never seen before among the prostitutes, but none of them knew the dead girl who'd looked like Rose. She was in the ground now, but images of her kept appearing in his head, both the timid little thing who spoke so hopefully and the corpse he'd examined on the slab.

But how many other faces had paraded through his mind over the years? He couldn't even begin to count them. He'd tried to give every one of them justice. They all deserved that. Sometimes he'd succeeded. Too often, it seemed, he'd failed.

He felt as if he was spending his days chasing ghosts. Vanishing cutpurses, a man glimpsed in the murk who let no word slip to anyone. He eyed everyone he passed, trying to compare them to the figure he'd half seen. That was madness, and he knew it. What he needed was some substance, even the tiniest piece, that small thread he could tug and unravel the cloth.

At least no more had died. But five was too many, far too many in such a short space of time. And it hadn't ended. Until he found the killer, he knew there would be more.

'I want one of the night men watching the bridge,' he told Rob. 'Do we have anyone reliable?'

'There's Flint. He doesn't drink too much and he follows orders well.'

'Can he keep his eyes open and stay at his post?'

'As long as you lay it all out clearly for him.'

The constable sighed. That was the way it had always been; those covering the nights seemed to be the lost, hopeless ones. But what could he expect? The job paid next to nothing.

'I want him to stay out of sight. And if he notices anything . . .'

'Yes, boss.'

Lister escorted Flint to a spot south of the bridge. Far enough away to keep hidden, but close enough to see, then run and break up any trouble.

'You understand?' he asked again. 'Stay here. This is where you'll be for the next few nights.'

'Yes, Mr Lister,' the man replied seriously. He tried hard, Rob knew, he wanted to work well. 'Stand here till morn, and if owt happens on t' bridge, go and break it up.' Flint smiled, pleased with himself.

'That's it.'

He went through it all once again, then left. At least he could be sure that the man wouldn't wander away during the night. Back at the jail, Rob talked to Crandall, telling him to keep the men alert as the inns closed for the night. Saturday was always bad. Men had been paid, they had a day of rest ahead of them. Drink would fire all the pent-up grievances and anger from the week. Fists and boots out on the cobbles. Knives.

'Bang a few heads together and drag them into the cells,' Lister said. But he knew full well that Crandall wouldn't be out there himself. Like his late relative, Simon Kirkstall, he was too delicate for a scrap.

Nottingham sat in the room off the stable behind the Rose and Crown with Jem. The storyteller had the place tidy, with sweet, fresh straw for the bed, a brazier burning to give some heat.

'That Molly, the landlord's daughter, she brings me food that's left over from the kitchen,' Jem said. 'Lovely lass.' He smiled as he looked around the small room. 'This isn't a bad place to spend the winter. Cosy enough, too. And folk seem to like the tales.'

'You need to come out to my house again,' the constable told him.

'Any time you want me, it'll be my pleasure. Did I tell you that three or four years back I went around with a magician?'

'Magician?' Nottingham said. He'd seen one at the market once, drawing a crowd that gasped and applauded his skill and showered him with coins.

'Oh aye. He did it all – card tricks, made stuff appear and disappear, everything. They loved him in the markets. We were always being invited to people's homes for the night. Grand places, an' all. He'd entertain the gentry and I'd tell my stories to the servants.' He laughed. 'He got the money but I got the better food and company.' He sighed. 'We had a little circuit – Thirsk, Malton, Northallerton, then into York.'

'Why did you stop?'

'George, that was his name, he died. It were in Malton. We were sleeping in a farmer's barn. Right as rain when we went to sleep, dead when I tried to rouse him the next morning. I've not been back since. Too many memories.'

Nottingham ate at the inn, watching people come and go. Conversation ebbed and flowed around him. John Reynolds, the landlord, was rushing hither and yon, up and down the stairs, serving food or clearing the tables.

Briggate was still busy with groups of men determined to enjoy Saturday night. He could hear some of them singing out of tune somewhere.

He realized he'd fallen back into the rhythm of the job without thinking, as if he'd never been away. Early mornings, evenings that stretched out late, too little sleep. But he'd done it for so long that it all returned as naturally as breathing.

As he walked he glanced at faces. They were all so young, so open and eager for life. He must have been that way once; it was impossible to recall now.

The whores were busy, bustling men away as soon as they were finished, ready for the next. He saw some of the night men on their rounds. There was nothing more for him tonight. No more secrets to be squeezed from today.

The church bells were ringing. The clouds lingered, making a drab, grey day. The cells were full: men brawling when drunk, two women who'd got into a scrap over a jug of gin. Tomorrow they'd all be up before the petty assizes, fined and released.

Rob Lister returned from the morning rounds and stood in front of the fire, soaking up the warmth.

'Quiet out there.'

'Sundays usually are,' the constable said. 'Be glad at least one day of the week is.'

'Emily took me to see the baby last night.'

'Were you scared to hold her?' He laughed.

'I was terrified I'd drop her.'

Nottingham nodded. 'I was like that the first time, too. You get used to it. At least she's alive. When we saw her in the church porch I didn't think she'd last the day.'

'She's thriving, according to Mrs Webb. Putting on weight. But she'll be there a while yet.'

'You're going to be a papa.' He lifted his mug of ale in a toast.

'And you'll be a grandfather. But this . . . I don't know, it just seems a strange way to do it,' Rob said.

'What's so odd? She needs a home. You can give her one. There's nothing bad about that.'

'I know.' But Nottingham could tell that the lad wasn't convinced yet; the hesitation in his voice gave him away. There was nothing he could say that would sway him; he'd have to come to terms with it himself. It was time to change the topic.

'Make sure we keep two men on Kirkgate this morning. I don't want the cutpurses trying to rob anyone on their way to church.'

'Yes, boss.' He frowned. 'I've been doing some thinking about these murders.'

The constable glanced up at him. 'Go on.'

154

'What if the deaths of the moneylenders were someone's revenge, and Kidd's murder came from an argument?'

'We searched into the idea of revenge and we didn't find anything. Show me something to convince me. And you're forgetting the murder of the whore and Four-Finger Jane.'

'Maybe they seem connected because they all came in a flurry,' Rob argued. 'It's been quiet ever since.'

Nottingham raised an eyebrow. 'You don't think five of them is enough?'

'No, it's not that.' Lister began to pace around the room. 'I'm just trying to make some sense of it . . .'

'Then you're talking about three different killers. One for the moneylenders, one for the pimp, and another for the girls.'

'Yes.'

'Come on,' the constable said. 'Don't you think someone would have given us a name in that case? Three different murderers? We'd be bound to know something by now. And you know what we've got. Silence.'

Rob sighed and stared out of the window. Nottingham watched, about to say more, when Lister tensed.

'The cutpurses,' he shouted and pulled the door open. By the time Nottingham reached the corner, a boy was running down Briggate, people moving aside to watch.

If Nick was here, Kate had to be somewhere close. Slowly, deliberately, he looked around. Then he spotted her, walking along Kirkgate towards the church, trying to blend in with the crowd on their way to service.

If he ran she'd only dash away and he wouldn't have a hope of catching her. Instead, he walked quickly, head down so she wouldn't see his face. But the girl never looked back. Just before the church, she slipped down High Court and out of sight.

The constable rushed. He turned the corner, but she was already gone. At the end of the short lane he looked both ways, but there was no sign of her. Should he gamble on one direction?

Nick was fast. Rob raced down Briggate and he couldn't gain any ground. Folk stared, stopping and turning to watch the chase. Then a figure stepped into the road, waving his arms to try and stop the boy. Tom Williamson, his face broad and serious.

The lad could have ducked around him and not even missed a step. Instead he deliberately aimed for the man, ramming against him and bouncing away, moving even faster than before.

Williamson fell, hands clutching at his belly. His wife was no more than three yards away, already beginning to scream. She pulled her children close and folded her arms around them.

Rob knelt, panting hard. Williamson's clothes were already soaked with blood. He tore them away, trying to discover how bad the wound might be. The merchant looked up, surprised at it all, biting his lip to stop crying out.

'We'll get someone to help you.'

A crowd had already formed around them, heads craning and gawking for a better view.

'You.' Rob pointed at a man. 'Fetch the doctor and send him to Mr Williamson's house. You and you, bring a door to carry him. I don't care if you have to kick it off its hinges. Move!'

He took hold of Williamson's hand and squeezed it lightly. The blood was still flowing and he tried to staunch it with the man's shirt. This was bad. Even pressing down on the flesh didn't help. Lister glanced at Mrs Williamson. Her face was white with shock and fear.

Everything took too long. The blood kept flowing. He had one of the women escort Williamson's wife home, telling her to prepare the place. Anything was better than having her here, seeing all this. He heard the swish of silk as she left.

The man was dying; the bleeding wouldn't stop. Where was the damned physician? And where was the boss? He'd expected the constable to be right behind him. Instead he was nowhere to be seen.

Finally two men appeared with a door and they lifted the merchant on to it. He didn't make a sound; his eyes were closed, his breathing low. Very gently, they carried Williamson to his house, no more than a hundred yards away. As they approached, Rob glanced up and saw Nottingham hurrying down Briggate.

The servants had a fire going in the bedroom hearth, the warmth just beginning to take hold as they eased the merchant on to the bed. Rob cut the rest of the clothes away, two fingers on the man's neck to keep feeling for a pulse.

By the time the doctor arrived, Williamson was barely alive. He did what he could, but the look in his eyes said everything; this was a hopeless task.

Rob stood back and let him work.

'Where were you?' he whispered to the constable.

'I saw the girl and went after her.'

'I hope to God you caught her.' But he saw the man shake his head sadly, never taking his eyes off Williamson. The girl was dangerous, but it was Nick who was the real threat. And unless the physician managed to perform a miracle, he was going to be a murderer.

But this was no day for wonders. After half an hour the doctor stood up and shook his head.

'He's gone.'

Fifteen

Nottingham moved, gently closing Williamson's eyes and pulling the covers over his body. He stood for a moment, staring down at the man who'd been his friend. Tom Williamson had always been so full of life, so happy to laugh at himself and the world. He was a man in love with his wife, who adored his children. His business thrived, he was an alderman – sooner or later he'd have had his year as mayor.

Now everything had gone. Stolen away from him.

Hannah Williamson sat in the parlour, clutching a shawl around her shoulders. Over the years her body had thickened, but there was still a childish look to her face, an innocence that wouldn't vanish. She didn't look up as the constable entered the room.

'I'm sorry,' he began. What more was there ever to say than that? She knew what those words meant. All he could ever do was listen to the pain and the anger. But she was silent, giving no more than a brief nod as she tried to hide her tears.

A few folk had assembled outside the house, clamouring for news. Nottingham walked past without a word, back towards the jail.

'Go home and tell Emily,' he said to Rob. 'She knows Mrs Williamson, she'll want to go and help.'

'Yes, of course.'

'Was there any way to prevent it?'

'No. Williamson tried to stop him.' Lister spoke slowly, seeing it all again. 'Nick could have swerved around him without even trying. He ran straight into him. It was no accident. He must have had the knife in its hand.'

'I want everyone out searching. Pull the night men back in. Make sure they're all armed.'

'Yes, boss.'

The constable took a deep breath. 'I'd better go and talk to the mayor.'

'Why?' Brooke asked. 'Can you tell me that, Richard?' He blazed around his office, his face red with fury. 'For God's sake, Tom Williamson was an alderman. And,' he added carefully, 'one of your strongest supporters on the corporation.'

All the way here, Nottingham's anger and frustration had been building to a head. A few sympathetic words would have tamped it down. Now he exploded.

'He was also a very good friend. Someone I'd known for a long time. Have you forgotten that? What do you think – that I wanted to see Tom dead?'

'No, of course—'

'We've been hunting that cutpurse and his girl for days. There are eight of us to cover the town during the day. Eight. Then you and all the others expect us to take care of everything else, too.' He stood, brought the keys from his pocket and slammed them down on the desk. 'Since you don't think I'm doing a good enough job, you'd better have these back.'

'Richard—'

'I've just had to stand and watch someone I like die, and I couldn't do a damned thing to stop it. Then I had to go downstairs and see his wife. Do you think that's a duty I enjoy? Well, do you? Do you believe I want it to happen?'

'Richard,' Brooke repeated, but his tone was softer now. 'Please.' He held up his hands. 'We're both on edge. Tom was a good man. We've just lost someone we both admired. We need his killer with a noose around his neck.'

'My men are going through Leeds again right now.'

'Good,' the mayor agreed calmly. The frayed tempers started to knit up. Now there was the grim determination to find Tom Williamson's killer.

'You'll need these,' Brooke said as the constable stood with his hand on the doorknob. He tossed the ring of keys through the air.

'Yes,' Nottingham agreed. 'I will.'

'Emily's with Hannah Williamson,' Rob said.

'Good. How many do we have out looking?'

'With the night men I could rouse, there are twelve. I put them in pairs.'

'Whereabouts are they?'

He pointed it out on the crude map of Leeds they had on the wall. New streets had been sketched in; every year the town grew larger.

'There used to be a camp in the orchard beyond Lands Lane,' Nottingham said.

'They checked it the other day. I thought we'd start there.' He'd expected the boss to complain about his meeting with the mayor. Instead he was close-mouthed, not even a glimmer of how it had gone. He stared at the map as if there was nothing more in his mind than the job at hand. The constable lifted an old cutlass off the desk and pushed it through his belt.

Rob selected one for himself. He'd had lessons when he was younger and proved to be good with a sword. Finally he was ready.

'Let's go and find them, boss.'

They walked without speaking, the swords banging against their thighs with each step. Out along Lands Lane, past the empty bowling green to Shaw's orchards. The trees were bare, only one or two forgotten apples left on the ground.

No sign of any camp here, but Nottingham hadn't

161

expected to find one. They'd be further out where nobody went. He led the way past a collapsed wall, scrambling over the stones, and along a thin path through the grass.

He could smell something, wood smoke in the air, and halted, trying to sense its direction. Lister pointed. He nodded and moved again. More slowly and warily now. This was it, the scent was stronger, a few smudges of soot drifting by in the air.

Now the constable knew exactly where to find them. A pair of dilapidated, abandoned buildings hidden away behind a small rise. No doors, much of the roofs missing, but they'd offer a little shelter against the cold. It was where he'd found Lucy a few years before.

Only one way in and out, he remembered. That gave them the advantage.

He unsheathed the cutlass. Rob did the same. They were close enough to see the two buildings now, what remained of them. Ivy covered the walls; the land was slowly claiming them back. Smoke rose from an empty doorway.

'Ready?'

Lister nodded and Nottingham took a breath.

There were five of them in the place, but no Nick or Kate. Two who were probably no more than six or seven, a pair of girls around ten, and a serious-looking boy who might have been thirteen. He stood as the constable appeared in the doorway, moving forward to try and protect the others.

'We're looking for a pair of cutpurses.'

'There's only us,' the boy answered. He tried

to sound grown-up, but Nottingham could hear his voice waver with fear.

The constable put up his sword. 'I'm the Constable of Leeds. Do you know them?'

'Yes.' The lad swallowed hard.

Nottingham softened his voice. 'What's your name?'

'Joseph.' He kept still and wary, out on his own for too long to ever lower his guard.

'Do you know where we'd find them, Joseph? They're murderers now.'

'I don't.' He glanced over his shoulder at the other, fearful children. 'They've been here a couple of times. They took what we had. Nick beat Matty when she wouldn't hand over her bread.' He nodded at a girl with bruises on her dirty cheeks. 'What will you do when you find them?'

'They'll be tried and hanged if they're found guilty.'

Joseph nodded soberly. 'Then I hope you catch them.'

'Where else might they go? The man they killed was a friend of mine.' It was worth asking again. Maybe the boy would be willing to give them something now.

'They do what they want.' He was trying to sound like a man, but tears were beginning to form in his eyes.

'What did he do to you?' Nottingham asked very quietly.

Without saying a word, Joseph pulled up his sleeve to show a long cut that was starting to heal. Quickly, clumsily, he hid it again and swiped the shirt across his eyes.

'If you see him, I need to know.' He looked at the boy, then the rest of them. One of the girls looked as if she might speak, but he continued. 'I know you don't peach. But this is different. They're killers. Please.'

The boy gave one small nod. Nottingham took a pair of coins from his breeches and placed them in Joseph's hand. Enough to buy a loaf and some cheese. That would keep them alive for one more day.

'Do you think they'll tell us?'

'Yes.' He didn't doubt it. Joseph would want his revenge on Nick. 'Where next?'

They returned to the jail as the light was fading. The men were already there, waiting to make their reports and finish for the day. No sign of Nick and Kate, but they'd be very cautious now.

'Send the night men round all the inns and lodging houses,' he ordered.

'They wouldn't be stupid enough to try and take a room,' Lister said.

'They might. They have money, they're looking to hide.'

'Don't you think they've left Leeds after that?'

'I don't know,' Nottingham replied wearily and ran a hand through his hair. 'That would be the sensible thing.' He gave a small, wan smile. 'But these two don't seem to think that way. Nick . . .' He shook his head. The boy had his taste of death now. He'd want more.

'What now, boss?'

He stared out of the window. Almost full night now. If the pair had found a spot outside the town it would be impossible to find them before daylight.

'Go through every empty house,' he ordered. 'I want all the men on this. All the gardens, everywhere you can think of. It's Sunday, there won't be much else to fill their time.'

Very few of the whores were out. This was always a bad day for business, with the inns closed and men tucked at home as work loomed in the morning.

They were women with a desperate look in their eyes, shawls pulled tight around their shoulders as they shivered in the darkness. They'd take a minute or two to talk on the promise of a farthing.

He remembered one of them. She'd been Cassie when he knew her three years earlier. Now, she insisted, it was Alexandra. The woman had been at Four-Finger Jane's funeral, saying nothing and vanishing as soon as the coffin was lowered.

'Charlotte,' he said.

'Gone,' she answered. 'But they all have now, haven't they?'

'Did you know her?'

'Not really. She wasn't here long. Nice enough but lost.' She gave a sad smile. 'I talked to her once. Too innocent, that one. That was her trouble. Men took advantage.'

'Do you know where she went?' Nottingham asked, but the woman shook her head. 'What about her pimp?'

'He's gone, too.'

This was taking him nowhere.

'Did you ever see the girl who took over Jane's place?'

'Grace, you mean? Dark hair, very pale, young? Here a day, that's all, before she was dead.'

'That's her.' At least she had a name now.

'I told her she should go back home. She wasn't made for this.'

'Where did she come from?'

'Ossett,' she said, 'wherever that is. Too late for her now, isn't it?'

But not too late for her family to know what had happened. He'd write to the constable there in the morning.

'Who killed her?'

'I don't know. If I did, I'd tell you.' She stared at him. 'There's too much death around.'

'I know,' Nottingham agreed. 'I know.'

Nottingham could feel the prickle at the back of his neck. Someone was following him. He could feel it. But every time he turned there was nothing. His hand rested on the hilt of the cutlass.

All he could hear were his own footsteps echoing off the buildings as he walked down Briggate, but he was certain. Just before the bridge he ducked into the passageway where Jane had died, pressing himself against the wall and drawing his sword.

Hidden in the darkness, he held his breath.

There, at the edge of his sight, a flash of white.

Nottingham brought the blade down. He felt it graze flesh. And then a woman's scream.

Sixteen

She had a hand clamped over the arm, but the blood ran through her fingers. The screaming had stopped as soon as she saw light glinting off the cutlass. Now she was shaking and shivering as if she was about to faint.

Kate. She looked small and frail, bruises blooming on her face.

'Where is he?'

'You've got to help me. He tried to kill me.' She raised her head so he could see the marks on her neck. Blood still dripped down her arm.

'Empty your pocket.' He kept the tip of the sword close to her neck. Maybe she was telling the truth; he wasn't about to trust her.

Her hand moved slowly. A knife clattered to the ground, a couple of coins.

'Is that all?'

'Yes.'

'Walk ahead of me. And don't try to run.'

'I'm still bleeding,' she told him.

'Then you'll bleed until we get to the jail.'

He glanced around, stooped, and collected the penknife. No sign of Nick. He wasn't about to believe a word she said until he had her safe in a cell.

The constable locked the manacles around her tiny wrists and ankles, the iron so heavy it weighed her down. He found a strip of linen and bound her arm.

'Where's Nick?'

'Can I have something to drink?'

In the lantern light he could see her properly. Her fair hair was dirty and matted. She'd taken a battering, one eye already swelling and turning black, fingermarks bright red on her throat.

'Once you tell me where he is.'

A scheming look came into her eyes. 'If I tell you, will you let me go?'

'If you don't tell me, you'll hang.'

Her shoulders slumped. 'We were up on that big hill above the river, off to the east.' Cavalier Hill. 'He'll have gone by now.'

He probably had, but he'd send the men up there at first light. The constable gave her a mug of ale. With the weight of the chains she could barely raise it to her mouth.

'Tell me about Nick.'

It came slowly, little fragments of memory that she stitched together. She'd met him a few months before in Doncaster. Her parents were dead, the pair of them lost in a fire. She found a group of children. Nick had been with them, there but always apart. He taught her to pick pockets while he cut purses. Soon the night watch was looking for them and it was safer to take to the roads. They went to Barnsley, to Sheffield, then drifted north.

'Leeds is rich,' she said. 'Nick said we'd do well here.'

'When did he start wanting to hurt people?'

'He's always been like that.' She stared down

into the mug, swirling the liquid gently. 'It was the other children at first. He'd hit them and torture them until they screamed. He hit me too, if I made him angry.' She lifted her head, 'But he always said sorry to me after. I used to be able to calm him down.'

'Not now?'

'No.' She spoke the word sadly. 'It would always pass.' Kate looked at him. 'Like a storm. Blow itself out. Now it's there all the time. When he started beating me tonight I didn't think he was going to stop until he killed me. That's why I ran.'

He could hear her sorrow. No, more than that, he thought: loss. She'd relied on him. Loved him, if she even knew what love was.

'What are you going to do?' Kate asked.

'I'm going to find him and arrest him for murder.'

'You'll have to kill him.' She sounded empty, hollow.

'If I have to, I will.'

'What about me?'

She'd put the boy before herself, he noticed.

'You'll go to the Assizes.'

'Will they hang me?'

'You didn't kill anyone. Probably seven years' transportation.'

The girl didn't say anything, just finished her ale and held out the mug. As Nottingham closed the cell door she asked, 'What if I help you catch him?'

'It might make a difference.'

He waited for more but she stayed silent.

* * *

169

'But you got her, boss,' Rob said.

The constable stared into the fire. He was weary, ready for his bed and wishing he could sleep for a year.

'I didn't do anything. She gave herself up. She's terrified of Nick.'

'It sounds as if she cares about him, too, doesn't it, Papa?' Emily said sadly.

'More than she realizes.' He didn't want to talk about the girl any longer. Even if she hadn't killed anyone she was still a part of it all, the robberies, the woundings, the killing, as guilty as Nick. And they were both alive. It was Tom Williamson who was going to be buried for doing his civic duty. He needed something brighter to finish the day.

'Have you seen the baby again?'

'I went this afternoon,' Emily told him. 'You need to see her, Papa. She's beautiful. And Annie came to school for the first time this morning.'

Nottingham glanced towards the kitchen. The door was closed.

'How did she do?'

'A bit lost,' she answered with a smile. 'But she's already made one friend there. That's a start. She needs to learn to be a girl again. She's forgotten.'

Nick had gone. Lister stood at the top of Cavalier Hill, staring down at the valley. He'd brought all the day men and spread them out as they climbed the slope carrying broad branches and sweeping through the bushes.

He'd found the remains of the camp, the ashes

170

of the fire cold. Nick probably left as soon as he realized that this time the girl wouldn't return. And on his own, the boy was going to be even more unpredictable and dangerous.

He kicked a stone and watched it roll downhill, gathering speed until it caught in a thick tuft of grass. It felt like the story of his life.

'Kate's offered to help us catch him,' the constable said when Lister returned.

'Do you believe her?'

Nottingham rubbed his chin. He'd taken off the bandage; the cut on his palm was healing.

'I think I do,' he replied after a moment. 'She's too scared of him now.' He raised an eyebrow. 'And we don't have anything to lose, do we?'

Rob had glanced through the door of the cell at the start of the morning. The girl was asleep, her legs pulled up. She looked so young, so innocent, it was hard to imagine she'd done so much. But she'd pay for it.

'How? We'll need to lure him out. And we have to make sure she doesn't run.'

'I haven't decided yet.' He let out a long breath. 'Oh, I forgot. I was talking to one of the whores last night. The girl we fished out of the river was called Grace.'

Lister grunted. What did a name matter? She was dead and buried. Knowing her name wasn't going to bring her back.

'She was from Ossett.' Nottingham tapped a piece of paper on his desk. 'I've written to the people there. They'll probably know her family.'

'You know that won't help us catch her killer.'

171

'No,' the constable agreed quietly. 'But what if fourteen or fifteen years from now, that little girl you and Emily are taking in decides to run off? Do you think you'd ever have a peaceful night until you knew what happened to her? Even if it's bad news?'

Rob could feel the shame creeping up his face. He turned away, staring out of the window.

'Yes, you're right.'

'Don't worry, you'll get used to thinking like a father. And believe me, daughters are the hardest of all.'

'Do you think we're doing the right thing? Taking her in.'

'That's for the two of you to decide,' Nottingham answered slowly.

Tom Williamson's funeral would take place the next day, as soon as the cloth market was over. A few more days and merchants would probably start making their offers for his business. Generous ones, he hoped; the firm was doing well.

And Tom would have his place in the graveyard, along with so many others who'd been friends, who'd been loved. Nottingham had been too busy to visit since he started back in the job; it was always dark on his way to and from work.

He owed his family some time.

One by one, he cleared the fallen leaves from Mary and Rose's graves. The grass was thick, the earth dark and heavy under his feet. It was odd, the sense of peace that he felt standing with them. For a moment or two all the cares could slip away. He could imagine them as they'd once been.

In his mind he could hear Mary's voice, her sadness at Williamson's murder, the joy of knowing they'd have a granddaughter. Five, ten minutes, that was all he needed to be able to leave with a sense of contentment.

But he still didn't know how they'd trap Nick. The men were out looking, but it was too easy for one boy to hide in a town of seven thousand people. Like trying to find a twig in a forest.

Nottingham stopped for a moment at the lych gate then headed away from Leeds, over Timble Bridge and up Marsh Lane. The day was quiet here, the town and all its noise behind him. As he opened the door of the house he heard the clang of a metal pot in the kitchen.

'Where's Annie?' he called out.

'Still at Miss Emily's school,' Lucy told him as she bustled through. 'What are you doing here, anyway? It's the middle of the day.' She folded her arms and stared at him. 'They haven't got rid of you, have they?'

'You should be so lucky. I just wanted to ask her a question.'

'She'll probably be here soon. I can find you—'

He shook his head. 'I'll go and look for her.'

The girl was dawdling. He spotted her on the Calls, moving from one shop window to the next and staring at everything for sale.

'You won't be home until evening at this rate,' he said and she turned, mouth wide in surprise.

173

'I'm sorry, sir,' Annie said. 'They just . . .'

'I know,' he agreed with a smile.

'It won't happen again.' Her face was bright red.

'A few minutes here or there don't matter. But there's something I need to ask you. Did Nick have a particular place he liked to go? A camp?'

He'd asked Kate the same thing that morning, but she only shook her head. At the time he believed her. Now he wondered if she was trying to protect the boy, to keep him free. He'd seen it often enough before, the way beaten wives would justify what their husbands had done.

'I don't think so,' Annie said after a little while. 'We kept as far away from them as we could in case he got in a temper.' She looked up at him. 'I'm sorry, sir.'

He'd never held out much hope. But apart from Kate, she was the only one who might know.

'It's fine,' he told her.

'There was one thing I remember,' she began as he started to turn away.

'What's that?'

'He talked about the den once and she started giggling. It was late and they thought we were all asleep. I might not have heard it right.' She blushed again.

'That's good. Take your time going home. I'm sure Lucy won't mind.'

'The den,' he said. Kate stirred and look up at him. She'd been lying on the bench, eyes open and staring at nothing.

'What?'

'Where is it?'

'I've never heard of it.'

'Don't lie to me.'

'Who told you about it?'

Nottingham ignored her question. 'Where is it?'

She shook her head. 'You'll never find it on your own. It's off that road that goes north.'

'Then you'll come with us. In chains.'

'I can't walk in them,' Kate said. 'Please.'

She'd learned to lie, but not quite well enough yet.

'You'll manage.'

Seventeen

Kate made a good show of struggling, taking her time over each pace, head bowed, body looking like it was weighed down. People stopped to stare as they passed, the girl in front with the constable, Lister and three of the men behind her.

Let her make a meal of it, Nottingham thought. As long as he found Nick, he didn't care. The cutlass slapped lightly against his leg.

Kate led the way past Town End, beyond a few straggling cottages, then stopped.

'Along there.' She tried to raise a hand to show the track.

'You lead,' the constable told her. 'And no shouting to warn him.' He nodded at the men; they drew their weapons.

It was a good half mile, from one path to another and a third, until they were deep in the woods.

'There's a clearing a little way on. That's what we called the den. We'd go there sometimes.'

It was definitely out of the way, Nottingham thought. No one would be likely to find it.

'Stay with her,' he said to Dyer. 'Make sure she doesn't shout.'

'What if she tries, boss?'

He stared at the girl. 'Then stop her.'

The constable walked ahead of the men. The grey day was dying, the air damp against his face. He listened for any sound, but all he could hear were soft footsteps behind him.

It was exactly as she said. He made out the small open space ahead and a shelter of branches. Safe enough, all the way out here. He gestured for the men to spread out. If Nick was here, he wasn't going to give the boy a chance to escape.

He stepped into the open. A twig snapped under his boot, the sound loud and sharp. Another step, then a third. Still no movement in the shelter. The sword felt heavy in his hand; he gripped it tighter. Nottingham waited, ready. He began to count, one, two, going all the way to twenty before he kicked at the branches.

They fell apart, toppling one on the other. No one inside.

He picked the pieces away. In the back corner the found a small pile of empty purses, strings dangling and a reticule. Nothing to indicate when Nick had been here last. No traces of a recent fire.

'No luck,' he told the men. 'I want all of you searching round here for him.'

'What about the girl?' Rob asked.

'Put her back in the cells.'

They marched away, muttering and grumbling as they moved. The constable stayed, standing and listening. The boy could be close and he'd never know. Finally he followed the thin track back towards the Newcastle road. He'd gambled; this time he'd lost. But it wasn't over yet.

'What do we do now, boss?' Rob asked. He'd waited at the end of the track, leaving Dyer to return Kate to the jail.

'I'm open to suggestions,' Nottingham said. He slid the cutlass back into its scabbard. 'We're chasing him.'

'What else is there?'

'That's the problem. He has the upper hand. But I don't know a way around that yet.'

Leeds was filled with people. As he approached the market cross he could hear the lowing and screams from down in the Shambles, cattle brought for the slaughter, the squeal of a pig as its throat was cut. Blood would be flowing down Briggate and the packs of dogs would be gathering.

Old Jem sat by the cross, resting on his pack. He looked up and grinned.

'That's why I moved up here. Can't hear yourself think down by there. Too noisy to draw a crowd.' He gave a small, soft laugh. 'Not that I'm having better luck up here.'

'One of those days. For both of us.' He explained, Jem nodding as he listened.

'I saw them taking that lass back in chains. I've seen the pair of them a few times. That boy, he has the look of the devil about him. His eyes are empty.'

'He killed Alderman Williamson. If you spot him again, I need to know.'

'Aye, I'll do that, right enough. He needs putting down, that one. Some people are just born bad to the soul, Mr Nottingham.'

'Thankfully only a few.' He clapped a hand on the man's shoulder and walked away. He smiled as Jem raised his voice and began a tale in his usual way:

'It weren't in my time, or your time, or the time of anyone alive today or yesterday . . .'

Rob was waiting on the Calls as Emily locked the door of the school and slipped the key into the pocket of her dress.

'Ready?' she asked and he nodded.

The baby was squalling and fractious, hitting out at him with tiny limbs as he tried to pick her up. How could anything so small be so loud, he wondered.

'She's not hungry,' Mrs Webb told him. 'She's not long off the teat, and I winded her. Does she need changing?'

He looked helplessly at Emily, who took the girl and checked her clout.

'Yes.'

She was clumsy at first, but surer than he'd ever be, he was certain of that, and soon the girl was happy again. Mary; he had to start thinking of her as Mary. He stared at the baby, the round, pudgy face and curious eyes, and tried to imagine how she'd look as she grew.

Rob stayed for a few minutes, holding the girl again and feeling her warmth as he cradled her. She fell asleep and he passed her to Emily, then left. There was too much work to take more than a few minutes away.

Kate was in her cell, sitting with her back against the wall and her knees drawn up.

'You must know where he is.'

'I don't,' she replied. Her voice was as dull and empty as her face.

'Help us and it'll go better for you,' Rob told her.

'That's what the other man said.' She raised her manacled wrists. 'But I'm still here and I'm still wearing these, aren't I?'

'You'll keep them on until we find him. Where else might he be?'

She shrugged. 'He might have left.' Kate turned her head and looked at him. 'He's smart, Nick is. If he's moved on, no one will ever catch him.'

'Sooner or later, someone will.'

'Not him.'

'He tried to kill you,' Rob said. 'Or have you forgotten that?'

'I remember.'

'Then where will we find him?'

'I don't know!' she shouted.

* * *

179

The pounding on the door roused him. Barefoot, carrying the cudgel, Nottingham went downstairs and opened the door to a freezing wind. One of the night men, wrapped in bundles of clothes like rags and holding his lantern high.

'What is it?'

'Sorry to disturb you, sir,' he said with an awkward lisp. 'But Mr Crandall said you and Mr Lister need to know. We found a body. Josh Bartlett.'

'Bartlett?' Rob hurried down the stairs, tucking his shirt into a pair of breeches. 'How?'

'Looks like someone stabbed him.'

'Where is he?' the constable asked.

'The tenter fields below Boar Lane. Already sent for the coroner, sir.'

'We'll be there as soon as we can.'

'He was certain he could beat anyone,' Lister said as they hurried into town.

'Apparently he was wrong.'

'There won't be too many who'll mourn him. Definitely not his girls. He was a nasty bastard, even for a pimp. Big, brutal.'

'And dead now,' Nottingham said. 'Three pimps gone, two murdered. Two moneylenders dead.'

'Or maybe someone just saw the chance of revenge on Bartlett,' Rob told him. 'He's dealt out enough punishment.'

'Maybe,' the constable said quietly. 'Maybe.'

Hoggart the coroner had already been and gone. The body lay face up. Even in the dark shadows from the lanterns it was easy enough to see the blood all across Bartlett's chest. Nottingham put a hand against the man's neck. Still a little warmth in his flesh; he hadn't been dead long.

'He told me no one had been threatening him.' Rob gazed down at the corpse.

'From the look of this, it took quite a lot to kill him. I can see six wounds. There might be more once we get him in the cold cell.'

'He liked to fight.'

'This time he lost.' Nottingham pushed himself upright, feeling the ache in his knees. He nodded at the two men waiting to carry the body to the jail. 'Where did he live?'

'Mill Hill,' Rob replied.

'See what you can find there. And hunt down the girls who worked for him. They should be able to tell us something.'

In the darkness the house felt strange, full of bitter, rancid smells. He'd brought a lantern and lit it with his tinder, waiting until the flame flared bright before moving around. The place was empty; Rob could sense it as soon as he entered.

He began upstairs, where he'd heard the woman sobbing the last time he'd been here. A bed with a dirty sheet, blankets tossed on to the floor. A jacket hung on a nail. No dresses, no sign of any female clothing.

The parlour was just as he remembered it, almost bare, a half-empty mug of ale sitting on the floor by a chair. All he found in the kitchen was a jumble of unwashed plates and the strong stink of rotten food. How could Bartlett have lived with that?

But it didn't matter now. He'd never be coming

back here. And it looked as if his whores had already fled.

Nottingham cut away the man's waistcoat and shirt. Six wounds, from shoulder to belly; impossible to judge which one had killed him. Bartlett's hands were ingrained with dirt, the nails bitten down to the quick.

He'd been powerful, well-muscled. But there were no fresh grazes or marks on his knuckles. It didn't look as if he'd fought back. That was curious. From what Rob said, the man loved violence. He lived by it.

And died by it, too.

He was still studying the body when Lister arrived.

'Nothing at the house, boss. His women have gone.'

The constable nodded and said, 'Take a look at him. Tell me what seems wrong.'

He waited, giving Rob time to examine the body.

'No recent bruises. Only some old marks on his hands. And those cuts are big. A sword, not a knife.'

'He didn't defend himself. He might not have had a chance.' He rubbed his chin. 'What was he doing down in the tenter fields, anyway? He was too big to drag there after he was dead.'

'Whoever killed him must have taken him by surprise. Probably the first cut put him on the ground and the rest were to make sure he was dead. I know him; he'd have been lashing out otherwise.'

'Search the area properly once it's light. I want

men out looking for his whores, too. We need to talk to them.' He glanced down at Bartlett's corpse again. 'Do you still think there's nothing happening here?'

'He had plenty of enemies.'

'Ones he'd meet in a dark field?'

Lister sighed. 'I don't know, boss. But if there's something, who's behind it? Tell me that.'

'I wish I could.'

Nottingham sat at the desk and rubbed his eyes. He had the sour dregs of ale in his cup and too many things filling his mind. Another few hours and he'd be attending Tom Williamson's funeral, once the cloth market was over.

Outside, a thin drizzle was bringing in the day.

He didn't understand what was going on in Leeds. He couldn't make head or tail of it. But it was there. He could feel it Someone was working, eliminating the moneylenders and the pimps one by one, and he had no idea who it could be. This didn't have the hallmark of anyone he knew. Not Tom Finer; these days the man cherished his respectability. But Rob was right about one thing: the town had changed in the last two years. More than he'd ever imagined.

He patrolled up and down Briggate twice, making sure everything was in order, then strode away as the bell announced the opening of the market. Earth was mounded in the graveyard of the Parish Church, ready for the burial.

At home, Lucy put food in front of him and stood by the table as he ate. Nottingham could

183

hear Annie in the kitchen, finishing her work before going off to the school.

'What is it?' he asked as he swallowed the last of the bread.

'I've sponged and brushed your good coat and breeches,' she said. 'And I darned the hole in your best hose.'

Nottingham nodded. There was more to come, he could tell.

'It's her. Annie.' She inclined her head towards the other room. 'Is she staying?'

'I thought that was already settled.'

'It's your house.'

In name, perhaps, but most of the time it never felt that way.

'Then she's staying. Emily said you'll need help once the baby comes to live here.' He couldn't bring himself to call the child Mary. Not yet.

'I will.' Lucy folded her heavy arms. 'But with two more people we're going to need more room.'

He'd never given it any thought. The house was simply the house. Home. But she was right.

'Go on,' he said.

'I talked about it with someone.'

'One of your admirers?' He smiled as she began to blush.

'Don't be so cheeky,' she told him, but the flush rose further up her face. 'He says we can easily add two more rooms.'

'And did he say how much it would cost?'

'I wanted to talk to you first.'

Nottingham didn't believe her. He knew Lucy;

she'd want everything in detail, down to the last penny. But he didn't have time to think about it now. He needed to be dressed and on his way to the service.

The Parish Church was full. Hannah Williamson and her children sat alone on the front pew. Behind her, all the members of the corporation, looking grand in their robes. Then the merchants and every worthy in the town. He saw John Reynolds from the Rose and Crown, the landlords of the Old King's Arms and the New King's Arms and the other inns around Leeds; even Harry Meadows from the Talbot, dressed in a dark, sober coat. At the back were the men who'd worked at Williamson's warehouse and others from the trade, the masters of the dyeing and finishing shops. He'd been a well-liked man. A respected man.

And his killer was still somewhere close. Whatever the girl claimed, the constable felt sure that Nick wouldn't run. Not yet.

The mayor spoke, then Alderman Atkinson. The vicar took this service himself, two of the curates beside him. The sermon lasted until people became restive, and finally the coffin was carried outside into a damp, biting wind.

Emily was waiting there. Nottingham buttoned his greatcoat and joined her.

'I left one of the older girls teaching the class,' she said. 'I wanted to come for this.'

There could never be any joy in a burial. He'd attended too many in his time. Nottingham waited until the first sod hit the coffin, squeezed his daughter's arm and walked away. A moment with Mary and Rose, then to see John Sedgwick. Lizzie and James kept the grave neat.

You'd have loved to be deputy now, he thought. You'd have enjoyed all this. Chasing down Nick. But would you have believed me if I said that one person could be behind so many of these crimes? He could hear the man's voice, arguing with him over a drink.

The constable shook his head and walked away. He was right. Even if he didn't have the evidence yet, he knew.

Rob searched all across the tenter field. They'd found Bartlett near one of the hooks used for stretching cloth. The earth was darker there, tinged with something dark and sticky when he touched it. The man had been killed here.

It was easy to imagine. The pimp was cocky, he'd have had no qualms about meeting someone, no matter where. His girls must have known before anyone else; they'd scattered like birds, not a trace of them left. The men were keeping an eye out for them as they hunted Nick, but he doubted they'd ever be seen again. Too frightened.

There were too many with reason to kill Josh Bartlett. He'd gone out of his way to make enemies, picked fights everywhere, and beaten anyone who crossed him. There might even be a few happy to claim the brief glory of the murder. Folk were strange.

There was nothing out here to give him a hint, only a chill on his hands. He thrust them into his pockets and walked back to town.

Could the boss be right? He hadn't believed it. But the longer this went on, the more he was forced to wonder. God knew they should have found one of the killers by now, at least had some sort of word. But everywhere he turned there was silence.

But wouldn't he have seen it building? Surely he would have spotted it . . . that was what he didn't understand. If someone wanted to move in, to try to take over the moneylending, the prostitution and God knew what else, why wouldn't he announce himself? To show he had the power.

He stopped at the baker and bought himself a pie, his first food of the day. He loved the job, but it was rare to have time to eat regularly. At the jail he glanced through the night report in case it offered anything on Bartlett's death.

He was still there, licking the last crumbs from his fingers, when Nottingham arrived in his good clothes. Of course: Tom Williamson's funeral. He'd heard the bell tolling then forgotten all about it.

'Anything?'

Lister shook his head. 'I'm going to see a man who might know something. But no one's been banging down the door to confess.' He sighed. 'Back to the beginning. How was the service?'

'Full. Emily came for the burial.'

'I don't imagine there'll be a dance now.'

'No. I think Hannah Williamson has more pressing things in front of her.'

After Rob left, Nottingham poured some ale and wandered back to the cells. Kate looked up as he stared at her through the door.

187

'You're dressed smart today.'

'We buried the man your Nick killed.'

She stayed silent, breathing in and out a few times, then asked: 'What's going to happen to me?'

'I already told you, it's for the court to decide. There's a prison under the Moot Hall. We'll be taking you there soon.'

'Will you kill Nick when you find him?'

'I told you that, too: not unless I have to. I'll arrest him and let the jury make up their mind.'

'He won't let himself be taken.'

'Tell me where I can find him,' the constable said.

'I took you there.' She banged her wrists against her thighs, a little gesture of frustration. The manacles rattled.

'You must have had other places.'

'What if I tell you and you catch him?' He heard the note in her voice. Hopeful, cunning. This was why the constable had kept her here. After all, she'd come to him out of fear. The longer she spent in a cell, she more she craved a favour.

'We might be able to agree on something.'

Dusk was falling. The air felt frozen as he breathed. Mist rose over the fields in the distance. Nottingham walked with Lister at his side, Waterhouse and Dyer behind. The fog muffled all the sounds, killing them before they could echo. They all had their cutlasses drawn, ready.

Kate had given them directions. In return, if

they took Nick, he'd agreed to let her go. No one would notice, and no one would care. People wanted the murderer, the rest didn't matter. The mayor had sent for him after the funeral, demanding to know what progress they'd made.

She'd sworn that this was their only other secret place. Now he had to hope that she was desperate enough to tell the truth.

Eighteen

South of the river, then east. The camp was close to the riverbank, she said, about half a mile along, hidden behind a large tree.

In the faded light could just make out the shape, a tall, sturdy oak that reached above its neighbours. Its leaves were all gone the winter, jagged branches stark against the sky.

They fanned out into a short line as they drew closer, trying to move quietly through the tangled grasses. Close to, Nottingham could make out a rough shelter of boughs. For a moment he thought he saw a tiny flash of movement inside.

'Now,' he shouted. 'Run.'

The men began to dash, shouting loud enough to stir the dead. Nottingham stood and watched, grasping the hilt of the sword tightly. The boy ducked out of his shelter, glancing this way and that. He had the little knife in his hand. No expression on his face: no fear, no anger.

Nick waited until Lister and the others were a

few yards away. Then he moved, fast as quicksilver. A feint to his right before darting off to his left, just out of reach of Rob's cutlass.

And suddenly the boy was sprinting, his legs a blur, eyes fixed on the constable.

He wanted to kill again. It was there in his eyes, intent, dark.

The men were following, but Nick had ten yards on them; they couldn't hope to catch up. One chance, Nottingham knew that was all he would have. He watched, not moving, until the boy was so close he could smell his stink.

Now, he thought, and stepped to the side, bringing up his weapon and feeling the blade slice into the boy's thigh.

Nick went straight down. His legs were still moving but they couldn't support him any longer. Then the constable brought his boot down hard on Nick's hand and kicked the knife away. Such a small, innocuous weapon. But so deadly.

The lad was clutching at his wound, moaning. Tears were running down his cheeks.

'Are you all right?' Lister asked. He was winded, bent over to catch his breath.

'Not a scratch.' The constable smiled. 'More than our friend here can say.'

'He was fast.'

'Bring him to the jail,' Nottingham ordered. 'Drag him if you have to, I don't care. And get a doctor to look at that wound. I want him alive for the gallows.'

He walked away.

* * *

The cells were empty by the time they hauled Nick in. Rob looked at the constable and raised an eyebrow.

The lad would survive. For now, anyway. He'd never walk properly again, the doctor said. But that hardly mattered. He'd never need to limp further than the dock and the gibbet.

Nottingham poured a cup of ale and sipped slowly. His throat was dry, scratchy.

It was over. But too late for poor Tom Williamson.

Lister locked the door to the cells, just the two of them in the office.

'You let her go?'

The constable nodded. The girl had simply stared at him as he unlocked her chains, as if she couldn't believe it was happening.

'What am I going to do?' Kate asked as she rubbed her wrists.

'I don't care,' Nottingham said to her. 'But you'll leave Leeds.'

'Where can I go?'

'Anywhere but here.' He dug two pennies from his pocket and put them in her hand. She looked at him again, then darted off, slamming the door to the jail behind her.

'She earned it. She told us where we'd find Nick.'

'Finally.' Rob spat out the word.

'No one's going to give a damn about her. Most people will have forgotten she ever existed.'

'So she gets a second chance?'

'For as long as she lasts.' He took another drink. 'I don't think either one of them has much of a soul. She never even asked about him, if he was alive or dead. They were a matched pair.' He turned his head towards the closed door. 'The only difference is that Nick liked to kill.' He slammed the mug down on the desk. 'Now, we have some other murders to attend to.'

The word had spread quickly. As Nottingham walked up Briggate the next morning to give his report to mayor, folk stopped to congratulate him and wish him well. But the news would be poor consolation to Hannah Williamson and her children.

'Good work, Richard,' Brooke said. He was seated at his desk, a small hill of papers in front of him. 'We'll send him off to York tomorrow. He can rot there until the Assizes. How did you find out where he was?'

'Someone gave me the information.'

The mayor nodded. It was done, one worry lifted from his mind. All the missteps and fumbles forgotten. For now, at least. And exactly as he predicted, no mention of the girl, as if she'd never existed.

Lucy had bought a capon at the market and stewed it for their meal. Rob wolfed it down, wiping the bowl with a piece of bread.

Emily was talking, something about the school, but his mind kept going back to the question: what would he have done if he'd been the constable? Would he have let her go? True, she'd told them where to find Nick. But she was guilty, too. She'd helped in the robberies, and she'd done it very willingly. That deserved punishment, not freedom.

But the boss had been right on one thing. Nobody had mentioned her during the day. All they'd cared about was Nick, wanting the tale of how he'd been taken.

'Rob?' Emily said.

He jerked up his head. 'What?'

'I was saying that Annie's taken to reading. She's already making out her words well in a book. And she's taken to numbers, too. I've never seen anything like it.'

'I was miles away. Sorry. That's wonderful.'

'You're as bad as Papa.' She gave him a teasing smile.

Rob glanced at Nottingham. He was quiet, looking at something in the distance, just as far away as he'd been himself.

Nick had been taken to the prison in the cellar of the Moot Hall. This morning he'd be escorted to York. When the assizes began in a few months, he'd be tried. Nottingham knew he'd be called to give evidence. But that wouldn't happen until December. He might not even be constable then.

The weather had changed and he was grateful. Warmer, with a faint breeze from the south that felt like a balm after the harsh cold. Another week and they'd be lighting the bonfires. With the drinking and the apprentices on the loose, the night would be long and rough.

But there was plenty to do before that. Finally he could give all his time to the killings that had crowded back into his thoughts since they arrested Nick. There was a pattern of some kind; there had to be. Yet try as he might, he simply couldn't make it out.

He walked up Briggate with his greatcoat unbuttoned. The shutters were down on the shops, servants and mistresses bustling around to buy this and that, smiling and chattering away. A pale, hazy sun had broken through the clouds, enough to raise the spirits.

Con was up at the market cross, rubbing rosin on his bow. He looked up and smiled as he heard the footsteps.

'Better weather today, Mr Nottingham.'

'Two days of this and we'll think summer's returned.'

'You found the boy. It was all the talk last night at the inns.'

'We did. Now it's back to other matters.'

Con frowned and raised the fiddle to his shoulder, plucking each string lightly, then adjusting one until the note pleased him.

'I haven't heard a thing.'

'No one has. That's the problem,' the constable said.

'I hope you find him.' He began to play a quick little jig and then he was lost in his own world.

Tom Finer wasn't in Garroway's.

'Already been and gone,' the proprietor said, wiping the sweat from his face with a handker-chief. 'Drank his coffee and left. Didn't even look at the London papers. He must have some business.'

The constable talked to a few people he knew,

but no one had anything to say. There was no word, nothing at all.

Old Jem was down by the bridge, close to the old chapel. He was in the middle of a story, acknowledging Nottingham with the briefest nod, never stopping his flow of words. When he finished, listeners put a few coins in his hat and wandered away. Jem pushed himself slowly to his feet.

'They're saying you're a hero for capturing that lad.' He chuckled. 'Happen I'll have to start telling a tale about your bravery.' He slipped the money into a purse and shouldered his pack. 'I'm just off to your lass's school.'

'I'll walk with you.'

'Leeds is getting all smart now,' Jem said as he glanced about. 'New houses, plenty of brass around.'

'For some.'

'Same as ever: for them as make the laws and the money. They're not likely to care about the rest, are they?' With a quick handshake he disappeared into the school.

How many times had he asked the same questions, Rob wondered. It seemed like dozens, all through the morning, until his throat was raw.

The ale at the White Swan felt like nectar, going down slow and merry as he ate one of the meat pies the landlord's wife baked. He'd almost finished when the constable sat on the other side of the bench with a long, low sigh.

'A mug of twice-brewed and a bowl of stew,'

he told the serving girl and turned to Lister. 'Tell me you've had some luck.'

'None at all. Half of them are sick of hearing about it. I think a few are trying to avoid me since they've heard the questions so often.'

'I know.' Nottingham nodded. 'But if we keep at it we might stir something up.'

'We haven't so far,' Rob pointed out.

'Someone killed them.' He counted them off on his fingers. 'Stanbridge, Smith, Jane, Kidd, Grace, Bartlett. Six of them in just a few days.'

'I know. Believe me.' He was about to say more when there was a commotion at the door. A moment later a frightened boy, no more than ten, was pushed through the crowd to stand in front of them, clutching a cap in his hand.

'I'm looking for the constable,' he said.

'You've found him,' Nottingham answered. 'What is it?'

'They sent me down from Mr Colly's dyeworks up on Mabgate, sir.' He stared down at the ground. 'There's a body, you see.'

The whole place fell silent as the crowd listened intently. Now a buzz of conversation began to fly around the room.

'A man?' He glanced at Rob.

'Yes, sir.' The boy looked down. 'I think so. I didn't see it, they just told me to come and fetch you.'

'Go back. Tell them we'll be there as soon as we can.'

The serving girl returned with the meal. Nottingham looked at it longingly, took a swig of the ale, and said: 'No time today.'

196

'If I had a penny for all the meals you've ordered and left . . .' she began.

'You'd have your own tavern. I'm sorry.'

The dyeworks were lined along Sheepscar Beck. It was no more than a few minutes' walk, but it was another world out there, almost in the country. Leeds felt distant, fields all around, brown now in the autumn, a few sheep grazing on scrubby patches of grass.

The stream ran in dark purples and blues, oily patches of it floating the water. But it was the stench that hit them as they approached. How could anyone work here, the constable wondered, then answered his own question. Because they needed to make money.

Colly himself was waiting at the door, an older man with a short wig and hair growing from his ears and nose. His eyebrows stuck out in dark, wild tufts and his clothes looked a size too small for his body.

'About time, too,' he said dismissively. 'This way. Well, come on then.'

He led them through a warehouse that held undyed cloth, then to a door to the bank of the beck.

'Down there.'

Stone steps led down into the stream, close to the discharge pipes for the works. The stink was overwhelming, but Colly didn't seem to notice it. Nottingham felt the bile rising in his throat and saw Rob turn away, trying not to retch.

The body moved slowly round and round in an eddy of the beck. A man, fully dressed, face down.

'Are you going to get him out or just stand staring all day?' Colly asked.

'Do you have a hook or a pole?' the constable said. He kept his eyes on the corpse; the figure didn't look familiar. Colly gave two sharp whistles and a man appeared. A minute later he returned with a long, heavy stick.

It took time to draw the dead man close enough to haul up the steps. In the warehouse, water pooled around the corpse as Nottingham and Rob caught their breath.

'Aren't you going to see who he is?' Colly asked. He was a few feet away, pacing anxiously around the room.

'All in good time,' the constable told him. 'You can help us by sending someone for the coroner.'

It was Rob who bent and turned the body, then looked up in shock.

'It's Warren.' The words arrived slowly. 'The bookkeeper.'

One of those who'd been to dinner with Stanbridge on the night he died. The man who employed John Wood.

Lister tilted back the head. The man's throat had been slashed. The same as the moneylenders. A quick search of his pockets only brought a few coins. No keys, no notebook.

'As soon as the coroner's been, get two of your men to take him to the jail,' Nottingham told Colly.

'But they'll miss work.'

'And you'll pay them for their time.' The constable stared at him until the man nodded his agreement.

* * *

'You take a look at his room,' Nottingham said to Rob. 'I'll go to his office.'

'Yes, boss.'

They hurried away from the works, scarcely breathing until the air was cleaner and sweeter. But the stink of the place seemed to cling to their clothes.

'What do you think now?' the constable asked.

'I don't know. I really don't know.'

There were two or three customers in Ogle's shop, one of them keeping the bookseller busy as the constable climbed the stairs.

Warren's office was unlocked, empty, papers scattered everywhere. Someone had gone through the place in a rush. No point in trying to gather everything up: it would take days to go through it all and he didn't even know what to look for.

He needed Wood.

'Who's gone up there this morning?' he asked the bookseller downstairs.

'Mr Wood was in first thing. He left almost immediately.'

'Is the door up there usually locked?'

'Of course. Mr Warren and Mr Wood both have keys. Why?'

God save him from inquisitive shopkeepers, he thought.

'Warren's dead. Where does Wood live?'

The man blanched. 'I don't know.'

'Nobody goes up there now except me or my men. Do you understand?'

'Yes.' The bookseller nodded. 'Of course.'

A last thought came to him: 'Did Warren have

a key to the shop, so he could come and go as he pleased?'

'Yes.'

Warren's killer had taken the keys, come during the night and gone through everything. What was he searching for? Could Wood have been the murderer? No, he had his own key and he'd have known exactly where to find everything. But why had he left so hurriedly?

The Turk's Head was quiet, men back at their work after dinner. Only the landlord, looking up hopefully as he entered.

'John Wood drinks here,' the constable said.

'Sits right over there and has his dinner.' The man nodded towards the bench by the wall.

'Was he in today?'

The landlord needed to think for a moment.

'Like as not. No, wait.' He shook his head. 'Not today.'

'Where does he live?'

'I don't know.' The man shrugged. 'You should ask Ezekiel Horton. They're friends; he could likely tell you.'

'And where will I find Mr Horton?'

'He works at Williamson's warehouse. The one as got hisself killed.'

It only took two minutes in the shop around the corner from Water Lane for Rob to discover Warren's address.

It was a pleasant, three-storey building, the front door polished and glowing in the faint sun. He knocked, waiting until a whey-faced woman

200

was facing him, her eyes quickly taking in his old clothes.

'No room here,' she said in a voice like flint.

'I'm Robert Lister, the Deputy Constable of Leeds.'

She'd started to close the door in his face. Now she stopped. She was perhaps forty, short and bony.

'What do you want?'

'I need to see Mr Warren's room.'

'Why?' She drew herself up. 'What's he done?'

'He's dead,' Rob told her. 'Murdered.'

He knew how the word hit people. But he wanted her shocked.

'He can't be. I heard him come in late and go up the stairs.'

'It's not even an hour since we pulled him out of Sheepscar Beck.'

She glanced up and down the street, watching for any nosy neighbours.

'You'd better come in.'

She led the way up the stairs, pulling a ring of keys from the pocket in her gown. At the top floor she stopped and tapped lightly on the door, as if she couldn't believe what he'd just told her.

'What time did he return?'

'I don't know.' All the acid had gone from her voice now. 'I'd been asleep for a while when I heard the key in the lock and the footsteps.'

'Just one person?'

'Yes.'

'Did you hear him leave again?'

'No, I'm sure of that.'

But she could have sunk back into her rest and

never noticed. Warren could have come home and gone out again. Or someone else could have taken his keys.

'Let me in there, please.'

Nothing had been damaged, but the room had been carefully searched. That had taken time; whoever did it knew he wouldn't be disturbed.

Still, Rob took the time to look around. Papers lay in piles on the table, scattered, not tossed around. But no one appeared to have touched the clothes that hung on nails or torn apart the bed.

The landlady was waiting outside.

'When you clean the room, keep all Mr Warren's goods,' he told her. 'We might need to look through them.'

A funeral yesterday, business as usual today. But that was commerce, where money was king. Moving forward, little time for mourning. Tom Williamson's warehouse was busy. Men hauled cloth on to a barge that bobbed on the river as a clerk stood by, counting each bale.

Nottingham waited until they were done, impressed by the ease with which they walked along the plank from towpath to vessel under the heavy loads. Finally, the clerk tallied his figures, shook hands with the captain and marched back into the building.

'Not the same without Mr Williamson around,' he said sadly. The man had worked for Tom for a decade or more, a thin soul who looked dour at the best of the times. Now his face wore its sorrow plainly.

'Nothing will be,' Nottingham agreed. 'I believe you have a man called Ezekiel Horton here.'

'Over there.' He pointed and shouted the man's name. 'Not done anything bad, has he?'

'No,' the constable said with a smile. 'Nothing like that. But he might know where someone lives.'

Horton looked puzzled as he gave the address.

'John said he wasn't doing anything wrong these days. He'd given that up since he started working for Warren.'

'Maybe he hasn't. But I need to see him and he's not at work.'

It was in one of the courts hidden away near the bottom of Briggate, close to the *Leeds Mercury* office. The only question, Nottingham thought, was whether Wood had fled yet.

He had his answer quickly enough. The room was unlocked. Neat enough inside, but stripped almost bare of clothes and anything personal. A pair of women's slippers, worn through on the soles, had been left behind.

'As soon as Wood saw the office had been ransacked, he must have gone home, packed up what he owned and left,' Nottingham said. 'He knew it wasn't a burglary. He realized Warren was dead.'

'Or he killed him. Warren's room has been searched, too. Strolled up the stairs in the middle of the night, calm as you please.'

The body lay in the cold cell. The constable had turned out the pockets. No keys, but everything else – a good handkerchief and coins – had been left.

He leaned back in his chair, picked up the mug of ale and sipped. The fire was blazing.

'Seven dead. Now are you starting to believe?'

'Perhaps you're right,' Rob admitted with a long sigh. 'I know none of it makes sense. But why would Wood run like that unless he was the killer?'

Nottingham shook his head.

'He could take something from that office whenever he wanted. I think he went to the office, saw what had gone and thought he'd better run before he was next.'

'Then what was it?' Rob asked. 'What did Warren have that was so important?'

'Until we find the man who murdered him, we're never going to know.'

Nineteen

Seven o'clock by the Parish Church clock as Nottingham crossed Timble Bridge and walked up Marsh Lane. Tonight, Rob would go around the inns and ask his questions, but they both knew it would be fruitless. Nobody would talk because nobody knew.

What had Warren been doing on Mabgate, anyway? What had lured him out there? He needed to stop beating himself with questions he couldn't answer.

Home was welcoming and cheerful. The food Lucy served was hot and filling, a reminder that he'd never had a chance to eat dinner. He felt weary, tired of so much death. He remembered when it was rare; now the bodies seemed to pile one on the other, day by day.

He shared the table with Emily and her books. As he finished eating she packed them away and placed the cap on the ink bottle.

'Papa,' she began, and he knew she wanted to talk about something.

'What is it?' he asked with a smile.

'You know, I've never had a girl who's picked things up as fast as Annie.' She pushed a strand of hair from her face, tucking it behind her ear. 'She said she's never been to school before, but it's hard to believe.'

'Maybe she's just bright.'

'She is,' Emily agreed with a fierce nod. 'I know it's only been a few days, but if she keeps on this way she'll be ahead of everyone by the end of next year. It made me think . . . in time, I could have her teaching the youngest girls and I could be with the older ones.'

He lifted his mug and drank. 'It sounds to me like you're expecting a lot from her.'

'I know, but . . .' Emily frowned for a moment then looked up. 'If she really is as clever as that, it's a pity not to use it. Don't you think so?'

'Perhaps she's the one you should talk to.' She opened her mouth to speak, but he continued: 'Not now. Closer to the time. When she's ready. *If* she's ever ready,' he added. 'It's very early days yet. She's barely settled here.'

'Yes,' she agreed. 'Of course. I don't want to force her.'

'I thought the idea was that she could help here while Lucy looks after your baby. She won't be able to do that as well as teach.'

'That's the problem.'

He understood, and Emily was right. But that was the lot of most women, with lives of home and hearth.

'See what she wants to do if the time comes. Not everyone's as ambitious as you, remember that.'

'I won't push her. I promise.'

'Remember that,' Nottingham said. 'Whatever she chooses will only be a waste if she believes it's a waste.'

'Yes, Papa.' She grinned at him. 'Why can't all fathers be like you?'

'Old and tired and ready for his bed, you mean?'

Lister prowled the inns along Briggate. He heard more about Tom Warren than he'd ever known. Sorting facts from rumour would take time. But if he believed all the gossip, the man had been a forger and a coiner and possibly far more.

By the time he trudged wearily home along the darkness of Kirkgate, he didn't know what to think. People seem to take a peculiar relish in blackening Warren's name. Why?

At first he was too deep in his thoughts to notice the footsteps that shadowed him. By the time he turned, the man was only ten yards away. A heavy greatcoat, tricorn hat pulled down to hide his eyes.

206

Rob reached into his pocket to grab his knife. 'What do you want?'

But the man didn't answer, just kept coming at the same steady pace.

'Stop.' He drew the blade. Just three yards away, the man halted, his breath blooming in the air. Big, broad, with an air of menace.

'Who are you?'

'I'm on my way home.' A deep, unfamiliar voice.

'Then off you go.'

He waited until the man had vanished from sight before walking on, listening closely and hearing nothing. He must be on edge with all the killings, Rob thought, seeing danger where there wasn't any. The man was probably telling the truth. Carry on like this and he'd start seeing ghosts. But he couldn't shake the feeling, the prickle of death at his back.

'I looked for you yesterday morning,' Nottingham said as he settled on the bench in Garroway's coffee house.

'I had business,' Tom Finer replied. He picked up the dish of coffee and drank.

'You'll have heard about Tom Warren.'

'I expect all of Leeds has by now.'

'He took care of your accounts, didn't he?'

Finer raised a thick eyebrow. 'He did, and I'll be needing them back from his office. When I went there yesterday, the bookseller wouldn't admit me.'

'Those were my orders,' Nottingham said. 'I'll see they're returned in good time. What can you tell me about him?'

207

'He was good at his job. I don't have the inclination to do it all myself.'

'His clerk was a forger. He's vanished, too. Everything gone from his lodgings.'

Finer rubbed his chin. 'Then that's your answer. He killed Warren and ran off with whatever he could.'

'No.' He didn't give a reason. 'Warren was involved in something.'

'Was he? What's your proof?'

'It's there.' No matter that there wasn't a piece of evidence yet; he knew it inside.

'Then my advice is to follow that, Constable.' He gave a faint, hard smile. 'But I'm sure you don't need me to tell you how to do your job.'

'If you know something, now would be a good time to say.'

'The man did my accounts. That's all.'

Nottingham stared out of the window, watching the wagons and coaches pass along the Head Row.

'You've built up a little empire here, haven't you?'

'I've invested in things that offer good returns.'

'Then you're clever enough to know that empires can crumble.' He brought out a farthing and flipped it in the air so it landed with a jangle on the table. 'Sometimes it can happen on the toss of a coin.' He started to rise.

'Do you know Michael Barthorpe?'

'No. Who is he?'

'A man might know something.' Finer picked up the dish of coffee and drank.

Damn him. Nottingham never heard the name Barthorpe. Now he had to find him and hope Finer had sent him after something worthwhile.

This had been a case of hints that led nowhere. Look for Charlotte, only to discover that the girl had gone. Information vanished into thin air.

'Michael Barthorpe,' Nottingham said as Rob walked into the jail.

'Who?'

'Someone said he could help us.'

'I've never heard of him.'

'It could be nothing. But we need to find him.'

'Yes, boss.' There was no point in asking who'd given the information; the man wouldn't say. 'I'll tell you this: hardly anyone had a good word for Warren last night. To listen to them, he'd committed everything but murder.'

'Do you think there's much truth in it?'

'Some of it, definitely. It ties in with what you told me about his clerk. But a strange thing happened on the way home . . .'

The constable listened, then asked: 'You didn't get a look at his face?'

'No.'

'Stay alert.'

The constable went through the correspondence. A letter from York, acknowledging receipt of Nick. That all seemed like history now, something that happened a lifetime ago. Where was the girl, he wondered? Perhaps she'd last out this year, next if she was lucky. But he doubted she was too long for the world.

Barthorpe. Rob spent the morning asking after the man. He was about to give up when someone directed him into Hunslet. He found the man bent over a potter's wheel in a small workshop, shaping clay into a cup as his feet worked pedals to keep the wheel turning. In the far corner a kiln threw out its heat, enough to keep the place warm.

'Michael Barthorpe?'

'That's me.' He slipped a flat knife under the base of the cup and slid it on to a tray before gathering another handful of clay and slapping it down. 'What can I do for you?' He gestured and the finished items on the shelves, all glazed brilliant white. 'Cups? Bowls? Every one good quality.'

'I'm Robert Lister, the Deputy Constable of Leeds. I want to talk to you about Tom Warren.'

'I see,' Barthorpe answered and looked over his shoulder at the kiln. 'We've half an hour before that lot's fired. Ask your questions.' He sat upright on his stool and rubbed his back.

He looked around thirty, bearded, his hair unkempt. But there was an openness to his face and warmth in his eyes. A scrawny body, but his arms were taut and muscled.

'How well did you know him?'

'Better than most, I suppose,' the man replied quietly. 'He was my cousin. His mother was my aunt. She's dead now.'

'So's he. People are saying he was a criminal.'

'It's true,' Barthorpe agreed. 'He was always good with numbers, they came to him easily. Me, I'm good with my hands.' He held up his arms for a moment. 'I like clay. Tom was a clerk, and he discovered he could copy anyone's writing. Between those two skills he found a way to make a living. A good one, if that's what you like.'

'Do you know why anyone would want to kill him?'

'No. But if that's how you make your money it's not too hard to imagine, is it? I didn't see him often. Me, I'm married, we have children, I'm trying to earn my way. He had . . . a different life, I suppose. But he came here three days ago and asked me to look after something for him.'

Rob felt his heartbeat quicken. 'What was it?'

'A package. He said he'd come back for it when he could.' He bent and washed his hands in a bucket of water. 'I'll fetch it for you. Not going to be any use to him now, is it?'

He'd hidden it up in the rafters of the work-shop. Small, just as the man had said, wrapped in oilskin with a heavy wax seal.

'You didn't open it?' Rob asked in surprise.

'It's not mine,' Barthorpe said. 'Why would I? But it's not going to be much use to Tom now. Maybe it'll help you find whoever killed him.' He gave a sad, wry smile. 'That would be some justice, I suppose.'

'Thank you. What other family did he have?'

'Two sisters, if they're still alive.' He shrugged. 'That's all.'

'There's a body to bury.'

'Then I'd better find an undertaker.' He sat at the wheel again and began to push the pedals. 'I have a family to support.'

Rob pushed the packet deep into his pocket, look-ing around as he left Hunslet. It was ridiculous, but since last night he'd had the niggling sense that someone was behind him. No matter how often he stopped and turned, though, he hadn't been able to spot anyone.

Traffic was waiting at Leeds Bridge. A cart had lost one of its wheels, the load spilling across the road. Men were arguing and shouting. Nothing new; it seemed to happen at least once a week. The town was becoming too busy.

The constable was composing a letter, dipping his quill in the ink and writing with careful slowness. It was one part of the job that he'd never enjoyed, a task he put off as long as possible; the words would never flow for him.

He was just sanding it, ready to send, when Lister appeared and tossed down the packet with a triumphant grin.

'From Michael Barthorpe,' he said. 'Warren left this with him a few days ago. They were cousins.'

Nottingham picked it up and broke the seal. Papers inside, not too many of them. He unfolded the contents and started to read, frowning as he understood what the documents meant.

'Take a look.'

'They're deeds,' Rob said after he'd gone through them. 'For two houses.'

'The property on Lady Lane, that's one of the places Tom Finer built,' the constable said.

'That other one is the cottage where Smith the moneylender lived.' Rob poured himself a mug of ale. 'If Warren owned these, what was he doing living in a room on Water Lane?'

'Maybe he forged the deeds.'

'Possibly,' Rob said, then shook his head. 'But why would he wrap up a pair of forgeries and leave them with his cousin?'

'Maybe someone was looking for them.' Nottingham shrugged. 'The first thing we need to do is find out if these are real.'

'We have Smith's account books here,' Rob said. He began poring through the pages, then stopped, his finger on a line. 'Rent to Mr Warren.'

'Go to Lady Lane, find out who's living in that house. I'll see if I can start to make any sense of the papers in Warren's office.'

All the account books had vanished. Ogle the bookseller swore he hadn't allowed anyone upstairs, but that hardly mattered. Mostly likely the killer had taken them. Nottingham spent an hour sifting through everything, trying to put it all in some semblance of order, but it was a hopeless task. Wood or Warren were the only ones who understood it all and they were gone.

He wondered how Tom Finer would take that news.

The constable left, frustrated, carrying a heavy bundle of papers. He had names on invoices, people who must have been Warren's clients. It was some small consolation.

Finer was at home, in the rooms he occupied looking down over the Head Row, just three doors away from Garroway's Coffee House.

The fire was burning bright in the grate, the room so close and hot that Nottingham's chest felt tight. But the old man seemed to be more alive in the heat, pacing up and down as he listened.

'I need those account books,' he said.

'I'll ask the man who killed Tom Warren when I find him,' the constable told him.

Finer snorted. 'I'd probably do better searching for him myself.'

'No,' the constable warned. 'You won't even start trying. Not unless you want to wish you'd never come back here.' He frowned. 'How did you know about Michael Barthorpe?'

'Warren mentioned him once when we were talking. Said they were related.'

'He's a potter. And you didn't tell me Warren had bought one of the houses you built.'

'That's how we met. What does it matter, anyway?'

'He visited Barthorpe and left the deeds to two places with him. Why would he do that if he wasn't scared?'

Finer's eyes widened little. So there were a few things he didn't know.

'I couldn't say. I hadn't seen him in a while.' He stayed silent for a long time. 'Do you know what this reminds me of?'

'What?'

'Amos Worthy. It was before Arkwright took you on, you wouldn't remember. When he wanted to control everything here, he took care of all the competition. One way or another, it didn't matter to him. All this is something he would have done.'

'I seem to recall that you were part of that competition,' Nottingham reminded him.

'Why do you think I left Leeds?' Finer said

sharply. 'He was going to kill me otherwise. Told me that to my face.'

Amos Worthy. He'd never be rid of the man. Dead and buried, but his shadow still lingered. He'd been the one who tried to save Nottingham's mother after her husband had disowned wife and child. He loved her, but she always turned him away. And then he'd tried for his joke beyond the grave with money left to Emily. But she had the final laugh, using it to help fund her school for poor girls.

'He's dead. That disease ate him until there was nothing left,' the constable said. 'I saw him go in the ground myself.'

'We'd better hope he is.'

The house on Lady Lane was just two years old but already it looked weary. The paint on the door was beginning to flake and crack, and the windows sat awkwardly in their frames. Cheaply built, never intended to last. Even as they went up, people had said how shoddy they looked. But Leeds was thirsty for houses. They were sold before they were finished.

A servant answered his knock, a harried woman with a heavily-lined face and a squalling baby in her arms. Somewhere behind her he could hear another child running about and a voice trying to keep order, followed by a hard smack, a short silence, then wailing.

'I'm the Deputy Constable of Leeds,' Rob said. 'I'd like to speak to your mistress.'

'You'd best come in.' She stepped aside. 'Go through. The children are just being fractious.'

The woman was in the parlour, a fire blazing. A young boy stood in the corner, rubbing a red cheek and blinking back tears.

'Deputy Constable,' the servant said, as if it was an explanation.

She was tall, half a head above him, with thick dark hair and quiet blue eyes with a quizzical gaze that didn't waver.

'I know we haven't met, sir. How can I help you?'

'I believe you rent this house from Tom Warren. Mrs . . .'

'Grey. My husband does, yes.' She wore a plain woollen dress, good quality, but carried herself as if it was a silk gown for the ball. He tried to place her accent. Yorkshire, but he didn't know where, with a veneer of breeding. No surprise. There was money here: the room was heavily furnished.

'I'm sorry to tell you, but he's dead.'

'I see.' Her expression betrayed nothing. 'Perhaps you should talk to my husband, Mr . . .'

'Lister.'

She gave the briefest nod of acknowledgement. 'He's the manager at Dryden's finishing house. You know it, I'm sure.'

'Of course.' Finishing cloth was skilled work. The manager would be handsomely paid.

'He can tell you what you need. But we've never had anything to do with Mr Warren, I can assure you of that. We simply pay him our rent.' She allowed herself a brief smile. 'Now, if you'll excuse me, we have a handful here. I'm sure you must have heard them.'

Grey knew nothing when Rob talked to him.

He frowned at the news, and asked a question or two. The family had moved from Halifax six months before when he took the manager's job. He didn't even know Leeds; all his time was spent at work or at home.

'Where do you want me now, boss?'

'See if you can make sense of all those papers from Warren's office.' Nottingham glanced out of the window. A thin, cold rain had started to fall, people hurrying past on Kirkgate. 'At least it'll keep you dry.'

'What are we looking for?' Rob asked.

'I wish I knew. Apart from all the account books, I don't even know what's missing. It's like a puzzle without a key.' He stood and slid his arms into the greatcoat. 'I stopped at Mrs Webb's house earlier. It was time I met my grand-daughter properly.'

'How is she?' Rob realized he'd barely given the baby a thought since he'd seen her, as if she wasn't quite flesh and blood yet, just an idea.

'Beautiful.' He smiled. 'Gaining weight every day. Doesn't even cry much, she says. That's a blessing. Emily used to scream her head off when-ever she was hungry. She's a bonny little girl.'

'I need to go and see her again.'

'Enjoy her while she can't do much,' Nottingham told him. 'As soon as she starts crawling, she'll run you ragged. It never stops after that. Mrs Webb said Emily's going to bring her over to the house for a few hours on Sunday.'

'Really?' She hadn't told him; perhaps she'd only arranged it early that morning.

'Between her and Lucy, though, you might not get close.' He tapped the bicorn hat on to his head. 'I wish you well with the papers.'

It was impossible, Rob decided after two hours. Without knowing what wasn't here, he couldn't even judge what was important. By themselves, the invoices and bills of sale meant little. All he'd achieved was a list of those who used Warren's services. A few papers looked as if they might have been altered, but he couldn't be certain.

He put more coal on the fire and watched the flames leap higher. Outside the rain was heavier, streaming down the window.

It was aggravating, fruitless work, but still better than being out in that.

Nottingham found Jem in his room by the stable at the Rose and Crown. A brazier kept the place warm, old sack stuffed into the cracks around the door to keep out the wind and the water.

'Hazard of the trade,' Jem said as he listened to the rain on the roof. 'But God made it, so there's no sense complaining.' He brought out a jug. 'That Molly slipped this out to me. Fancy a mug?'

The constable shook his head. 'I can't stay long. You heard about the body in Mabgate?'

'Course I have. You couldn't hear much else this morning.' He grinned. 'You know how folk are. They love a killing.'

'Anything interesting?'

218

'Not so you'd notice. Someone was talking about a man named Groves. Said he'd be happy to see Warren dead.'

Solomon Groves. A name dredged up from the past.

'What else?'

'No more than the usual blether. Are you sure you won't stop for a drink, Mr Nottingham? It's cats and dogs out there.'

Twenty

The draper's shop smelt of roses. Nottingham wiped the rain from his face and looked around. Hose, handkerchiefs, stocks that glistened in the candlelight. Little had changed over the years.

He heard footsteps and Groves came bustling through from the back room, halting as soon as he saw his customer.

'Mr Nottingham.' A smile quickly hid the dismay. 'Are you looking to buy?'

'Not today,' the constable told him with a smile. 'Just a word with you, Mr Groves.'

'Of course.' But he looked uneasy, as if he'd rather be anywhere else.

'Tom Warren.' He said the name slowly, watching as the man blinked a few times.

'A terrible shame. I heard about it. So much death these days.'

'I agree. But it's strange, last night someone

219

was saying you won't mourn Mr Warren too much.'

'Me?' But the way he tightened his grip on his coat collar told the truth.

'You,' Nottingham insisted. 'Why might that be, I wonder?'

'Did you know him?'

'We only met once.'

'He was a very unpleasant man.' Groves's face reddened.

'Blackmail?' It was just a guess, but as soon as he spoke the word, he saw that he was right. The man's face tightened.

'Yes.'

Something else to add to the list of Warren's crimes. He didn't need the details; the knowledge was enough.

'That gives you a reason to kill him.'

'I—' Groves' face lost all its colour.

'Don't worry,' Nottingham told him. 'I don't think it was you.'

'Thank you. I couldn't. Never. Not that.' He took a few short breaths. 'He kept asking for a little more money, you see. Just a little at first, but lately . . .'

'You're free of him now.'

'I am.' He sounded as if his life had begun again with Warren's death.

'Who else might be happy to see him gone? Do you know?'

'No. I'm sorry.' The man's problems had probably been his whole world. Now he might be able to glance outside a little.

'Then I'll wish you good day.'

* * *

220

He was drenched by the time he reached the jail, water dripping from his hat and coat. The rain teemed down harder than ever. Drops bounced up from the cobbles, a thin river of it ran down the middle of Kirkgate.

'You had the best of it today,' Nottingham said as he shook himself like a dog. 'What did you manage to find in Warren's papers?'

'Nothing.' He put down the quill and rubbed his fingers. 'With no accounts, I don't even have an idea what to look for.' He gestured at the papers. 'I can go through them till Doomsday and these still won't tell me a thing.'

'We're back where we started, then.'

'I've made a list of his clients from all the bills of sale and invoices. But I've no idea if it's complete.'

'Is Tom Finer's name there?'

'Yes.'

That was good. Outside, the last of the light had faded, only the sound of the rain and a few carts moving slowly.

'We might as well go home. We're not going to achieve anything else today.'

The rain blew out overnight, but it left the ground sodden. The piles of wood for the bonfires were all wet; at this rate they'd be hard pressed to get a single decent blaze from them.

His boots squelched in the mud as he walked down Marsh Lane. The clouds still hung heavy, hiding the stars and the moon. But the bitter cold had passed; that was something. Somewhere a fox barked as it stole through the darkness.

They had a list of men who did business with Warren. That was a place to begin. But he was certain that the killer would have taken everything with his name on it. The best they could hope for was to uncover a hint and trust it led them somewhere.

It was slow work. When he met Rob in the White Swan at dinner time, Nottingham saw that he'd had no success, either.

'All they want to know is where their accounts are,' Lister said.

'I've had the same,' Nottingham told him. 'One man demanded to know what we were doing.' He smiled and shook his head. 'I offered to check his ledger after we find it and he shut up fast enough.'

'It's taking us nowhere,' Rob said. The killer was three, four, five steps ahead of them and probably laughing at the way they were flailing around.

'Who gains from all this?' the constable wondered.

'No one. Not that I can see. That's the problem. There's no new moneylender in town, no rumours of any fresh pimps arriving. Since Josh Bartlett was killed, half the whores have gone, according to the night men. They've all become too scared.'

'Then someone's waiting for the right moment. He's putting everything in place.'

'Boss . . .'

Nottingham raised his hand. 'Hear me out. I don't understand how Warren became part of this, but it's exactly the same method, the same murderer. He's waiting until he's ready to step in and take charge of everything.'

'It seems too calculated.'

'We're dealing with someone who has a plan. Someone ambitious. I was told yesterday that it was like something Amos Worthy would do.'

'But Worthy's dead. I've told you, times have changed here.'

'Maybe not as much as you think.' He sat, thinking. 'Stanbridge had dinner with Warren before he was killed. Who was the other man with them?'

'Mark Ferguson.'

'Go and talk to him again. Chances are he's terrified now. In his shoes I would be.'

'I will. I'll enjoy that.'

'You said the other moneylender deals with businesses.'

'Probably half the merchants in Leeds borrow with him. That means plenty of aldermen. Everything's absolutely legal.'

Nottingham nodded. 'He's probably safe enough, then. Killing him would cause too much outrage. I don't think the murderer's ready to flex his muscles that far. Not yet.'

'And we still don't know how to catch him.'

'No,' the constable agreed. 'We don't.'

Ferguson kept neat rooms above a shop on Boar Lane. Not the most fashionable address, but well appointed inside. A servant took Rob's hat and greatcoat, leaving him in the parlour staring out at Holy Trinity Church across the street, its Meanwood stone still glittering white and the wooden spire climbing to the sky.

'I hadn't expected to see you again, Mr Lister.'

Ferguson stood in the doorway. A short, curled periwig today, a crisp stock and an elaborately embroidered waistcoat topped tight breeches and hose intended to show off his legs. There was a mix of resentment and fear in his voice. Good, Rob thought: he could build on that.

'I felt it was worth a visit. After all, you've been unfortunate in your choice of dinner companions. Stanbridge dead, then Warren murdered. I thought I'd better see that you were still with us.'

'What?' Ferguson's eyes widened in disbelief. 'What do you mean? No one would want to kill me.'

'I'm sure you'd know more about that than I would. But a man who preys on widows must make enemies.' He gave a half-smile.

'I think you'd better leave.' Scared, but more confident when he was secure in his own home. It was easy enough to undermine that.

'If you wish. Who do you have to protect you?'

'Protect? Why would I need that?'

'We don't know yet who's behind the killings. He's clever. It could easily be someone you know and trust. I just wondered if you'd hired someone to keep you secure.'

'Of course I haven't. I don't need anyone like that.' His eyes flashed with anger and fear.

'Joshua Bartlett thought the same thing. He was a big man, a fighter. But someone managed to lure him out to the tenter fields and kill him. If it can happen to somebody like that . . .'

'What do you want?' Ferguson asked, a desperate edge creeping into his voice.

224

'Your memory. I need to know every name that was mentioned when you dined with Stanbridge and Warren.'

'I don't know. When they talked business, my mind drifted.'

'Then I suggest you think, Mr Ferguson.' A heartbeat's pause. 'Your life might depend on it.'

Rob was content to wait, to give the man time and let the pressure build. No doubt the man was attentive enough if the talk turned to women or ways of making money. Anything else, though? He wasn't so certain.

'I can't remember. They might have talked about people.' He stared helplessly. 'I stopped listening to them.'

The best chance they had and he turned out to be a man with a head full of air.

'Keep thinking about it. I want to know if any name comes to you. It's important.'

Ferguson nodded quickly. 'Am I in danger?'

'You may be,' Rob told him. 'In your position I'd assume I was.'

At least that would give him something to think about. Rob smiled as he clattered down the stairs. Maybe fear would give him a spur.

Nottingham walked. Often the rhythm of it, the movement, helped him think. Did all this remind him of Worthy? Not of the man he'd known. But by the time he became constable, Amos Worthy was already established. He had a web of aldermen in his debt and he was beyond reach. All he'd ever been able to do was thwart the man here and there. Only death had been able to beat him.

Could there be another in his mould?

Finer seemed convinced. But he would happily send the law off in the wrong direction while he exacted his revenge.

Yet Nottingham could feel it, that one man on his own was behind this. So far, though, he'd left no trace. Not someone who'd been in Leeds for years, he was certain. Anyone with those ambitions would have made his move when Kirkstall took over as constable.

And he didn't know the ones who'd come since. He didn't have their measure. Rob was right; the town had changed. Yet even he couldn't come up with a likely name. Whoever was doing this was very skilled at making himself invisible.

More than that, he knew things. He heard things very quickly. How? How could his ears be everywhere? And how had he been able to tempt people like Bartlett and Warren to places where he could kill them?

He realized he'd walked out past Town End and into the countryside. The fields were brown where they'd been ploughed, rising away to green on the hills where a few sheep grazed. The air was heavy with smell of damp earth and the puddles on the road deep enough to jolt a cart. Not even half a mile outside Leeds and this was a different world. Quieter, slower. More disturbing, in its own way. He felt comfortable among the noise and the voices, the women crying their wares, the bustle of Briggate. It was what he'd known all his life, his music.

Nottingham turned and walked back slowly to town. He didn't have any answers, but perhaps the problem had a shape at last. Yet the man behind it all was still no more than a shadow in the mist.

He'd become used to Annie serving the food, as if she naturally fitted into the place. She was still shy, always looking down, unsure if she was doing the proper thing. But she'd settle. Lucy was looking after her well. The girl was beginning to fill out a little, more than the skin and bone she'd been when she arrived. And the fear that haunted her face had disappeared.

After the meal, Emily called her in and set a book out on the table, going over the page word by word, helping her pronounce the words then put each sentence together. His daughter had patience, Nottingham thought. But she was right: twice through and the girl was reading it as if it was the most natural thing in the world. Emily looked at him and raised her eyebrow questioningly. He nodded. The girl had a quick mind.

Sitting by the fire, the soft drone of reading in the background, the constable laid out his thoughts and questions for Rob.

'How could he have known that Four-Finger Jane had been asking questions for me? And what did he say to Warren and Bartlett? With all the deaths, they should have been on their guard.'

'He's somewhere he can hear things,' Lister answered. 'He has to be.'

'One of our men?'

Rob shook his head. 'They don't have the wit for it, never mind the drive. But he might have heard it from one of them.'

Men drank and talked. It wouldn't take much to draw information from them.

'What about the other question?'

'Josh Bartlett wouldn't have been afraid. He probably never gave a moment's thought to my warning. He was greedy. So was Warren.'

'Dangle the possibility of easy money in front of them . . .'

'They'd be there with their tongues lolling out,' Rob said.

Nottingham remained silent for a long time, frowning and staring into the flames of the fire. Finally he pushed himself to his feet.

'I think we need Jem and his stories tomorrow,' he said. 'Time for a bit of liveliness around here.'

The temperature dropped harshly through the night. Even before dawn, the cart tracks in the mud had dried into hard ruts. Every step was tricky; judge it wrong and a man could break an ankle.

At the cloth market, buyers and sellers completed their business quickly, eager to get out of the cold. It was a rushed affair, over long before the hour had gone by, men already taking down the trestles to carry to the Cloth Hall for the afternoon's trading.

And further up Briggate, fewer had come to sell their wares. Less shouting and haggling. People simply wanted to buy what they needed and return to the warmth. Nottingham spotted a few children, pale and icy and hoping for any kind of scraps. But around the Shambles the

228

packs of dogs still gathered, quick and snarling after anything tossed away.

He found Jem outside the Moot Hall and gave his invitation.

'Maybe I should come early. Not too many wanting to stop and listen today. Can't blame them, neither.'

'As early as you like. Give Lucy a good tale and she'll probably warm your ale for you.'

'How can I resist an offer like that?'

No Con today, but the weather was too bitter for his fingers. Too raw for anything, and it felt as if it was growing harder with each hour. Just the cusp of November and it felt like the middle of January.

At midday he was in the White Swan, grateful for the fire and all the bodies around. The meat pie filled his belly and the ale washed it all down neatly. It had been a wasted morning, and he knew it. Hardly a soul around to give him answers, and he didn't even know what questions to ask.

Had he lost the knack of the job? Grown too stale and dull in the last two years? He was missing something, some link in the chain of things. So was Rob, and he was young and sharp. But he lacked experience; Brooke had been right in that, at least. Together, though, perhaps they could beat the man behind all this. They had to. It was as simple as that.

He was dragged from his thoughts as Michael the landlord slid on to the bench across the table. A burly man with a perpetual frown, his hair

229

was greyer now and wilder than ever, with thick, spreading whiskers.

'You look like a man with a weight on his mind.' He had a mug grabbed in a large, scarred fist, and took a deep drink as he looked around.

'Too many of them.' Nottingham managed a wan smile.

'You ought to own a place like this. If it's not the customers giving problems, it's the people I buy from. Wanting their money before they'll deliver or trying to short-weight me.' He rolled his eyes. 'Still, you do hear a few things here and there.'

'Oh?' This was why Michael had come over. Not to complain, to pass information.

'Had a man in last night. Henry Meecham, you know him?'

'No.'

'He looked like he'd been to a few other places first. Slurring his words and not making sense half the time. But he had money to pay for his ale and he didn't look like he was about to start a fight.'

'What did Meecham say?' He knew Michael's way; he needed to be eased along, and even then he'd take the long road.

'That he'd seen a killing in Mabgate.'

'What was he doing up there?'

'I didn't ask him. But he sounded certain enough about it.' He took a clay pipe from the pocket of his apron, tamped down the tobacco with his thumb, and lit it from a taper. 'I thought you might want to know.'

'I'm grateful.' The constable could feel his

230

heart thumping in his chest. 'Where do I find him?'

'That's the trick with Henry. You never know where he'll sleep it off.'

'Doesn't he have a home?'

'Not that I know of.' Michael shook his head slowly, hair flying around. 'Mostly where he passes out.'

Nottingham felt the hope starting to trickle away like sand in an hourglass. Meecham was a wandering drunk. Once he found the man and had him sober, they'd still need to separate what he'd seen from the visions in his head.

'Is there anywhere he favours?'

'I just serve them, take their money, and listen when they talk. I thought you'd like to know.'

He finished the ale and stood, reaching for coins to pay for his meal.

'On me, Mr Nottingham.'

'Then I thank you twice.'

Twenty-One

'Henry Meecham.'

'What about him?' Rob asked.

'Where would we find him?'

'If he's not drunk in the cells, he could be anywhere.' He narrowed his eyes. 'Why? What's he done?'

'Witnessed Warren's murder, by the sound of it,' Nottingham said.

231

Lister glanced out of the window. It was growing dark early and the night would be brutally cold.

'I'll get the men on it. They all know him by now.'

'Get him in here for his own safety. I don't want him dead overnight. From anything.' If Meecham was going around Leeds talking about what he'd seen, the killer could easily hear it.

'Yes, boss.' He pulled on his greatcoat and looked wistfully at the fire. Nottingham was already waiting at the door.

'Tell me about Meecham,' he said as they walked down Briggate, heads buried in their collars.

'There's not much to say that you can't guess. Drinks whenever he has money. Works at this or that until he makes a little, then he goes to sup it all. I don't know why he'd be out at Mabgate, though. He usually likes to stay closer to town.'

'That's what he told Michael at the Swan.'

'Then let's pray we can find him.'

They went to the inns, but no sign of Meecham. Nobody had seen him since the night before. Lister went to pass the word to the men, and the constable returned to the jail to leave a note for Crandall. All he could do was hope Henry Meecham was still alive and that his memory would be sharp once he was sober.

He'd left orders to send word as soon as the man was found. At home, as he listened to Jem's stories, he stayed alert, hoping for a knock on the door.

232

The old man stayed close to the fire, soaking in its warmth. Annie sat on the floor, wrapped up in Jem's words, transported into the tale of Jack and his adventures up the beanstalk. Emily was cuddled up with Rob, and Lucy stared into the distance, smiling as she listened. He was the only one not lost to the magic.

Jem finished and coughed. Lucy rushed to refill his mug and give him bread and the last of the cheese. They'd eaten well, some beef from the market, potatoes, and more, talk dashing all around the table.

Nottingham had sat back and watched it, taking pleasure in the eagerness and the noise. It took him back to another time. If he closed his eyes he could almost imagine himself there . . .

'You're quiet.' Lucy nudged him and whispered in his ear. Jem had started again.

'Am I?'

'I've been watching you. You've hardly said a word all night.'

'I've just been enjoying it all.'

'Maybe,' she said doubtfully, 'but not all of you is here.'

He smiled. She knew him too well.

'I'm hoping to hear about something.'

'Work?' Lucy asked and he nodded. 'I'll tell you something, going back to that job has done you the power of good. You're alive again, you've got that spark in your eye. We were all worried you were just going to fade away.'

He'd wondered that himself. Wished for it at times, that his image would grow paler and paler until one day he was no longer there. But she was right: being constable again had brought him firmly into the present. Duty and responsibility had given him something worthwhile. He was solid again, substantial.

As soon as the knock came, he was on his feet and opening the door. An icy chill outside, and one of the night men saying they had Meecham safe at the jail.

'Keep him there. Warm him up and give him food. I'll be along shortly.'

Two more minutes and he was marching towards Leeds with Rob at his side. There was ice forming on the puddles and cobbles; in the morning people would slither and slip and break their bones.

Nottingham pushed his hands deep into the pockets of his greatcoat. Meecham might hold the thread they could pull, the one that would lead them to the end of this. He didn't speak. No need; they were both thinking the same thing.

Too many of the night men had gathered at the jail. He knew why; they wanted to be warm. But as he glared, they began to leave.

'How is he?' the constable asked Crandall.

'Freezing. I put a brazier in the cell and gave him a pair of blankets.'

'Something to eat?'

'The dregs of the stew from the Swan. It's burnt but—'

'Good enough.' He turned to Rob. 'You've dealt with Meecham before?'

'Too often.'

'Then you talk to him. I'll just listen.'

* * *

234

Henry Meecham wasn't old, probably not even forty yet. But he had an ancient air, deep weathered creases on his face, most of his hair gone. He seemed like someone who'd turned away from life and only found joy at the bottom of a cask.

But he'd finished the food. That was a good sign, Rob thought, and the brazier took away the worst of the chill in the room.

'Well, Henry, a meal and a fire. We're treating you like royalty now.'

'You are, Mr Lister. I'm right glad of it, too.' He slurred his words, but Rob had never heard him do anything else, as if his voice never quite surfaced from the drink.

'You were in the Swan last night.'

'Were I?' He listed his head, eyes narrow in surprise. 'Happen I were.'

'You told the landlord you'd been up on Mabgate. What took you out that way?'

'Used to work there. Five years a dyer, I were.' He held up his callused, dirty hands. 'I'd go home all colours.'

It was as much of an explanation as they were likely to hear, Rob decided. Maybe some odd memory had taken him back. It didn't matter.

'What did you see there?'

'I must have fallen asleep in the grass. I heard some people talking.'

'How many?'

'Two of them. Sounded like just two, any road.'

'Do you know who they were?' He held his breath, hoping for a worthwhile answer, and

235

glanced at the constable. Nottingham was listening intently, staring at the floor.

'I thought I knew one of them,' Meecham answered. 'Big, burly. The way he held himself. Only I didn't see his face.'

'Do you have any idea who he was?'

'No.' He shook his head. 'It was like it was on the tip of my tongue. But it wouldn't come.'

'What happened? Tell me what you saw, Henry.'

'They were talking. Then the big one, he did something and the other one fell down.'

'Go on,' Lister said quietly. 'After that.'

'The big one, he went through the other man's pockets. Then he kicked him into the beck and walked off. That were it.'

'What did you do?' Nottingham asked.

'Nowt,' Meecham snapped as he turned his head towards the voice. 'What would you do? I stayed right there. I must have fallen asleep again. Next thing I knew I heard the feet and people were coming to work. Once they'd gone past I left.'

'I need you to remember everything you can about the big man. The killer.'

'I've told you. Can I have a drink? I need a drink. I'm parched.'

The constable returned with a mug of ale and the man cradled it carefully before sipping.

'What was he wearing?'

'A coat. The moon came out for a moment while I was watching and I saw it. It looked like one of the pockets was missing.' He pawed with his right hand. 'And he had a hat. Three corners on it.'

236

'What about his face?'

'I told you. I never saw it.'

Another quarter of an hour and they didn't get any further. Nottingham locked the cell door behind them.

'We'll try him again in the morning.'

'I don't think he knows any more than that,' Rob said.

'You're probably right.' But they had something. Not much, but better than the murky shape he'd seen going to kill Jane. Time and sleep might jog something in Meecham's memory. 'We'll try anyway.'

'He'll probably wake in the night, shaking and seeing things. That's what he usually does.'

'Then Crandall can deal with it. He might as well make himself useful for once.'

On the way home, they kept a brisk pace against the cold.

'How long do you think Meecham will live?'

Rob weighed the prospects. 'This winter, next perhaps. We'll probably find him frozen to death one morning. I'm not sure he even cares.'

But with the morning, Meecham had nothing to add. He shivered, even with the brazier burning, reaching for the mug of ale as if it was balm.

The constable let him stumble out into the early morning. He'd given them something. Only a few shreds, but it was more than they'd had before.

Sunday. People would parade to church in their best clothes. No coats with missing pockets today. He wondered how much he could trust the man's words: what had he seen and how much had he imagined? Meecham had witnessed the killing, yes, but as for the rest . . . But he'd take the small something he'd been given and try to build on it.

At least, now Nick had gone, no one was muttering that the streets of Leeds were dangerous. The mayor was happy. These other killings didn't affect ordinary folk. Let criminals kill criminals, and the town might be better for it.

Most would hardly even notice if someone took control of the crime here. It wouldn't touch their lives. Their worries were for themselves and their families.

He was the one responsible for keeping them safe. Sometimes it seemed as overwhelming as the very first day he'd taken office, all those years before. He'd been young enough then to believe he could do it. He'd learned quickly that it wasn't possible; it never would be. Some things you had to accept. Any town worth its salt had an underbelly to keep it sharp. The trick was keeping the right balance.

By late afternoon he felt weary. He'd spent half the day walking around in the cold, looking at men in their coats. One or two with missing pockets, more than he'd ever imagined. But none who matched the rest of Meecham's vague description. Too short, too thin; one who limped awkwardly.

He went home in the last of the light. The final day of October. Bonfires were piled up for Gunpowder Treason Night next Friday. More would appear. A night of mayhem, if the wood was dry enough to burn well. And always the danger of fire spreading.

The sound of a baby's cry greeted him. He'd forgotten that Emily was bringing the little girl for a few hours. Mary. He had to learn to use her name.

With coal piled on the fire, the room was close. Emily walked around, holding the child close, rubbing her back to calm her as the others watched. Nottingham removed his coat, held out his arms and gently took Mary, carefully cradling her head and seeing the relief on his daughter's face.

It didn't take long. A few words, a snatch of a lullaby, and she quieted, staring up at him. He sat, keeping her in his arms. He'd never had time to do much of this when his girls were small. He'd been working all hours, proving himself worth the job.

She was a sweet little girl, her eyes blue and wide, something on her lips that might be a smile. A small hand taking hold of his thumb. He saw Rob watching him, a look of pure terror in his eyes. He'd learn; everyone did.

Finally, Mary slept and he tenderly put her back into the basket on the floor, covering her with the blanket.

'How did you manage that, Papa?' Emily pushed a strand of hair behind her ear and looked anxiously down at the girl.

'Practice,' he told her with a smile, even if it wasn't completely true. As he gazed around the room he realized that he was the only one who'd had any part in raising a child. Annie was still just a bairn herself. Lucy was so capable that he often forgot she was still young. Emily taught girls, but by the time they reached her school they could speak and run and laugh. As for Rob . . . the lad had a good, open heart when he wanted. They'd all learn. They had no choice.

The meal was food left from the night before, cut and stewed with this and that. But it was warm in his belly and that was all that mattered. After they were done he stood over the child while Emily wrapped herself in a cloak and Rob shrugged into his greatcoat. Yes, it would be good to have new life here.

'Make sure she stays warm on the way back to Mrs Webb,' he said, then the door closed behind them.

'You're clucking like a hen,' Lucy told him.

'Maybe,' he agreed. 'But you weren't there when we found her. She was so cold I thought she'd die.'

'She has a powerful set of lungs.'

'I daresay you were the same.'

'I'll learn,' she said. 'Won't I?'

'Good training for when you have a few of your own.'

She snorted and disappeared into the kitchen, leaving Annie standing shyly with her book.

'Miss Emily usually helps me with my reading now,' she said.

'Well then, we'd better look at it.'

Families, he thought. Families.

* * *

Rob watched the constable leave the jail. Monday morning and the world was alive with its bustle and noise. Nottingham had simply said he wanted to talk to someone, then left. No explanation. But that was his way. Cryptic and cautious.

No deaths reported overnight. At least there was that.

But there would be more before this was over. He felt it in his gut. One man behind everything? Warren's murder had tipped the balance; he'd come to believe the boss was right. Why hadn't he spotted the signs for himself? We see what we want to see, Nottingham had said, and it was true. Everything had been there; he simply hadn't been able to make a pattern from the pieces.

So much for doubting whether the man could still do the job. Even after two years away, he was still sharper than Rob could ever hope to be.

'Do you have my ledgers yet?'

'You already know the answer to that.' The constable sat across the table from Tom Finer, waiting as the man rolled up some documents and tied them with a red ribbon.

'The deed on some land just south of the river. A fair price. Someone needing money quickly.' He gave a thin, satisfied smile and glanced out of the window of Garroway's at the people moving on the Head Row. 'An investment. There will always be more people. There won't ever be more land.'

'And you'll make money on it.'

'If I'm lucky.'

'You can't have found Warren's killer yet. We don't have any fresh bodies.'

Finer raised a thick eyebrow. 'Why would I leave him to be found?'

'You don't know who it is yet.'

'You'll have to wait and see.' Another brief smile. 'But you're still groping in the dark. You wouldn't be here otherwise.'

'I just wanted to remind you that this is something for the law to solve.'

'The law hasn't done very well so far. How many dead now? Six, is it? That's hardly a success.'

'We're close—'

'Which means you're nowhere at all,' Finer said. 'You might as well keep your bluffs for someone who'll believe them. The only thing you've managed to catch is a young cutpurse.'

Nottingham didn't reply. What could he say? It was true.

'And don't start suggesting we work together. You want justice. I'm after revenge.' Finer shook his head. 'The two don't meet. Now, if you've said your piece, I have work to do.' He tapped the document. 'Money to make. Legally.'

He hadn't held much hope of co-operation, but as he turned up his collar against the chill wind, there was one crumb of satisfaction: Finer was no further along in the hunt than he was. The old man would have been smug if he'd succeeded.

He spent the morning walking. It kept the blood

turning and gave him the chance to look at the men on the streets. No one who came close to Meecham's description. Only one missing pocket. And nobody who matched the half-glimpsed figure he'd seen in the mist.

Twenty-Two

'Boss?' Rob came into the jail with an older man. He was large, chins jiggling over his collar as he walked. Not prosperous, but no pauper either, wearing a waistcoat covered in food stains, but a coat that was impeccably clean. The man glanced around the room through a pair of spectacles. Forests of hair sprouted from his nostrils and ears, grey and thick. 'This gentleman wants to talk to you.'

'Mr Pargiter,' Nottingham said. 'I haven't seen you in a long time.' He gestured to a seat and Rob watched as the man made a performance of lowering himself.

Pargiter had come up to him outside the Moot Hall, demanding to see the constable.

'Can I help you? I'm his deputy.'

'No. I need him.' He carried a walking stick, and banged it on the ground to emphasize his words.

He knew Pargiter; all of Leeds did. Someone never short of an opinion and ready to air it, wherever he was. He was happy to let the boss deal with the man.

* * *

243

'You're looking for the man who killed Warren.'

'We're looking for a murderer,' Nottingham agreed. Rob leaned against the wall, poured a mug of ale, and listened. 'Why, do you know who did it?'

'No.' A bang of the stick on the floor for emphasis. 'Of course not.'

'I see,' the constable said slowly. 'Do you have any information that might take us to him?'

'No.'

'Then I don't understand why you're here.' Rob caught Nottingham's weary glance and gave a quick smile.

'Because you're doing everything wrong, as usual. You were just the same when you were in office before.'

'And what are we doing wrong?' The constable's expression hardened.

'You should be cleaning out all the filth in this town. That's where you'll find him. It's simple if you care to look.'

Rob turned away to hide his grin. The man was a menace. He knew how to run everything except his own business. That had struggled for years. Even his sons couldn't make a success of it because Pargiter would never give them the chance.

'That's your advice, is it?'

'It is,' the man said firmly.

'Then I suggest you leave right now, before I put you in a cell for trying to impede justice,' Nottingham told him.

'What?' The man went goggle-eyed and colour rushed across his face.

'Now.'

Very slowly, Pargiter rose. At the door he waved his stick. 'I shall be writing to the *Mercury* about this.'

Rob raised his cup in a toast. 'About time someone told him.'

'Let him say what he wants.' He sighed. 'Are we doing something wrong here?'

'No. We're doing everything we can. What do we have to go on? A man with a coat pocket missing? I counted three of them this morning. And we're relying on the word of a drunkard.'

'I know, I know. We need more.'

'We do,' Rob agreed. 'But where are we going to find it?'

He'd enjoyed throwing Pargiter out of the jail. The man had deserved it for years. But the satisfaction didn't last. Doing everything wrong. That niggled and ate at his mind as he walked.

The weather was warmer again, as if it couldn't choose between one thing and the other. He could hear the clear notes of Con's fiddle at the top of Briggate, exactly what he needed to calm his soul.

It was a lilting air, full of promises and light. He stood a few feet away and listened, letting the music pour through him. Con held the final note until it became a whisper. Nottingham moved forward and threw a coin in the hat.

'That was beautiful.'

'I heard it once, a long time ago. I thought I'd see if I could remember it.'

'You did.'

'In parts, maybe.' He shrugged and he adjusted the tuning on the violin, plucking at a string until his ear was happy. 'I heard something else, too. I hoped you'd come by.'

'What?'

'It was just a snatch. Two men stopped and listened for a moment. But they kept on talking. One of them said their da had told him it would all come to a head on the fifth. Then the other one laughed.'

'That was all?'

'They moved on after that, I could hear them walking away.'

'It could be nothing.' Most likely it was an innocent fragment, nothing to do with murder.

'Perhaps it is,' Con agreed. 'Their da, so it was a pair of brothers talking. It stayed with me, that's all. The one who talked, he sounded young. Twenty, somewhere around there.'

'Did you recognize their voices?'

'No.' Con frowned. 'And you know me, Mr Nottingham. I remember the way people speak and walk. But they were new to me. They weren't from Leeds, you could tell that. Not too far away, maybe, but not here. I just wanted to tell you, that's all.'

He put a hand on the man's arm. 'I appreciate it. I'm glad you did.'

Did it mean anything? He wandered down the Head Row and along Vicar Lane, trying to hammer the words into the picture he had. A family? He'd imagined one man, working alone. Still, it was possible; a family would hold their secrets close, not letting a word slip.

He could feel his heart beating a little faster at the thought. Why hadn't he imagined that?

In all likelihood, the words had nothing to do with this. A family affair, a phrase that had wandered out from behind closed doors. And not being from here – what did that mean? So many of the faces he saw every day were new. Families arrived all the time, trundling in with their possessions and their dreams. Young men, girls, everyone hoping the town contained the gold they hadn't managed to find yet.

'I think you're making something out of nothing,' Rob told him as they sat in the White Swan. Only bread and cheese on offer today, the cook ill. 'They're just words.'

The constable pared away a piece of rind with his knife.

'Maybe, but it's something to consider. The family part.'

'No,' Lister said after a few moments. 'I know I didn't believe you at first. I was wrong about that, I admit it. But we'd know if there was a family like that here. How could they hide it? It has to be one man.'

'Let's keep an open mind. On everything.' He broke open the hunk of bread. 'Remember what I said about seeing what we want to see.' He chewed for a moment, then washed the food down with a swig of ale. 'How do you feel about fatherhood now?'

'Still terrified. She's so small, so . . . fragile.'

'They grow. Faster than you can believe. You'll turn around and the next thing she'll be walking.'

247

He grinned. 'Then you'll be fending off her young men.'

'But how do you know what to do?'

'You don't. No one does.' The confusion on Rob's face made him smile. 'People will show you. They'll offer more advice than you'll ever want, and one half of it will contradict the other. But you learn as you do it. And Mary will have a family around her.' He wondered about the girl who'd left her baby in the church porch. Was she alive or dead? How scared had she been, alone and with a new life in her arms? She probably couldn't even care for herself, never mind anyone else. 'Don't worry. You and Emily will be good parents.'

'I hope so. It's just . . .'

'I know, believe me. Bigger than anything you ever imagined.' He pushed the empty plate and drained his mug. 'Come on, we have a killer to find, whether it's one man or a family.'

It will all come to a head on the fifth. Gunpowder Treason Night, with the bonfires flaring and crackling and everyone running wild. A perfect time. On Friday. And already Monday was sliding away into darkness.

Perhaps it really was nothing, just talk about something else.

But . . .

He trudged down Kirkgate, stopping at the church. A little time with Mary and Rose, telling them about the baby, hearing his wife's soft laughter and seeing her smile. Then, before he

248

left, a visit to John Sedgwick. His deputy for so long, the one who knew what he was thinking before he realized it himself.

Would the two of them together have done any better on this? But there was no answer in the empty graveyard.

A brighter morning, the sky clear and still full of stars as he walked down Marsh Lane, not even the first hint of dawn on the horizon. He hadn't been able to sleep, troubled by too many thoughts.

Whether the remark Con heard meant something or not, it had infected him with urgency. November the second today, and sand running out of the glass every minute.

He was the only man on Kirkgate. He could easily have been the only one awake in Leeds, as his footsteps echoed off the buildings. At the jail he skimmed through the reports, hoping for anything that could be useful. But nothing more than the normal drunkenness and fights, and a complaint of adulterated ale from the Talbot.

Nottingham sighed as he built up the fire, waiting until it caught and the flames began to leap.

Coming to a head on the fifth . . .

He was still weighing the words when Rob arrived, stifling a yawn. The young man had been out late, going around the inns once more, talking, listening for any scrap. But as Nottingham looked up hopefully, he shook his head.

'I want you to go around those pimps you know,' the constable said. 'Tell them to stay indoors on the fifth and keep their doors locked.'

'Boss . . .'

'And that moneylender, the one you say is above board, tell him the same thing.'

'Thompson. We can't. Not on a few words that probably have nothing to do with killing.'

'What if they were talking about that and we end up with more bodies? Warn them. Make it sound serious. I'd rather be wrong and have them all alive.'

'Thompson's going to ask why we haven't caught the man yet. And he has the ear of some important people in town.'

'Then let him complain. Maybe we'll have the murderer by then. The murderers. Tell him we're trying to save his life. Maybe that will make a difference.'

'What about the whores?'

'I'll go and talk to them.' But he already knew it would be a hopeless cause. With so many men out, drinking and celebrating, it would be a busy night for them, with money in their purses. Most of them would take their chances. The ones with pimps would have no choice. At least he could warn them and try to keep them on their guard . . .

'Stay at home?' Thompson said in disbelief. 'Why?'

'Because things might turn dangerous on Friday,' Rob told him.

'Dangerous? What in the name of God are you talking about?'

He tried to explain, seeing the man's anger rise.

'My daughters have been pestering me for a week to go and see the fires. Now you're saying

I have to tell them no. Whose idea is this? Yours or the new constable's?'

'We think it's best.' Even if he didn't believe it, he owed the boss his loyalty.

'If you're so certain, why haven't you arrested anyone yet? Don't be so ridiculous.' He slammed a hand down on his desk. 'All you're doing is spreading panic.'

'We're trying to keep people safe.'

'I'll be talking to some friends of mine about this,' Thompson said.

'That's up to you.'

'Yes,' the man replied coldly. 'It is. And now I have some work to do.'

Exactly as he predicted, Rob thought as the servant showed him out. But he'd done his duty. It was no better during the rest of the morning. The pimps barely listened. One laughed in his face. And who could blame them? If they were cowed by faint threats, they wouldn't last long.

He didn't believe it himself. He couldn't believe it. It wasn't evidence, it wasn't even rumour. Just a few flimsy words a blind fiddler had overheard and blown into something important. Yet the boss chose to take it seriously. He'd revised his opinion of the man once, acknowledged he'd seen something others couldn't believe, and been right. But this was caution based on nothing . . .

Nottingham didn't go around the whores. They'd never accept it from him; they'd simply think the law was trying to keep them from earning a living. Instead he went to Lands Lane and knocked on Lizzie's door.

'Mr Nottingham,' she said in surprise. She wore a stained apron over an old dress, her hair caught up under a cap. 'Come in.'

Isabell stood by the table, dressed like her mother, small fists pressed down into bread dough.

'We're in the middle of . . .' Lizzie gestured.

'I'm sorry. I've come at a bad time.'

'No, no . . . there's ale if you want it.' She held up flour-covered arms. 'Help yourself.' 'It's lovely to see you again.'

'There's something you might be able to do for me,' he told her. He explained as she kneaded, showing her daughter what to do. James would be off at the bluecoat school, gaining more education than his father had ever enjoyed.

'But if you're willing, I want you to be very careful,' he finished. 'Just talk to one or two that you know and let them spread the idea. The people behind all this, they're ruthless.'

Lizzie said nothing, watching Isabell shape the bread into a loaf. She took it, placed it on a wooden shovel, and slid it into the hot oven.

'Half an hour,' she said to the girl and smiled. 'Now go and clean yourself up. Look at you, you're a mess.' As the girl climbed the stairs, Lizzie's expression grew more serious.

'Do you believe it?' she asked.

'I don't know,' Nottingham admitted. 'But the more I think about things, it seems possible. The women might listen to you.'

'I can tell them but they're not going to listen. They'll earn good money on Friday. I used to look forward to it, back when . . .' She shook her head to toss away the memory.

'Only if you're willing.' For a moment he saw Grace, the girl who looked like his dead daughter. 'But be careful. The people behind this are ruthless.'

'I'll do it,' Lizzie said. 'I can pass the word to a few. After that it's up to them.'

'I wouldn't ask for more than that. Thank you.' He stirred on the chair. 'Did I tell you I'm going to be a grandfather?'

Home, and what had they accomplished? A day and an evening of walking, watching, of talking to men and to women. Following ideas that all seemed to lead nowhere. Nottingham turned his key in the lock of the house on Marsh Lane. It was dark inside, the banked fire giving just enough of a glow to make out a jug of ale and a cup on the table.

His mouth was dry and he swirled the drink around, letting it go down his throat like honey. From the kitchen he heard Annie start to snuffle and cry, then Lucy, soft and soothing. 'Go back to sleep. It's only a nightmare. You're safe now.'

'Does she have them often?' he asked. 'The nightmares.'

'A few times.' Lucy glanced at the back door. It was closed, Annie in the garden, feeding crumbs to the birds. 'She dreams she's back there. I had the same thing when I first came here. It'll pass once she's properly settled.'

'Do you think—' But he had to stop as the girl returned, picked up the broom and started to sweep the flagstones. Her reading book lay on the table, open to where she'd been studying first thing. Annie was bright, she was eager, a good worker. He'd been lucky with the waifs he'd brought into the house. Before he knew it, the months would pass, Mary would be weaned and living here. A rag-tag bunch. But a family, as surely as if they were all blood. His wife would have been pleased by it.

The cloth market began without problem, but when had it been any different? The wool trade was the lifeblood of Leeds; no one wanted problems here. The merchants moved around quietly, all of them elegantly dressed, flaunting their wealth and power.

He knew he looked like a scarecrow in comparison. Thick, darned woollen hose, old, baggy breeches, and a heavy, tired coat long out of fashion. No shoes with glittering buckles but boots with hobnails. Clothes to keep him warm, to take all the wear that came with the job.

Nottingham walked by the trestles. He was about to leave when he saw John Brooke marching down Briggate, pipe clenched tight in his mouth, nodding his hellos to the merchants and clothiers. He wore a tricorn hat so beautifully blocked that it seemed to shine, and a greatcoat elegantly cut to flatter his figure.

The man would want to talk, no doubt about that. He'd only taken a few paces when the mayor put out an arm.

'I was hoping to catch you, Richard. I've been hearing a few things.'

'Oh?' he asked, as if he didn't know what was coming.

'Thompson's been complaining to a few people. Is it true that Lister suggested he and his family don't go to the fires on Friday?'

'It is. I thought it best.'

Brooke waited for an explanation. Let him ask for it, the constable thought.

'I take it you have good cause,' the mayor said finally.

'A possibility,' he replied carefully.

Brooke stared at him, trying to assess how serious he was.

'Unless you're positive, I don't want anyone spreading rumours. People enjoy themselves on Gunpowder Treason Night. We've already had to cancel the dance because poor Tom Williamson was killed.' He made it sound like a reproof.

'I won't say a word to anyone else.' That was true enough. Thompson and the pimps had been told. Any other word would pass to the whores through Lizzie. His part was done.

'Make sure you don't. And keep the apprentices in line on Friday. Crack a few heads if you need to. Last year they almost ran riot.'

The mayor didn't mention the deaths. But whores, pimps and moneylenders barely mattered to him. They weren't upstanding citizens who complained to the corporation.

'I'll make sure everything is in hand.'

The traders were preparing for the Tuesday market. Goods brought in by cart, on packhorses, or in bundles carried on their own backs. The Shambles was already busy with the sharp swoosh of cleavers as butchers hacked at their meat. A steady stream of women eager for the freshest cuts. Not that it would be likely to go off today; there was a brisk chill in the air.

He passed Jem sitting on his pack outside the Moot Hall and in the middle of a tale. The old man raised his hand in greeting. By the market cross, Con was in full flow, notes sparking off his fiddle. But he stopped in the middle of the melody, put up his bow, and called out, 'Mr Nottingham! Mr Nottingham!'

The constable turned quickly. Con never interrupted his music. 'What's so important?'

'I heard them again, the two I told you about.' He was close, his words a whisper in the ear. 'Late yesterday, just as I was finishing.'

He didn't doubt the man. Con had never mistaken a voice or a footstep. If he said it was them, then it was.

'What were they saying?' he asked urgently, keeping his voice low.

'Nothing important. I tried to follow them, but there was a press of people just there.' He gestured down Briggate. 'By the time I was past it, they'd gone.'

'Thank you,' he said, although it didn't help at all. They could be anywhere in Leeds.

'If I hear them again—'

'Don't do anything,' Nottingham warned him. 'It could be dangerous.'

The blind man nodded and looked like he was

256

about to speak. Instead, he put his fiddle up to his shoulder again and began to play.

The constable listened for a few seconds. The music was a sweet, soft air that promised spring. With winter arriving so early this year, they'd all be ready for that.

While he was up here he decided to stop at the Talbot and discuss the anonymous complaint he'd received about watered ale at the Inn. It was likely nothing, every single tavern had them, sometimes two or three times a year. Part of his job was to investigate, because some tradesmen did offend – bakers sometimes put chalk in their bread along with the flour to make up the weight and increase their profits. But a few hours in the stocks outside the Moot Hall quickly discouraged them.

It was still early but the inn was already busy, groups of men standing around and talking. Every market day would mean good money. The rich smell of stewing meat came from the kitchen and Harry Meadows stood with a smile on his face as he surveyed his kingdom.

'Mr Nottingham,' he said with pleasure, 'what will you have to drink? There's a fresh brew in the barrel.'

'Nothing today. I need to talk to you.'

'Oh?' He raised an eyebrow. 'Is something wrong?'

'It's better if we talk in private.' He liked Meadows. The man was genial and open. And he had no desire to ruin his reputation over a single complaint.

For a second the man wavered, then nodded. 'In the back.'

It was a passageway, the floor tiled, the walls made of stone. Crates of wine were stacked on the floor, next to a case of clay mugs. Beyond that he could see two women working in the kitchen, one close to Meadows's age, the heat from the stove making perspiration run down her face as the other ladled out bowls of food.

'What is it?'

'It's very likely not worth mentioning, but I've had a complaint that you've been watering down the ale.'

For a moment the man was silent. But Nottingham could see something flash quickly behind his eyes. Anger? Fear? The air between them felt sharp. Not too surprising; it was an accusation no innkeeper wanted. Then Meadows was in control again.

'Me?' He waved a hand toward the barrels. 'Try anything you want. Be my guest. Pour it yourself if you like. Nothing's watered here. Never has been and it never will be.'

'I believe you,' the constable said with a smile. 'Only one person has said anything—'

'Who was it?' Meadows asked.

'I don't know. But it's part of my job to look into it.'

'Of course. But taste the ale, Mr Nottingham. It's good, I promise you.' The man took a breath. 'I'd appreciate you keeping this private. I don't want folk thinking I'd do anything like that.'

'You're doing a good trade.'

'Better each week. And I'm going to have the

258

cockpit open this Friday night. A good cock fight after the bonfires. It should be full. Come as my guest,' he offered.

'Thank you, but it'll be a hectic night for me.' Out in the bar, men were clamouring to be served. 'You're in demand.'

There wasn't a landlord in Leeds who hadn't been accused of watering his ale; every one of them faced the same thing, and most of the time it meant nothing. He'd done his duty. Now he had more important things on his mind.

Twenty-Three

'What are you trying to tell me?'

Rob was in the Nag's Head, nursing a mug of ale. He'd been listening to Ralph Harding for the last five minutes. The man had something to say, but he was going all round the houses to get there.

He was one of the informers that Lister had cultivated, and the tips he'd given had usually been good. Where he heard things Rob didn't know, and he'd never ask. That was the man's own business. But he'd sent a message and that meant he had something to say.

'These murders,' Harding muttered. He worked loading barges on the Aire, a heavily-built man with thick arms and powerful legs. A few days of dark stubble covered his face, and his hair grew thick and wild.

'What about them?' He stared at the man.

A sly glint came into Harding's eye. 'What's it worth?'

'You know me, Ralph. That depends on what it is. I've always been fair with you.'

'Aye,' Harding agreed. 'Right enough.'

'Tell me what you know.'

'Someone was saying summat last night.'

'If you've dragged me out for gossip . . .'

'Nay, Mr Lister, it's not like that. I heard him talking myself. He didn't think anyone was close enough to listen, but I've got good ears.'

'Get on with it. I don't have all day to sit here.'

'Right. Well, one of them said—'

'How many were there?' Rob interrupted.

'Two. Young, the pair of them. Had their heads together but they didn't keep their voices down. One said they were free and clear, that no one knew who was behind the killings.'

Rob took another drink. His throat felt dry.

'Go on,' he said.

'The other said that Friday would see it over. Their da had everything planned. Then they laughed.'

'What did they look like?'

'Just young. About his age.' Harding pointed at a man aged about twenty standing close to the window. 'Fair hair. Nothing to notice, really.' He shrugged.

The man might be able to listen, but he might as well have been walking around with his eyes closed, Rob thought.

'I want to know everything you can remember, Ralph,' he said. 'Every last thing. Any names?'

But there was nothing, as if he'd listened but scarcely bothered to glance at the pair.

'Now, that's got to be worth summat, Mr Lister,' Harding said with a grin as he finished.

Rob took a penny from his pocket.

'If you'd paid more attention it would be twice that. Use your eyes as well as your ears.'

Rob walked quickly back to the jail, hoping that Nottingham was there. But the place was empty.

He knew what Harding's words meant and it galled him; he'd been so certain that the boss was wrong this time. But *what* was going to happen on Friday? How could they stop something they didn't know?

'It's confirmation.'

The constable listened carefully as Rob recounted what Harding had told him. He sat with his hands steepled under his chin, frowning.

'You were right.'

Nottingham sighed. 'I'd be happier if it did us any good. So far we know that whoever's in charge of all this has two fair-haired sons, and they're all in on it. And we have until Friday to catch them.' He looked at Lister. 'It's threadbare, isn't it?'

'It's still a little more than we had before,' Rob said.

That was true. One more tiny piece. But not enough, and time was falling away in front on them.

'It looks as if we're both going to be out late asking questions.'

* * *

But no answers. Not the ones they needed, anyway: Someone muttered to the constable about a coin clipper as he sat in the Turk's Head. That was good to know. He'd deal with it once this threat was done.

By the time he walked home the sky was clear, the moon bright, and thousands of stars shining in the sky. The cold had returned, and his breath bloomed like a small cloud.

His head ached. Not from the ale, but from all the words he'd heard during the evening. Too many of them, and not a single one that could help him find the man and his sons.

In bed, he lay listening to the small sounds of the night and trying to slough off the day. Perhaps Rob had discovered something.

Lister pushed his hands into his pockets as he strode down Kirkgate. He felt as if he'd been in every tavern in Leeds and learned nothing. A few drinks to keep his throat moist, but his head was still clear.

Someone was running along the street towards him. Rob turned, one hand grabbing the cudgel. It was probably nothing, but the last, strange night-time encounter had left him wary.

The sound grew closer. He could make out the shape of a man. The moon caught the face. Fair hair and an intent expression.

'Constable's man,' Rob called out. 'Stop.'

But the man kept coming. Light glinted on something in his hand. Rob drew the cudgel, ready.

It was easy enough to step aside in time. He remembered the lessons his fencing master had given him when he was younger. As the man passed, Rob brought the cudgel down hard. It missed the man's head but caught him between the shoulder blades. No more than a glancing blow. Not even enough to bring him down.

The man stopped and turned. Young, big and broad, a cocky grin on his face, and a long knife in his hand.

He was quick, feinting one way, then striking another. But he was untrained. He might as well have signalled every move. If it came to brute strength, he'd win, but Rob wasn't about to give him that chance. A cudgel was more than a match for a knife. With no one around to help him, it had to be.

He waited, parrying, slipping away, seeing the other man's frustration rise. Good. Let him make mistakes; Rob would be ready.

The opening came and he swung the club down hard. The man twisted away, but he was too slow: it stung on his wrist and made him drop the blade.

With a angry roar he kicked out. The toe of his shoe hit Rob on the kneecap before he turned and ran off.

Rob didn't follow. He couldn't. It was all he could manage to stay on his feet. Christ, it hurt. If he tried to move, pain shot up his leg. His foot could hardly take his weight. Very slowly, breathing hard, he bent and picked up the knife. It was very ordinary, cheap, but the steel had been ground to a deadly edge. He slid it in his pocket and took a step.

It was enough to make him gasp. He didn't fall

down, but it made him feel sick to his stomach. He forced himself, clenching his jaw. Another, then one more.

The fight couldn't have lasted more than a few moments, not even a minute. It had seemed like a lifetime. He'd know the man when he saw him again, and he had no doubt about who it was.

Rob let the leg drag. It seemed easier that way. Each yard felt like a small victory. By the time he reached Timble Bridge he had to stop and rest. The knee was swollen when he put his hand on it, half as big again as it should have been.

Sheer effort of will carried him home. He'd had worse injuries, two that could have killed him, but nothing like this. Someone told him once that the body quickly forgot pain. He'd be glad to be rid of the memory of this. By the time he opened the front door he was panting, just grateful it was over. He had no idea how long it had taken. He'd simply concentrated on getting here.

The stairs were hard. His knee wouldn't bend at all, so he had to hop up them in a sharp clatter of noise. Emily was the first awake. She lit a candle, standing on the landing, looking down at him.

But she didn't panic, didn't scream. She'd seen things like this her entire life. Nottingham appeared in another heartbeat. Without a word he came and helped, taking Rob's weight. He was stronger than he looked, Lister thought. The man had worn down to sinew and muscle.

Soon he was lying on the bed, breeches and hose removed. It wasn't a pretty sight. His knee was misshapen and ugly. But it was a beautiful relief not to have any weight on it.

Emily knew what to do. She vanished, coming back with a bandage and a basin of cold water. She soaked the cloth, wrung it out, then wrapped it around his leg. Rob closed his eyes, settling back. The sharp agony was starting to recede and he could breathe more easily.

'What happened?' the constable asked.

'I met one of the sons.' He went through it, seeing everything in his head. 'He thought he'd be able to beat me.' Rob gave a wry smile. 'If he hadn't been so scared, he probably would have done, too. I couldn't have given him much of a fight with this.'

'You're alive,' Nottingham said. 'And that will go down in a day or two.'

'Friday's not far away.'

'I hadn't forgotten.' He smiled. 'But you'll be more use to me if you're rested and able to move. Try to sleep.'

Try? He thought he might not wake until next year.

He'd lied. He needed Rob now. His knowledge, his persistence. His sense of doubt. It was always better to have someone willing to question him and make him think. Wednesday. Two more days, and he was no closer to finding the man and his sons.

Attacking the deputy constable? They were

265

either growing bold or wild. Too sure of themselves, that they'd win. But it wasn't over yet. It had barely begun.

Tom Finer had his usual seat in Garroway's, the coffee dish in front of him already empty. He was reading the London paper and put it aside as Nottingham sat down.

'You look worried.'

'Someone tried to kill my deputy last night.'

'Tried?' His eyes flashed. 'How is he?'

'Quicker than his opponent,' Nottingham said with satisfaction. 'But the man got away.'

'Is it . . .?'

'Someone young and big with fair hair. I've heard there are two men around like that. They're talking about their father and saying Friday is when everything will happen.'

'Then you've heard more than me.'

Was Finer lying? He didn't know; it was impossible to tell. The man always had so many things working and moving, wheels within wheels. He might already know about the family and be taking his steps to kill them. That would be completely in character for him.

'What have you learned?'

'Nothing at all.' He gave a thin, sour smile. 'And that's with the offer of money.'

He didn't believe that. Finer knew something. He was just keeping it to himself. But was it more than he'd already discovered?

'It'll happen once the bonfires are lit,' Nottingham said.

'Stupid remark. Of course it will. All that noise and confusion. You'll have people drunk and shooting off their guns to celebrate. Your men will all be busy. What better time for mayhem?'

'I wonder what they're planning to do.'

Finer shrugged. 'We talked about Amos last time.'

'I remember.'

'This is exactly the kind of trick he'd love.'

By the time Nottingham had first become constable, Amos Worthy already had the crime in Leeds firmly in his grip. Anyone who challenged him found he'd just signed his own death warrant. But he'd never known the young Worthy, when he was still trying to push out everyone else.

'What do you mean?'

'To take advantage of what's going on to get rid of an enemy or two. They'd disappear and no one would ever know what had happened to them.' He glanced around the coffee house. 'How many pimps are left?'

'A few.'

'Easy for three men to handle in a night.'

'They've all been warned.'

'And how many of them will listen? It's all a guess, anyway. I don't know what they intend any more than you do.'

He wasn't lying this time.

'Then I'd better get to work.'

Finer was staring out at the Head Row, watching the people and the carts as they moved.

'I think the worst thing for a man must be to survive winter and die in the spring,' he said.

'Are you ill?'

'No.' He gave a weary shake of his head. 'But

267

when you reach my age, you tend to think about death. The shadows grow longer.'

Rob tried walking. But his leg gave under him as soon as he put any weight on it. He needed to hold himself up to stop from crashing to the floor.

Lucy bustled into the room. 'Back into bed,' she commanded. 'I thought I heard you moving around.' She watched as he settled and pulled the blanket over his body.

Not even a cut; that was the damnedest part. The man's knife hadn't touched him. Just a kick and he was crippled until the swelling in his knee went down. A day or two, the apothecary had said when he visited. But that was too long. The boss needed him out there now.

'I know what you're thinking,' Lucy told him. 'But there's no point. You can't help him when you're like this.'

'Then what am I supposed to do?' He'd never been one to lollygag around.

'What Miss Emily told you.'

Rest, she'd ordered. Easier said than done. An hour of lying here was enough. He felt trapped, useless.

'Read a book.'

Emily had left two for him, and the new edition of the *Mercury*. He'd leafed through them, but he'd never been one to lose himself in a story. He couldn't even settle enough to go through the paper.

He was angry at himself. If he'd been faster, landed that first blow properly, dodged the kick . . .

No point in playing what if. Regrets weren't going to help him mend any faster. But he'd seen the man. Next time he'd take him down.

By dinner, Nottingham realized just how much he relied on Rob. He'd talked to the people he knew and learned nothing more. He was going round and round in circles.

Lister was familiar with the people who'd come during the last two years. They were the ones he needed now, and they were all strangers. He sat in the White Swan, eating a meat pie and trying to think his way forward.

He was drawing closer. But not close enough yet, and time was running out. He could feel the men, the father and his sons. Sometimes he believed he could almost see them out of the corner of his eye. But when he turned his head, there was nothing.

They'd felt confident enough to attack Rob. That angered him. It worried him. They must believe they were going to win. How?

'Someone said they'd seen you come in here.'

He looked up, dragged from his thoughts as Jem stood by the bench, the pack sitting high on his back.

'Were you looking for me?' He gestured at the bench and the old man sat with a sigh.

'Aye.' His eyes twinkled. A serving girl came by and the constable nodded. She returned with a mug of ale and put it down in front of Jem. 'Good health.'

'What is it?'

'People are saying your Emily's man was hurt badly last night.'

'Who's saying that?' The only person he'd told was Tom Finer and he'd given no details.

'It's the gossip.' He raised an eyebrow in question.

'Not true,' Nottingham said.

'I haven't seen him this morning.'

'You probably don't see him most days, Jem.' He laughed, but to his own ears it sounded false. 'Someone attacked him. That part's true. But Rob saw him off and the man escaped. Who started this? Do you know?'

He shook his head. 'I'd tell you if I did. But it's what folk are saying. They're starting to wonder what's going on when people go after the law. If I were you, I'd get him out and around this afternoon so people can see it's all lies.'

'He's not here. Rob's doing something for me.'

'Get yourself out there and tell them, then.' He took a long drink. 'There's something going on around here, Mr Nottingham.' He raised a hand before the constable could object. 'Don't go telling me it's all in my head. I can feel it. Like someone's tightening a cord around the neck of the place.'

He wasn't going to insult Jem by denying it. 'How many do you think know that?'

'A few, mebbe. Happen one or two think something's wrong, but they can't put their fingers on it.'

Better ignorance than panic, he thought. And word hadn't reached Brooke yet or the mayor would be breathing down his neck and demanding answers. All he could hope was that it stayed this way.

'I appreciate you telling me.'

'Word to the wise, that's all.' Jem gave a cracked smile. 'You've allus been good to me when I've been here.' He stood and hoisted the pack. 'They'll be wanting more tales.'

Alone, the constable finished his food and ale. He'd parade himself in a few minutes and lie about Rob. Do whatever was needful to quiet the talk. People would still mutter and murmur, of course. There was nothing he could do to stop that. But it would grow even stronger if they saw Lister trying to hobble around.

There were questions. Fewer than he'd imagined, and they seemed to believe his answers. But it wasn't bringing him any closer to the man behind it all. He was clever, Nottingham admitted reluctantly. Finer was right, it was as sly and devious as anything Amos Worthy had ever thought up. And with six dead so far, it was every bit as brutal.

That total would rise unless he stopped it. But he didn't know how.

'How's your knee?' Nottingham asked.

Rob had struggled into his clothes and made his awkward way down the stairs. It had been painful, it had taken time, and he was glad he'd done it all while no one was watching. The stick that the constable sometimes used helped him. But he moved slowly, tentatively, as if it was something he was just learning.

'Better than it was.'

'He's going to need another day, Papa,' Emily said. 'More, if he's going to be any use to you.'

271

They'd finished the meal, plates pushed to one side. He noticed that Rob had barely touched his food; a few bites of meat and nothing more. But he understood how frustration could dull the appetite.

'They must have been watching the jail and saw you didn't come in,' he said later as they sat by the fire. Nottingham had seen the effort it took for Rob to move. Emily was right: it would be another day, at the very least, until the lad was fit enough for duty.

'If I'd—'

'Don't blame yourself,' the constable told him. 'You did what you could. He was lucky, that's all.'

He slept, the warmth of Emily's body next to him. In his dreams he relived the fight time and time again. Sometimes he won, with the other man on the ground in front of him. Sometimes he lost, waking with a start and a gasp as the knife pierced his skin. Then he'd lie, wide-eyed and terrified as the cobwebs of it all cleared from his mind, until it seemed safe to rest again.

Rob woke to full light, alone in the room, no sounds from inside the house. He groaned as he tried to ease himself out of the bed. He tried to stand, catching himself before his leg gave way, groping for the stick. That helped. His knee wasn't so swollen this morning, but it was stiff; a dark bruise had blossomed on his skin like a flower. Very carefully, he dressed. Everything took longer, each action seemed to ache its way out. He felt like an old man.

Twenty-Four

At least Rob had given him a few names. He went from one to the other, but they had nothing to tell. Maybe it was the truth; maybe they didn't trust him.

He'd exhausted everything. There was nowhere else to turn. He walked, feeling the chill of the wind on his flesh. Wind had swirled the leaves into drifts and piles, oak and elm and ash. He kicked through them, hoping it might bring the same joy he'd loved as a boy. But there was no pleasure, not even for a moment. It was simply one more thing to slow him down.

Nottingham leaned on the parapet of the bridge, staring down as the river surged below. Small boats were lined up by the warehouses, and men moved back and forth to load them. Leeds was busy turning wool into money, cloth leaving for places all across Europe, the American colonies and who knew where else.

He'd done everything he could, followed every small nudge of hint. He'd talked until his throat was raw. And he still didn't have the answer. He hadn't failed yet, not with November the fifth still to come tomorrow, but this . . . it felt as if he had.

'Don't do it, Richard.'

He started at the voice by his shoulder. Joe Buck, grinning at his own joke. He hadn't heard

273

anyone approach, far from the world going on around him.

'You don't look like a happy man,' Buck said. He was as elegant as ever, with a brilliant long silk waistcoat under his dark coat, the silver buckles shining on his shoes.

'I'm thinking, that's all.'

'Dark thoughts. You were miles away.'

'People seem to say that about me too often,' he answered with a wan smile.

'I heard about young Lister. Is it as bad as they're saying?'

'No.' The constable could trust Joe to keep a confidence. 'A blow to his knee. He should be back tomorrow.'

'Let's hope so, for your sake. It'll be madness when they light the bonfires. Makes me glad I stay clear of it.'

'We'll manage. We always have,' Nottingham said.

'Will you?' The question made him turn his head.

'Why, have you heard something?'

'Just the usual. The apprentices plotting their riots. They say they're going to topple the statue from the Moot Hall.'

'They say that every year and they've never come close yet.'

'There are other rumours, too,' Buck said.

'Oh?'

'That something's going to happen.'

'Anything in particular?'

'No. But folk are scared. They sense it. You know what it is, don't you?'

'Not enough of it,' he admitted. 'That's the problem.'

'Is it to do with those killings you were asking me about?'

'Yes.' He laid out what more he knew. It seemed like nothing as he told it, bare, baked bones with no meat on them.

'Makes me glad my business isn't violent,' Buck said. 'I'll ask around, but folk would probably have told me if they knew anything.'

'At the moment I'd be glad of crumbs.'

'It all sounds like something Amos Worthy would have enjoyed.'

Nottingham gave a small, dry laugh. 'You're the second person to say that.'

'Some of us remember. Have you made sure he hasn't come back from the dead?' Joe laughed. 'I wouldn't put that past him, either.'

The constable smiled. 'Even he can't manage that.' Wearily, he pushed himself up. 'If you come across anything . . .'

'I'll send word. I promise.' Buck stood for a moment, staring. 'Take care of yourself. We're not as young as we'd like to believe we are.'

He knew that all too well, the constable thought as he walked back to the jail. He felt it in every ache and pain of life.

Rob stumped around the house, grateful for the stick. Every step still took effort, but it seemed a little easier. He was in the garden, hobbling up and down the path, when Lucy returned with her basket.

'What do you think you're doing?' she asked.

'Making sure I'm ready for tomorrow.'

'And you'll be no use at all if that knee swells up again, will you? I have ears, you know. I know what you and Mr Nottingham have been talking about. He's going to need you.'

'That's why I'm doing this,' Rob said.

'You've done it,' Lucy told him. 'Now go and sit down and rest it.'

She watched as he limped by her and settled in the chair. It felt good, easier, to have the weight off his knee, but he wasn't going to admit it to her.

'He's scared, you know,' Lucy said.

'Scared? The boss?' He'd never said anything, there hadn't been a sign of it. Just Richard Nottingham with his impassive face and long silences. The man he knew.

'He'd never let anyone see it. And you can wager he'd never tell anyone, especially you.'

'Why not?'

'Because he respects you, what do you think? He doesn't want to show any fear, because it might make him look weak. You're just the same. You keep it all behind your eyes.'

'Me?' He didn't believe her.

'The two of you are peas in a pod. Sometimes I think that's why Miss Emily loves you, because you're like her father.' She was quiet for a moment, as if she'd said too much, then quickly smoothed down her apron. 'That's what I think, anyway. You take care of that leg. So you're ready for tomorrow night.' She bustled away into the kitchen.

At first he didn't know what to think. He was

completely different from the boss. He admired him, he had since he first became a constable's man, but they were nothing alike.

Rob sat, thinking, trying to understand why Lucy believed that. She was sharp, she had a good eye for things. But she was wrong on this. She had to be.

The day was fading and still he knew nothing more. He felt as if he'd wasted it, rushing around like one of those chickens after the farmer had cut off its head. Going nowhere at all. But he couldn't give up. This evening he'd go round the inns once more, hoping that someone might have even one small drop of information.

With darkness, the cold seemed to creep back in from the west, the skies clearing. There'd be a frost tonight, Nottingham thought as he strode up Briggate. No men with a pocket missing from their coats. Who knew if Henry Meecham had even really seen that? It could have been the drink addling his brain.

Men had gathered round the fire in the New King's Arms and the Turk's Head, but no one he recognized. The same at the Talbot when he stopped there, only Meadows giving a cheery wave.

The Rose and Crown was busy, conversation coming from all the small parlours. He saw Molly Reynolds carrying a tray full of mugs up the stairs, her father John busy as he filled more from the barrel.

'You're making money tonight,' the constable said.

'Earning it,' Reynolds replied. 'No idea why they're all in here. Some days it's just that way.' He grinned. 'Not that I'm complaining. And we'll do good business tomorrow. The bonfires always make people thirsty.'

'I hear the apprentices are planning their rampage, same as ever.'

'And they'll get as far as usual. They'll either end up falling down drunk or fighting each other, or your lot will crack their heads.'

'Have you had any word about anything else?'

Reynolds finished filling the mug and set it down.

'Should I have?' he asked.

'A few people seem to be talking.'

'Some folk are never happy unless they hear the sound of their own voices. I suppose one or two seem worried.'

'What are they saying?'

'Nothing, same as it ever is. It's all blether, anyway. They don't know, so they have to conjure something out of nowt.'

If only that was true, Nottingham thought. But he'd know what it was soon enough.

He stayed alert on the way home. If they felt they could go after Rob, he was a target for them too. But no footsteps trailed behind him, and the only figures moving were in his imagination.

The streets were empty, just the echo of his boots for company as he went through the lych gate at the Parish Church. The day had already been long; a few moments more would make little difference.

He stood by Mary's grave, and for once he felt himself without words. The peace of her company would be enough. And Rose. He pictured her with her own child, then with Emily's Mary.

He didn't need daylight to find his way around the churchyard. A few steps and he was standing where John Sedgwick lay.

I could have used you tomorrow, he thought. Rob won't be able to do much. That was always the way, wasn't it, you and me together? Then we'd laugh about it later over a drink and count our wounds.

He'd stopped to see Lizzie early in the evening. But she'd been all apologies. No one knew anything, or they were too scared of something to open their mouths. He'd thanked her, given Isabell and James a farthing each, and left.

Worthy was buried on the other side of the church, not far from the wall by High Court. A small, simple stone. *Sacred to the memory . . .*

Why do they keep mentioning you, he thought? You're dead. I saw your corpse, I was here when they put you in the ground and I shovelled the sod on to your coffin. Wasn't that enough to be rid of you? Why do you keep coming back?

Twenty-Five

He slept, waking often, then closing his eyes and falling back. But as he stood and ate a chunk of bread, he felt as if he hadn't rested at all.

279

Nottingham drank the rest of the ale in his mug and stood for a moment, taking in the room. How many years had he lived in this house? His daughters had grown up here. His wife had died here. So much of him was in this place.

He turned at the sound. Rob edging awkwardly down the stairs, holding on to the wall with one hand, the stick in the other.

'Boss . . .'

'How well can you walk?'

Lister hobbled a few paces. He moved slowly, and Nottingham could see the strain on his face with each step.

'Better than it was,' Rob said. 'The swelling is going down.'

'Stay at home today.'

'But—'

'Come once it's dark. If people see you in the daylight, tongues will start working. Tonight's when I'm going to need you. Rest today.'

He could see the disappointment on the lad's face, but he knew it made sense. There was no sense in fuelling gossip. And by evening he'd need every man who could help.

His boots rattled on Timble Bridge and he stopped to hear the soft sound of the beck. Then up Kirkgate, past the buildings he knew so well – Ibbotson's house, Haxby, Pease, Cookson, every single one of them. This was his town. He'd seen it in so many different ways – from privilege, from poverty, as beggar and thief and constable. It ran through his blood.

Crandall was still at the jail, finishing the night report.

'Anything worth telling me?' Nottingham asked.

'Some boys were out, trying to stir up some mischief.' He shrugged. 'I suppose the apprentices will be saving themselves for later.'

'We'll have our hands full. Including you.'

'I thought it would be best if I stayed here and sent people where they're needed.'

The constable smiled. He'd expected something like that.

'No,' he replied. 'Everyone out there tonight.'

He saw Crandall's face fall. If he was going to remain in his job, he needed to learn.

'Yes,' the man said. 'Of course.'

'Good. Go home and sleep. I'm sure you need it.'

Alone, he put a little more coal on the fire, letting it burn until the room felt warm. The cold gnawed on him these days, and heat brought comfort to his bones and his joints. Today he'd go around once more and ask his questions. But he'd learned better than to hope for answers. Tonight would bring its reckoning and he'd have to be ready for it.

Slowly, he went through all the papers waiting on his desk. Outside, he could hear Leeds waking and beginning to move around. Voices, the trundle of an early cart, then a steadier flow of people and goods coming and going.

He'd put the last document aside when the door opened and Mayor Brooke entered, sweeping his hat off his head and tucking it under his arm. He dropped a letter on to the desk.

'This came yesterday. It's for you. About the boy who killed poor Tom Williamson.'

The constable read it quickly. The trial would be held next month and he was expected to attend as a witness. He hadn't given Nick a thought since they sent him to the Assizes in York. But it seemed he hadn't heard the last of the boy yet. For a moment an image of Kate flickered through his mind and he wondered if she was still alive.

'It should be Rob Lister giving testimony. He saw it happen.'

'You know how they work, Richard. You're the Constable; they want you. It's just for show. They'll hang him at the end of it.'

'Yes.' He remembered all those journeys on horseback to York. It always seemed to be winter when he had to travel there.

'Are you prepared for tonight?' Brooke asked.

For a moment, he thought the mayor was asking about the trouble ahead. But his face was open and hearty. The rumours and the sense of unease hadn't reached him yet.

'The day men will stay on and I'll have all the night people. The same way we've done it for years.'

'The talk is that the apprentices are planning something.'

'They always do, and every time it comes to nothing.'

'Don't give them an inch.' He grinned. 'Folk want to know there's law here.'

'My men have their orders.'

'That's what I want to hear. Let people have their fun but make sure it doesn't go too far.'

Tonight, Nottingham thought, that might be easier said than done.

'I'll take care of it.'

'Good.' He looked around the jail, appraising it – the stonework, the dirt, the untidiness of it all. 'Are you settled in the job?'

'Sometimes it's as if I'd never left.'

'The corporation is still casting around for a new constable. A few have applied. Between you and me, none of them seemed particularly impressive.'

'I'm sure you'll find the right man.'

'I hope so.' He sighed. 'Until then, this is yours.'

Perhaps he'd take those words back soon. It would depend what the night brought.

'I'm flattered.' It was what Brooke would want to hear.

The mayor rubbed his hands together.

'I'd better get to work. They're building a fire by the bridge. I'll be there. So will most of the members of the corporation. I trust you'll stop by when you have the chance.'

'If I have the time. It'll be busy.' He understood what the man was saying: make sure it's well guarded. He'd keep Waterhouse and Dyer there to stand watch on everything and stamp out any trouble.

Garroway's was quiet, only a few customers sitting and reading the London papers. Finer was at his usual table by the window, an empty coffee dish in front of him. It was impossible to read anything on his face. Maybe that was why he'd been so successful; he never gave away what he was thinking.

'There's a cold snap coming,' Finer said. 'I can feel it. My wrists ache.'

'We had a frost, that's all. And it looks set to be fair.'

'It'll change. You mark my words. A day or two and our teeth will be chattering.'

'What else do you know?' Nottingham asked.

'Nothing to help me find those ledgers. Have you learned anything?'

The constable shook his head. 'No.'

'Are you ready, then?'

For what? That was the question. While the fires blazed, something was going to happen. Something unknown. How could he be ready? All he could do was act once it started.

'As much as I'll ever be.'

'You were never one for planning, even when you started out as a constable's man. You let things happen and then you plunged in.'

'That's what I was paid to do.'

'A little thought and you could have nipped things in the bud. Stopped them before they began.'

'And what could I have done about this?' Nottingham said mildly. 'Tell me that.'

'Maybe more than you did. You ran from killing to killing. You never even thought there could be much more to it until I pointed it out.'

That was true. But he'd been out of this for two years. He'd lost his touch, his sharpness.

'Then what do you suggest?'

'You're on the back foot. When it comes, you'd better be ruthless. No talking, no arrests.' He stared, eyes cold. 'Kill them. All of them. The way you did when someone killed that deputy of yours.'

'John Sedgwick.'

Finer waved the name away as if it meant nothing. 'Treat them that way. You don't have any choice. Anything less and they'll murder you.'

Bitter words, he thought as he walked back down the Head Row. Con was by the Market Cross, playing a lulling air as the constable passed and greeted him with a nod. By the Moot Hall, Jem had drawn a small crowd, gathered close and caught up in his tale.

Leeds. Home.

Down by the bridge men piled up heavy branches for the fire, bundled faggots of wood ready to be added later. The town seemed to be hushed, full of anticipation and excitement. For most people, tonight would be a great celebration.

He'd loved this night when he was small, moving from one fire to the other with his parents, seeing how the blazes cast shadows that looked like devils to his eyes. Later, on his own and sleeping anywhere he could find, they gave the chance of a few hours' warmth. Some sweet bonfire toffee, if he could steal it, or food that a family had left to roast in the embers. He'd taken his own girls, watching the same wonder on their faces that he'd once possessed. Young Mary's turn would come, then her children and all the ones that followed. Long after he was dead and forgotten.

The day seemed to crawl past, as if someone had weighed down the hands of the church clock so that they barely moved. By dinner Nottingham felt as if he'd spoken to half of Leeds. He'd gone to all the fires, making sure none was too close to houses; the last thing the town needed was sparks drifting and causing a fire.

The White Swan was doing a sullen trade as men kept money back for the night's drinking. No press of people as he sat and ate, wondering what else he could do during the afternoon. He needed to feel he was making some progress, that he had some small hope of stopping everything that was coming towards him.

But by the middle of the afternoon, what little faith he possessed in that was slipping away. Another two hours and it would grow dark. Later, people would finish their work and the bonfires would be lit.

He walked, looking in vain for a man with a coat pocket missing. The day had stayed mild; there would be plenty of folk out tonight, and enough of them would end up drunk and rowdy to cause trouble.

Con had gone from the market cross, but Jem was still sitting by the Moot Hall. His voice sounded dry as old leather now, cracking and rasping as he spoke. He had an empty mug at his side. Nottingham slipped into the Rose and Crown, bought another, and took it to him. With a grin, he said, 'Bless you, sir,' and barely broke the pace of his tale. Small kindnesses, the constable thought. Maybe someone would have a favour for him.

But as dusk slipped in, there was nothing. The men assembled at the jail, everyone reporting for their duty. Those who worked nights looked resentful at starting so early, trying to hide their yawns. The day people seemed brighter, harder. At least they'd have extra pay this week, although they'd probably earn it in cuts and bruises tonight.

Nottingham gave them their assignments. Two men at each of the big fires, ready to deal with any incident before it could blow out of hand. The rest would cover the town. That should be enough to control the apprentices.

'I'm sure the cells will be full in the morning,' he said. 'But make sure you're not the ones with sore heads. Dyson, Waterhouse, I need to talk to you before you go.'

'What about me?' Crandall asked.

'Take charge of the men who are roving around. Make sure that if anything starts to happen, you send word to me immediately.'

He issued cutlasses to the pair watching the bonfire that Brooke and the corporation would attend.

'Use them only if you have to,' he ordered. 'With luck, the sight of weapons should be enough to deter any trouble.'

'Yes, boss,' Dyer answered. They were clever enough to restrain themselves.

After they'd gone, another sword lay on the desk, waiting for him. Nottingham unlocked a drawer in his desk and took out three pistols, powder and bullets.

Rob arrived after darkness had fallen. He was breathing hard, sweating and leaning heavily on the stick as he moved, but he looked ready.

'Any word?'

'Nothing,' Nottingham replied, and saw the man's face fall. 'How's your knee? No lies. I need the truth.'

'It still hurts,' Lister answered after a moment, then raised his head. 'I can walk.'

'You'll be no use with a sword. Take these.' He pushed two of the pistols across the desk. 'Make sure they're loaded and primed.'

Rob looked up as he worked. 'What about you, boss? Are you armed?'

The constable patted the pocket of his greatcoat. 'Already done. And I'll have the cutlass.'

As the constable locked the door of the jail, he could sense the eagerness in the air. The streets were full, people already starting to gather although the fires wouldn't be lit until the Parish Church clock struck the hour.

He could feel his heart beating hard. But he felt certain it wouldn't happen for a while yet. Not until the families had enjoyed the blazes and gone off to their homes, and the real drinking and merriment began. There was still time for some word to come, for him to be able to stop it before it began.

The fires were beautiful. Rob had loved them from the first year his father had taken him out to see them. It was magical to see Leeds alive and alight at night, as if the whole town was burning.

Emily had come home as he was preparing to leave. As she took off her cloak she'd watched him make his aching way from the kitchen and

288

he thought he'd never seen such sadness in anyone's eyes. But she didn't try to stop him. How could she, with her father out there? Instead she held him close and told him to come home when it was done.

She wasn't going to attend the bonfires. In the end he persuaded her to go with the Webbs and take Mary for a few minutes. The baby was a true Leeds girl; she should start as she'd carry on.

The constable moved at Rob's slow pace down Briggate. The blaze already towered into the sky, light brighter than day reflecting off the buildings. The town smelt of wood smoke.

He waited as the constable exchanged a few words with the great, good men and their wives. Nods to Waterhouse and Dyer, who circulated with their eyes alert.

Then they were away, back up the street. It hurt to walk, each step still took effort, but he had to be here. He owed it to the boss. Time after time he'd been right on this when Rob had doubted him and even thought he wasn't fit for the job any more.

His palm was clammy on the stick as he pushed it down to take his weight. It was close now. Whatever was going to happen would begin soon; an hour or two at most.

They didn't talk. Nothing they said would have seemed adequate. There was enough noise all around. Somewhere in the distance a man fired off a musket and Rob felt a sudden shock. But it was nothing more than celebration.

The glow of the fire reached up Briggate,

casting shadows around the whores standing in the passageways that led through to the yards. Some held fans coyly over their mouths. Others smiled and beckoned.

He wondered about the pimps. None of them had listened to his warnings. They'd probably all be drinking and waiting for the small hours to take the money off the girls.

It seemed to take an age to reach the market cross. He lumbered, he knew it, an ungainly beast. Rob stood next to Nottingham, looking back, their view blocked by the Moot Hall. The whole night crackled and sparked. Voices rose here and there, a harsh burst of laughter. Rob pushed a hand into the pocket of his greatcoat and curled around the handle of the pistol. He'd never been a good shot, but one hit was all it took. He could manage that.

At first he barely noticed the shout. It was part of the wash of sound. Then it came again, a strange wail that seemed to rise. Without even thinking, he began to move. But Nottingham was already ahead, pushing through the crowd, parting them with his shoulder.

It was no more than a few yards, just outside the Rose and Crown. People were pushing themselves back in horror to leave a space around the scene. Nottingham saw Jem on his knees, howling as he held Blind Con. The fiddler was on the ground, a trickle of blood seeping from the edge of his mouth. There were wounds on his chest and his stomach. He tried to paw at them, as if he could brush them away. The violin lay where it had fallen, body smashed and strings hanging loose.

'What happened?'

'Con came to visit me. He'd just gone and I saw he'd left his gloves.' Jem held up his hand, something gripped between the finger. 'I went after him. As soon as he stepped out on Briggate a man was waiting. Two blows and he run off.'

Nottingham look around. The people who'd gathered were silent.

'What did he look like? Where did he go?'

'Young, fair hair. He went into the Talbot.'

Rob had arrived, taking in the scene and hearing the last remark.

'Get him inside,' the constable said. He turned his head and saw John Reynolds, the landlord, watching. 'Send someone for the doctor.'

Con wasn't going to live; he knew the signs all too well. But at least he could be spared the indignity of dying on the street. Two men came forward to lift him and Jem picked up the broken fiddle. Nottingham looked at Lister and nodded.

Twenty-Six

The Talbot was a babble of confusion as they walked in, weapons drawn. A heartbeat later, they were surrounded by silence.

'Where is he?' Nottingham shouted. 'Fair hair, he had a knife.'

Mutely, someone pointed to the door that led to the kitchen. Suddenly the pieces all fell into place.

Harry Meadows had even told him. He'd said he had two sons. It was there, if he'd had the brains to see it.

He crashed through to the kitchen, hearing Rob hobbling behind. The room was empty, the door to the yard hanging open, the back gate unlatched.

Nottingham ran up the stairs. One room was locked. He brought his boot down hard until it splintered. Inside, two women cowered against the wall. One older, one still young. The wife and the daughter.

'Where are they?' Just fear and silence. He raised the cutlass.

'The churchyard.' The woman's words came out in a croak.

'Which one?' He took a step forward and saw her flinch.

'St John's.'

'Don't try to leave.'

Rob was searching, scattering everything off the table.

'St John's churchyard,' the constable said. 'Come in the back way.'

He raced back up Briggate, legs jarring with every stride. Nottingham knew people were stopping to stare as he shoved through the crowd and across the Head Row. A hundred yards ahead another bonfire was burning close to the grammar school, people laughing and cheering as another big branch collapsed.

At the lych gate, he stopped to catch his breath for a moment, then walked into the churchyard.

The glow from the blaze threw strange, flickering shadows across the churchyard. In the light he could see three figures standing close to the porch. He kept walking towards them until he was able to make out their faces. Harry Meadows stood in the middle, outlined against the darkness.

He fitted the memory in his mind to the figure who'd disappeared with Four-Finger Jane. But Nottingham didn't know the young men with bland faces and fair hair who flanked. Each of them stood over a bundle on the ground. They all held swords.

'I wondered how long you'd take,' Meadows said. All the joviality was gone, the landlord's false face vanished. 'People said you were clever.'

He didn't reply, just stared at them. Let Meadows waste his breath. Every word gave more time for Rob to arrive.

'You see these?' He kicked one of the bundles; it gave a muffled, frightened cry. 'Two of the pimps. The third's already dead. These two will be in a few minutes. We were going to leave them for you. Now you can have the pleasure of seeing them executed. You ought to pay me: I'm doing your work for you.'

'Killing's your work, not mine.'

'What's the line between work and pleasure?' Meadows asked. 'And when we're done with these two, we'll add you to the list.'

He said it so simply, as if it was no more than a fact, a matter of no concern at all.

The constable tightened his grip of the hilt

on the cutlass and took a pace closer. In the distance, something fell with a dull crash into the fire and a wave of shadows sped past across the churchyard.

'Stay there. After all, we want you to have a good view.' Meadows smiled and chuckled. The right-hand pocket was missing from his old coat.

The man turned to his sons. 'Are you ready?'

One of the bundles struggled, a final attempt to escape. But he'd been tied too firmly.

'Then it's time.' He kept staring at the constable.

The young men were as efficient as butchers. A single deep stroke across the neck, then moving back to watch the blood gush over the flagstones. The bodies twitched and fought, but there was no hope. In the space of a breath it was over.

'What do you think?' Meadows asked. 'Quick. It was almost painless, really. Humane. And my boys were like artists, hardly got a drop of blood on themselves. Excellent, wouldn't you say?'

Nottingham stood, not letting himself show anything. Finer had been right, he thought. They had to die. All of them. And he had to stay alive. He raised his blade.

'Good,' Meadows said. 'It's time for you now.'

The young men moved, fanning out. Their eyes were cold and dead.

Which one would come first? It didn't matter; the other would be close behind, attacking him from both sides. And that would leave the middle open for Meadows. He'd want to have the final blow.

Rob should be here by now. Hidden in the dark,

behind a gravestone, preparing his shot. Pray God he was.

Nottingham swung the cutlass in an arc, keeping the men back. Once, twice. But soon enough, they'd keep coming.

His mouth was dry as dust. His head was pounding. He tried to swallow, but it felt like a lump in his throat. Nottingham swung it once more. The young men's expressions were empty, eyes staring, no hint of how they'd move.

The shot echoed loud off the buildings. One of the young men crumpled. His sword fell, a sharp, brittle sound as it bounced on the stone and into the grass. His brother turned. Before he could do anything, Nottingham thrust the cutlass deep into his belly. He felt the soft yield of the flesh and pushed it home.

The man's mouth opened but no sound came. The constable pulled and the blade came free, a rain of blood pouring from the wound as the man tumbled to his knees.

'Neatly done,' Meadows acknowledged with a nod. There was nothing in his eyes to show that he felt anything for his sons. No pain, no grief. He didn't even give them another glance. 'But they made it too easy for you. Now it's just you and me, and I'm better than they could ever be.'

He didn't move. Nottingham knew the trick: let the opponent make the first move, catch him as he came.

Off in the distance, an owl hooted as it hunted. The bonfire glowed bright for a moment, red and yellow light picking them out in the churchyard, stark against the blackness.

'Not scared, are you?' Meadows taunted.

But he was proof against words. They washed over him. It would take more than that to make him do anything rash. The constable held his ground, ready.

Meadows took a half-step to his right, pushing the point of his sword forward. It was a test, a feint. The man wanted to see what his opponent might do.

He could feel the pulse in his veins. Nothing else existed in the world except the man facing him. Meadows had a thin smile on his lips, even with his sons both dead just a few feet away.

It was time to end this game.

Nottingham raised the cutlass, ready to slice down. Meadows lifted his blade to parry the blow. It left him open. With his left hand, the constable brought the pistol from his greatcoat, thumbed back the hammer and pulled the trigger.

He was too close to miss. The bullet caught Meadows in the middle of his body, spinning him backwards as his chest seemed to explode. For somewhere in the night, the flash from a muzzle and the roar of a gun.

The man jerked forward like a puppet. For the smallest moment he stood, staring at the constable, mouth wide, his face coiled in – anger? pain? Then he fell, changing shape from flesh to ghost.

The constable stood. Smoke still curled up from his pistol and the harsh stench of gunpowder filled his nostrils. All three of them dead.

Slowly, the world seemed to creep in around him. The sounds of the revellers, the crackling of the fire, the woodsmoke and smudges of ash floating down through the air. He raised his head and blinked, turning to see the two young men behind him and the older one in front.

It was over.

He didn't even notice Rob was there until the young man clapped him on the shoulder. He was grinning.

'You did it, boss.'

He had. But it didn't feel like a celebration. Just an ending of something awful. Five dead tonight. Six, if the boast about the other pimp was true. The threat might be over, but a butcher's bill like that was hardly a cause for joy.

'We did it,' he heard himself say. The words seemed to come from someone's else mouth. 'I told you when I started that I was going to rely on you.'

'I'll call the men to come and take them away.'

'Yes. And we need to put Meadows's wife and daughter in jail.'

'I'll take care of that.' He began to turn away, then stopped. 'That last shot . . .'

'What about it?'

'I didn't fire it.'

There was still a night to keep under control. As the families and the good folk drifted home, the mayhem began. The apprentices, the drunks.

He stopped at the Rose and Crown. John Reynolds looked at him and shook his head. Con was dead. No surprise. But he'd needed to hope for something; a miracle, perhaps. Now the beautiful music had gone from the world.

* * *

The bonfires had all burned down to cinders and ash. The town was silent, finally overtaken by the night. People slept. Even the drunks had stopped their yelling. Rob hobbled down Kirkgate, weary and aching. His knee had swollen again during the evening, tender and sore as he placed his weight on it.

The apprentices had been persistent, grouping and regrouping, in the mood for a fight. They'd had their battle. Now more than a dozen of them lay dazed in the cells, the others in their beds, nursing bruises and cuts as they dreamed.

Every minute had been full. He'd been too busy to think about Meadows and his sons. Now, in the quiet, it poured back into his mind. He'd killed a man. Not his first and it wouldn't be his last. He didn't like it, it would weigh on him for months. But sometimes it became part of the job. And with those three, they'd done Leeds a service. They'd needed to die.

Who had taken that final shot at Meadows? He'd been waiting, ready to pull the trigger if the boss needed it. Then he heard the bang, saw the flash from the corner of his eye, and watched Meadows stagger and fall. By the time he'd been able to struggle between the headstones, the gunman had vanished.

Mrs Meadows and her daughter were in a cell at the jail, sharing with three other women blind drunk from the celebrations. At first he was surprised to find that they hadn't run. But then, where could they go?

He wanted nothing more than to tumble into sleep, not to have to think for hours on end. The boss had stayed, ready to talk to the Meadows women. He wanted reasons. Rob wanted rest.

A light burned behind the shutters on Marsh Lane. He could hear soft voices inside. As soon as he turned the doorknob, they stopped. Emily and Lucy turned to look at him.

Then she was there. He could feel her breath on his face.

'Are you hurt?'

'No. Just . . .'

'Papa?'

'He's fine. Not a scratch on him.'

Suddenly Emily was holding him up. He was too tired to stand.

Twenty-Seven

The smell of coffee was too rich, too strong. As soon as he entered Garroway's it surrounded him. Nottingham sat on the bench across from Tom Finer.

'You won. The news is all over Leeds.'

'I suppose we did.' He was still too numb to think of it as a victory. He'd been awake all night, helping to control the apprentices, then talking to Marjorie Meadows and her daughter until his throat felt raw. He had a bruise on his arm from a club and some of Harry Meadows's blood on his coat. 'You were right about Amos.'

Finer looked at him, trying to understand. 'What do you mean?'

'Meadows was Worthy's son. His bastard.'

'He probably sired dozens of those in his life.'

'Maybe he did.' The constable tried to rub away the ache at the back of his neck. 'But this one came back.'

'Worthy threw the woman out as soon as she told him,' Mrs Meadows said. 'Gave her a little money and told her to get out of Leeds or he'd kill her and the bairn.'

He could hear her husband's anger and resentment in the words. He'd brought her and the girl from the cell to the office, given them ale and let them warm themselves by the fire before he started his questions. But there was really only one thing he needed to know: why?

'Where did they go?'

'Here and there, the way he told it. Richmond, Malton. They ended up in Settle. When he was old enough, she told him all about his father. Every bad thing she knew, until Harry hated him.'

'Was Mr Meadows a publican? Was that true?'

'He was.' She raised her heard proudly. 'And we did keep a good inn. But Harry, he couldn't keep away from the thieving. Just small things. Nobody ever found him out.'

'If you were doing so well, why did you come to Leeds?' Nottingham asked.

The woman pulled the shawl more closely around her shoulders, though the room was warm.

'That was Harry. He always had it in his mind that he was going to show his father. He was going to be bigger and better than him. That was going to be his revenge.'

'But Amos Worthy is dead.'

'Harry came here five years ago,' she continued. 'He brought our boys. He wanted to see his father, see what he'd done. They even had a drink with him, but Harry never told him who he was. When he came home, he was angry. He told me he was going to topple his father, to take everything away from him. But he'd do it when he was ready. Once our boys were big enough to help him.'

'Then he must have been disappointed to arrive and find Amos in the ground.'

'He was.' She gave a curt, single nod. 'But he wasn't going back. He said he'd build something bigger than his father ever had. He'd make sure people remembered Harry Meadows, not Amos Worthy.'

'What about you? What did you do?'

She lifted her head and stared at him. 'He was my husband.'

As if that was explanation enough. And perhaps it was, he thought.

'What's going to happen to us?' Mrs Meadows asked.

'You helped him,' the constable told her. 'Both of you. You'll be tried. I don't know what the court will decide.'

The girl began to cry and her mother folded her close. How many dead – seven? eight? nine? – and they'd done nothing to stop him. As he locked them in the cell it was hard to feel any sympathy.

He ordered Waterhouse and Dyer to take the revellers over to the petty sessions. They'd have their minute before the magistrate, to be fined and turned out with sore heads and wounds. Good riddance to them.

Nottingham sat at the desk and sipped from a mug of ale. It was light outside. He could hear men starting to sweep up the ashes from the bonfires. Another hour and there'd hardly be a reminder that they'd ever burned. The days moved on, and soon enough the cloth market would begin on Briggate.

With a sigh, he put on the old bicorn hat and went to make sure everything was well.

'That was it?' Finer asked in disbelief. 'He wanted to show he was a better man than Amos?'

'That was all.' He understood. Somehow, it didn't seem to be enough of an explanation for all the killing. It was such a small thing. There should have been more. But at least he finally had the truth.

'What about my ledgers?'

'Once we find them, I'll see they're returned to you.' But not before he'd examined them closely to discover exactly what the man was doing.

'A little bird said you were willing to face three of them by yourself.'

Nottingham raised an eyebrow. 'You have some very observant birds. But it's wrong. Rob Lister was there, too. And he wasn't the only one.'

'Oh?' Finer asked. His curiosity was piqued.

'There was someone else, someone who fired

a pistol at Meadows. I don't suppose your little bird would know anything about that?'

'Now, what would make you think that?' He stared blandly at the constable.

'Because I know you.'

'Then you have your answer.' Finer stood, buttoned his coat, and tied the muffler around his neck. 'My ledgers,' he said. 'Don't forget.'

'I told you.'

'Amos.' Finer shook his head. 'The past never dies quickly here, does it?'

John Brooke was in his office, poring over papers, as Nottingham entered.

'I heard what happened at St John's last night.' He sat back in his chair. 'You did a good job.'

He'd done what was needful, nothing more. If he could have stopped it earlier, he'd have done it gladly.

'No,' the constable answered. 'Too many died. Far too many.'

And Con among them. Pointless deaths, every one of them, simply to satisfy one man's ambition to prove he was better than his father.

'But it shows we were right to appoint you as constable again.' The mayor smiled. 'With this and the cutpurse, you've shown yourself well.'

'Maybe.' He shook his head. 'I'm tired. I haven't been home since yesterday morning.'

'Then go and sleep, Richard. You've earned it.'

'Yes,' he agreed dully. 'I'll do that.'

Nottingham stopped at the Parish Church. He glanced at Worthy's grave, wondering if the man was laughing himself hoarse somewhere. He'd have appreciated the joke of a bastard come to usurp his father, only to find him dead.

But Nottingham spent his time at the two headstones standing side by side. Rose and Mary. He talked to his wife, letting it all spill out, the sorrow, the regrets, the failings. In his mind she still looked exactly the way she had on her last morning alive. She didn't age, she was fixed in time, she had a beginning and an end. He was the one moving forward, slowly and reluctantly.

He stayed until the chill pulled at his face. Then he turned, walked back to Kirkgate and over Timble Bridge.

Twenty-Eight

Christmas Day, 1736

He sat with his granddaughter in his arms. The baby was sleeping, her head resting in the crook of his arm, tiny fists bunched together as if she was fighting rest. The day, all the people, had overwhelmed her. Soon enough Emily would gather up little Mary and take her back to the wet nurse. But she'd become a regular visitor, slowly growing used to her home, her new family.

Family. He had them around him. His rag-tag family, not built on blood, but something more solid. Emily and her lover. Lucy the servant. Annie,

304

coming out from her shell now she was starting to believe that no one would send her on her way. Lizzie and her children, James and Isabell, playing by the fire, a sudden flare-up of argument between brother and sister quieted with a mother's word. And Jem, snoring away now he'd paid for his supper with a few tales to hold everyone spellbound.

They'd dined well on a piece of beef, a gift from one of the butchers in the Shambles. It had surprised him, gratified him; he'd brought it back yesterday for Lucy to cook. She looked at him thoughtfully and asked, 'Where did you steal it?'

'Get away with you,' he laughed. 'Any decent constable would catch me if I tried to run these days.'

He'd returned from York three days before, after testifying against Nick the cutpurse for murder. He stayed for the verdict, although it was never in doubt. The judge put on the black cap and Nottingham glanced around the court-room, half-expecting to see Kate there, waiting. But there was no girl, only Nick, no flicker of an expression on his face as he listened to the sentence.

Only two nights away, and fine company at the Starre Inne, but it felt good to be home, to be surrounded by everything he cherished. Some were missing, but they'd never be too far from him. And with Annie and tiny Mary, there was new life, the wheel revolving.

'I think your daughter needs changing,' he said to Emily, and she took the baby from him.

'I can do it,' Rob offered, and the constable saw her stare at him in astonishment. 'I ought to know how, at least.'

The lad's knee had mended without harm; a few days of rest and he was good as new. But the young healed quickly, he thought. Their hearts as well as their bodies.

They'd barely mentioned Meadows or the night in the churchyard. What was there to say, anyway? They both knew what had happened.

Things had been quiet in Leeds, nothing more than petty crimes that were solved by the end of the afternoon. It was as if a hush had descended on the town with winter.

Nottingham had searched Meadows's rooms above the Talbot. He'd found plenty of papers from Warren's office, but never Tom Finer's ledgers. The man had never asked for them again.

Lizzie yawned, stretched, and stood.

'We'd better go home before I fall asleep,' she said as she gathered her children. 'Thank you. For everything.'

'Believe me, it was my pleasure,' he told her. 'You're always welcome here, you know that.' He dug two farthings from his breeches pocket for James and Isabell.

'We'll walk with you,' Emily said. 'Mary needs to go back to Mrs Webb.'

The door closed. All that remained was the sound of Lucy and Annie washing the pots in the kitchen and Jem snoring softly in the corner.

Peace.

Afterword

The inns in this book existed. The Talbot did indeed have a cockpit, and the fights were a big attraction. Garroway's was there, the only coffee house in Leeds at a time when the drink was rare and expensive, as was tea. Gunpowder Treason Night, as it was called, celebrated the smashing of Guy Fawkes and the Gunpowder Plot to blow up Parliament – the exact opposite of how it stands today.

Richard Nottingham, too, was real, and he was the Constable of Leeds, although there's no mention of him retiring and coming back to work. In fact, there's precious little mention of him at all in the records, just a note by a member of the Town Waits (musicians) of him marching in a parade, and even there he's wrongly called Deputy Constable. No portrait, no headstone, so little left. We know he married in 1676 (to Jane Wood, not to someone named Mary), and he died in 1740, but I've been unable to discover any record of his birth so far. They had several children, most of whom lived; the oldest, Elizabeth, married the second son of a baronet. As Richard held the office of Constable until 1737, he must have been a good age when he retired.

However, all that blank canvas gives me the luxury to invent his life and his family. And hopefully, he lives on a little.

I'm very grateful to Kate Lyall Grant for being willing to bring Richard out of retirement, and to everyone at Severn House for all the work they do; it's truly appreciated. In Lynne Patrick I have a wonderful editor, and my agent Tina Betts does a splendid job. All those in libraries and bookshops: like every writer, I thank you. My partner, Penny, gracefully puts up with plenty of silence as I work.

Above all, thanks to those who've read and loved the previous books and asked me if there will ever be more. Without that, Richard would still be enjoying many quiet days. Thank you for your support.